PETER LOON

Also by Van Reid

CORDELIA UNDERWOOD

— *or* —

The Marvelous Beginnings of the Moosepath League

MOLLIE PEER

— *or* —

The Underground Adventure of the Moosepath League

DANIEL PLAINWAY

— *or* —

The Holiday Haunting of the Moosepath League

Van Reid

PETER LOON

A Novel

V I K I N G

VIKING

Published by the Penguin Group

Penguin Putnam Inc., 375 Hudson Street, New York, New York, 10014, U.S.A.

Penguin Books Ltd., 80 Strand, London WC2R 0RL, England

Penguin Books Australia Ltd, 250 Camberwell Road, Camberwell,
    Victoria 3124, Australia

Penguin Books Canada Ltd., 10 Alcorn Avenue, Toronto,
    Ontario, Canada M4V 3B2

Penguin Books India (P) Ltd, 11 Community Centre, Panchsheel Park,
    New Delhi – 110 017, India

Penguin Books (N.Z.) Ltd, Cnr Rosedale and Airborne Roads, Albany,
    Auckland, New Zealand

Penguin Books (South Africa) (Pty) Ltd, 24 Sturdee Avenue, Rosebank,
    Johannesburg 2196, South Africa

Penguin Books Ltd, Registered Offices:
Harmondsworth, Middlesex, England

First published in 2002 by Viking Penguin,
a member of Penguin Putnam Inc.
10 9 8 7 6 5 4 3 2 1

ISBN 0-670-03052-X

LIBRARY OF CONGRESS CATALOGING IN PUBLICATION DATA AVAILABLE

This book is printed on acid-free paper.

Printed in the United States of America
Set in Bodoni Old Face with Didot display and Bodoni and Caslon ornaments
Designed by Carla Bolte

TO HUNTER AND MARY

My heart, my love,
my always!

CONTENTS

THE BACKCOUNTRY SETTLEMENTS IN THIS BOOK WERE REAL PLACES, though their names were changed in the course of incorporating them into townships. Eighteenth- and early nineteenth-century New Milford is now the town of Alna, Balltown was divided into Whitefield and Jefferson, and Plymouth Gore became Washington. Some boundaries are not so neatly described, so that Patricktown seems to have become part of Windsor and part of Somerville, and Sheepscott Great Pond is more or less present day Palermo.

PETER LOON

By the end of the eighteenth century, many common folk in the United States believed that the American Revolution had not fulfilled its promise, and that the true war was but half done. The subsistence farmer and the laborer asserted that a relatively small number of families—wealthy, and long-established in the New World—controlled the political arena, the courts, and even the official interpretation of recent history. Many veterans of the Revolution believed that this rule by the few and the wealthy was no more than a new face on the Old World's system of aristocratic privilege.

Several armed rebellions were mounted as the nineteenth century drew close, particularly in the northern states, and often against that "old devil" taxation; but these small insurrections were quickly put down by either federal or state authority.

In the District of Maine (then part of the Commonwealth of Massachusetts), men known as the "Great Proprietors" claimed vast tracts of territory on the strength of old King's Grants and often contradictory Indian deeds. Their claim of entitlement was a direct extension of the very system of European aristocracy that the United States of America had ostensibly turned its back upon.

Meanwhile, the poorer folk, who were clearing the great forests of the northeast, believed that unsettled land was the right of any who could physically wrest it from the wilderness, and they used sometimes brutal tactics to drive off and intimidate the proprietors' land agents and surveyors. These bands of settlers who organized themselves against law and authority called themselves first the "White Indians" and then the "Liberty Men."

1

How Ezekiel Peter Black Came to Sheepscott Great Pond and How His Young Daughter Was Courted

IN THE FOURTH YEAR OF THE AMERICAN REVOLUTION, A MAN NAMED Ezekiel Peter Black came to the settlement of Sheepscott Great Pond, in the District of Maine, with his daughter Rosemund. There was a great deal of speculation regarding Black and his daughter, these stories being fed by the appearance of the man himself, who was taller than other men and powerfully built; he was swarthy skinned and his beard and his long hair, worn in a queue, were blue-black. It was rumored that his father was Black Peter himself, the African slave who rose up against his tormentors and became a pirate, and that this Ezekiel Black had himself harried the southern coasts and got his daughter by the kidnapped wife of a plantation owner in South Carolina.

Rosemund was twelve years of age when she was brought to Sheepscott Great Pond, and people thereabouts had never seen beauty like hers. Her hair was not as black as her father's, but it was long and thick, and her eyes were almost black and her lips (even when she was a child) were full and red. She considered her neighbors with a certain unmasked sense of superiority, and even her father, who himself walked like a king among other men, treated her always as his equal.

Adding to the speculation about Black's past was the amount of *coin in hand* he carried to Sheepscott Great Pond, and his neighbors were greatly encouraged to accept him on his own silent terms when he purchased their labor in the clearing of his acres and the raising of his home. Two young men in particular were furthered in their own substance by the wages they earned in working for Ezekiel Black. Silas Loon and Obed Winslow were fast friends who all but lived on the Black homestead while it was yarded, raised, and planted.

Silas and Obed were not the only young men to pine after Rosemund as she thrived from child to girl, but they were of an age with one another and only a year or two older than Rosemund herself, and from the moment they both saw her, which was the same moment, they could see the blossom inside the bud. They ingratiated themselves with her father with honesty and hard work, and Rosemund would sometimes allow them to speak to her at the end of the day.

Homesteading in the Maine wilderness was a hard bargain, however you looked at it. The ground was stony, the summers were humid and filled with storm, the winters were deep with snow, and perhaps worst of all were the black flies in spring, and the mosquitoes in warmer months—horrible swarms, huge and hungry that made work bitter and defense useless. But as a rule, those who came stayed, and the children of those who stayed cut new farms and new settlements out of the deeper precincts of the forest.

When Silas and Obed were seventeen and Rosemund was fifteen, the two young men struck out on their own—one to the north and one to the west—and began to clear the land they would lay claim to. This was in a season when the agents of Henry Knox and the other proprietors were increasing their presence in the wilderness and demanding payment for land that the backcountry folk had settled. Undeterred by the presence of land agents and surveyors, the young men went to Ezekiel Black and spoke to him, taking turns.

"We both flatter ourselves in thinking we have your regard, Mr. Black," they said to Ezekiel Black.

The father said directly, "Honest labor, even when recompensed, merits regard."

Then the young men said, "And we further flatter ourselves, that your daughter thinks none too poorly of us."

Mr. Black might have expected this, for his expression never altered. His arms were crossed before him. "I believe she finds your company tolerable," he replied.

"We both of us love your daughter, Mr. Black," they told him. He said nothing.

"We are friends to the end of our days, and will not fall out, even for love," they continued. "So it is that we come to you, each begging your Rosemund's hand, and if you discover virtue in us and if you choose one of us for your daughter's husband, the other will quietly abide."

"I will not drive you away," said Mr. Black, "but I would not presume to choose a husband for Rosemund. She is too young besides, but when she is of age I will not refuse her if she chooses one of you. Go back and work your own land. Her love may not take the form of the biggest house or the most acres, but it would not hurt your suit, either of you, to have them when the time comes."

With that, they parted amicably and no more was said on the subject between them for some months.

In the late summer of the following year, Ezekiel Peter Black was countenanced with less agreeable company in the form of a surveyor working for Henry Knox. Surveyors were not well-liked in those parts; they were considered heralds to the official claims of the proprietors, and since one could not claim what one hadn't measured, they were more than usually driven off. Black discovered this surveyor at the eastern extremity of his own claim. The border between Sheepscott Great Pond and Davistown was in some dispute and the man was laying lines in preparation of an agreement between the two representative patents.

Black was mounted on a big black horse and must have made an impression upon the surveyor. "If you're dividing *my* land from that of Henry Knox," said Black, "or any other man, you have your stakes too far west."

"I'm dividing what belongs to Henry Knox from the Plymouth Patent," said the man.

"Your stakes need be further east," said Black, "and what lies west of them from here to that hill yonder is mine." He pointed over a recent deadfall at a green ridge.

"The Patent will soon take it up with you, once matters with England are solved," said the surveyor, and he did his best to appear careless by returning to his work.

Black replied "And if Henry Knox claims an inch that I consider mine, I will take it up with him, *and* the Patent soon after. So if you would save your *master* large grief for little gain, you'll move those stakes."

4

"Are you threatening me?" said the surveyor, bristling suddenly with all the office he imagined he possessed.

"I wouldn't threaten you, but I might climb down from this horse and pound you if I didn't want you to go back and tell Henry Knox and whoever else you serve that any claim to my land will rally my presence at their door."

"I shouldn't worry they'd be frightened."

"I shouldn't worry I'd give them a moment to think on it."

The surveyor was aghast that bald threats could be levied against men such as Henry Knox and the Great Proprietors. "While you're safe in your little house in the woods, men like Henry Knox are fighting the British for your rights!" he declared.

"Men fight the same battle for separate reasons," said Black, "and I am sure that Henry Knox has had little thought for me in his war. If he is willing to fight the British for this land, I am willing to fight him for it."

The conversation did not go on much longer, but the end of it was that the surveyor was allowed to gather his gear and leave in peace, if not peace of mind. Black did not dignify the man's work by pulling his stakes. "Any thief can drive a stick in the ground," he would say.

There was a story people told, years later, that Ezekiel Peter Black paid a visit to Henry Knox, though the truth was that the Plymouth Patent claimed the land Black had settled. The story told better with Knox in it, however—the hero of Dorchester Heights and Washington's Secretary of State.

Knox came into his own parlor one day, it was said, (there in his mansion in Thomaston), and Black was waiting for him, unbidden. Knox's favorite dog was lying at Black's feet like a best friend, and Black offered Knox the view of a pistol, muzzle first, as evidence of his claim. "I just wanted you to know," Black was to have said, "that you will have less warning of my presence in your home, than I will of your presence within ten miles of mine." Then Black got up and left, and by the time Knox had shaken himself from his apoplectic state, the settler had made good his escape. Knox, people said, had shot the dog.

But Ezekiel Peter Black was dead before he might have performed such a feat, despite what people said. Several days after his encounter with the surveyor, he collapsed in his own rough parlor and Rosemund was only barely able to drag him into bed. He shivered, as from ague, and sucked in his breath like a drowning man. Rosemund took horse to the nearest neighbor and soon the Black's homestead was scene to a deathwatch.

Silas Loon and Obed Winslow came, of course, and got nearly the last mortal words from Ezekiel Black. "You will marry my daughter, and be honorable," he said, but there was no clue in his words or his gestures, which one of them he thought he was speaking to. Try as they might, they could not bring the man's mind back to the question of his daughter's hand. Rosemund was called in, and she was left alone with her father, and soon he was dead.

Some said the surveyor had poisoned Black somehow, and there were tales that the conversation between the two had been a deal more friendly and that the surveyor had offered a jar of rum, from which he himself did not drink. But Rosemund had heard the true story of the encounter from her father's lips and she said it wasn't so.

Silas and Obed fretted what to do, and days later, they went to the farm nearest the Black homestead, where Rosemund was staying for a while, and told her that her father wanted her to marry one of them. "We give you to choose," they told her, "assuring you that you will do nothing to our friendship, however you decide."

Rosemund was overwhelmed, and could say nothing, and her courting fell out in this way: Silas and Obed gave thought to what chore they were pretty equal at, and took themselves out to the woods and felled a straight pine. Then, with a belt, they measured the trunk in two places, and at two points where the tree equaled itself in girth they commenced to drive their axes. Obed, it happened, fell upon a knot, where an old broken branch had healed over years before, but Silas's portion was clean as threshed hay. So Silas won and, half in delight and half in sorrow, he took Rosemund to wife when she was yet sixteen years of age, and Obed, who found circumstance harder to bear than he could have imagined, said goodbye to Silas with a shake of the hand and a tear in his eye, and left Sheepscott Great Pond.

In later days, many in the settlement were sure that, had Rosemund found courage to speak, she would have married Obed. It may be that some decisions in life should not be left to chance, or a strong arm.

2

*Of Rosemund Loon's Strangeness, and Silas Loon's
Death, and How Their Son Peter Was Sent
in Search of an Uncle "By Marriage"*

ROSEMUND WAS ONLY JUST SEVENTEEN WHEN HER AND SILAS'S FIRST
child was born. It was a difficult confinement, and the neighbor-
wives attending thought she might die. One of them wetnursed
the child, who was named Peter, while Rosemund hovered in and
out of the grave for three days. She did recover, but seemed more
puzzled than pleased with the baby.

Silas Loon, despite pride in his own claim of land, had never
been able to ask his wife to leave the Black homestead, and so had
sold his own place for livestock and feed and commenced married
life on his wife's property. Despite his presence, and his improve-
ments, Silas's new home was always known as the Black place.
Obed Winslow's cleared land and cabin were squatted by a new
family soon after Obed left Sheepscott Great Pond.

It seemed as if Obed had never left, his continued presence at
the Black homestead was so real to Silas. It might have been as
real to Rosemund, but she never spoke of it; she never spoke
Obed's name once he was gone, and rarely spoke Silas's name as
long as they were married.

The husband was ever conscious that Rosemund might have had Obed for a husband, but for chance or the Grace of God, and mindful that she might have been better off. Consequently, there was nothing denied her, and gifts were given and favors performed that she had never asked for or imagined. Her father had treated her as an equal as long as she could remember; and others, daunted by her beauty, had deferred almost reverently to her. Now her spouse treated her as more than equal, and suspected himself less than equal to the honor of being her husband.

Rosemund was not so much unkind as she was simply unaware; and eventually folks decided that she was *touched*. Such beauty came with a price, it was said, and no wonder she could look at her reflection in the pond and be a little mad. People did not think poorly of her, exactly. Once, a year or so after Peter was born, she was out walking in the forest, which was her wont, and she was attacked by a man who thought she was a wood nymph, she was so beautiful. She managed to brain him with a rock before he much had his way, and folks said she had grit, but she remained unaffected by the encounter. The man was thrown into a makeshift jail and died there soon after.

Other children came. Some survived birth and some of those survived infancy. Rosemund did as she pleased, which sometimes included fierce hard work in the gardens and fields, but as often took in a walk along the stream below the house or a visit to the hill her father had pointed out to the surveyor. She met Indians sometimes, and could speak more of their tongue than most settlers thereabouts. She wandered off with some Indian women once and Silas and his neighbors had to go looking for her. She never showed more than a passing sort of interest in her children. She was *touched,* folks were sure, and signs of her queerness only seemed plainer as the years passed. She had strange humors about her; she kept her children from church, disdained talk about land, and would sometimes laugh at jests that no one else understood.

The Loon children never heard of Obed Winslow. Peter and his brothers and sisters grew up in the presence of a pipe dream, it seemed. Some mothers, they knew, could be hard where life was so hard, but Rosemund Loon was like a ghost in the house. She might pick up a crying child and dust him off, but there was always the sense that she was merely quieting him for her own sake, for the sake of the dreamlife she lived, beyond the experience of those around her. Some thought that her first born, Peter, shared some of his mother's othermindedness.

A new century was born. When he was seventeen, Peter wasted no time cleaving from his family, but went north of his father's interrupted homestead of years before, where a new family had recently taken up living, and began to clear his own acres. His father came to help him after the harvest, and one bright October day a twisted hackmatack swung to the wrong quarter as it fell and it crushed Silas. Peter got his father home, carrying him the entire way, and Rosemund tended the man until he died the next morning.

To his brothers and sisters, Peter seemed more like his mother than ever as he stood out on the porch after their mother broke the news to them. He seemed confused, unable to decide between falling down or fleeing. His father had always been good to his children when he had the opportunity to deal with them at all. He had been the steady influence in their lives and it was difficult to make sense of their fate, now that he was gone.

The next night, long before sunrise, Peter woke to find his mother standing by his cot, looking down at him. There was a lantern in her hand, the light of which must have wakened him; it lit her face from below so that she seemed almost sinister. Peter wondered if she knew he was awake and tried to pretend otherwise, but she spoke in a near whisper.

"Peter," she said, and the use of his name sounded strange from his mother. "Peter."

"Yes, Ma."

"There is something you need to do," she said. Then she said, "There is something *I* need you to do."

This seemed stranger still, his mother needing anything from him. "Yes, Ma," he said.

"I need you to find your uncle."

Peter thought about this. As far as he had ever known, his mother had been an only child, and his father's brothers were all dead. "Uncle?"

"I need you to find your uncle," she said again. She was fully dressed and there was the scent of some autumn flower about her. She had just come in from one of her walks by moonlight. Peter could see a sliver of milky light lying on the floor beyond her.

Peter thought it polite to sit up, but he did not want to close space with her. His father was dead; his father's body lay on the table in the next room. His mother stood over him in the middle of the night demanding that he find an uncle of whom he had no knowledge. "My uncle?" he said finally.

"Your Uncle Obed," she said. "I need you to find your Uncle Obed."

"Who is Uncle Obed?" he asked.

She did not answer but lifted an arm to show him that she held his clothes. "You can eat before you leave," she said.

He sat up then, blinked, and looked more closely at her. "But they'll be burying Pa."

"Your Pa would want you to find your uncle."

"I expected I'd be needed here," said Peter in his confusion. "I expected I'd need to dig a place for Pa."

"The neighbors will take care," she said.

Peter's youngest brother stirred in the bed next to him. His mother shook the clothes at Peter just once and he complied by putting them on. He found his tall moccasins by the bed and tied them on. They were narrow for his feet and he had slitted the outsides of them. He followed his mother out to the main room where his father's remains lay on the table covered by a sheet, then to the back of the house where the one fireplace barely glowed.

"You better eat first, then bring this with you," she said, pointing first to a plate of victuals on the plank table, then a cloth sack.

Peter peered into the sack, and from the light of the lantern he could descry some hard biscuits and apples. "Am I leaving now?" he asked.

"You'd better get a push on before first light," was all she said. She sat opposite him.

The truth was, he hadn't eaten much for dinner, and guilty as it made him feel with his poor father in the room behind him, his stomach felt empty. He'd eaten through about half the plate when another question occurred to him. "Where is he?" His mother's face was hidden behind the glare of the lantern on the table, and when she didn't speak, he leaned to one side and said, "Where is this Uncle Obed?"

"I'll show you," she said. "Eat your breakfast."

Peter didn't know if it was breakfast or dinner, yesterday or to-morrow, but he finished what had been put in front of him with rather more relish than he would have guessed. When he was done, his mother brought him his father's coat and hat, then led him outside. Peter insisted on stopping at the table in the parlor and paying last respects to the man who had sired him and given him every advantage in his power.

Peter Loon felt oddly aware, pinned like tailor's work to the hour. A half-remembered moment of tenderness from his father rose up like a grasping hand and clutched Peter's heart and his throat, and he backed away, almost frightened by the fierce emotion that threatened to overtake him.

"Peter?" called his youngest brother Amos from their bed. It seemed hard, leaving his brothers and sisters like this. He sensed that they found him a comforting presence, with their father gone and their mother so ghostlike. "Peter?" came the voice again and Peter answered with a quieting *hush*.

He stepped out of the house, onto the short porch. Rosemund Loon—still holding onto her beauty despite her thirty eight years, most of which had been spent in this hard wilderness—tugged at her husband's coat so that it snugged more closely around her son's shoulders. She snatched the hat from his hand and put it on his head.

"Where . . ." he began.

With a ruthless sort of grip upon his shoulder, she turned him quickly about, and pointed south and east. "He went in that direction."

"My uncle?"

"When he left, he went in that direction," she said again.

"But when?"

"There can't be that many people in the world," she said. "You're bound to find him, if you look. He went south and east. He could be in the next settlement, for all I know, but I don't think so. His name is Obed Winslow."

"Winslow?" Peter had not lost that sense of complete awareness born at his father's silent side. He drew himself up to his height. "How Winslow?" he said. "What name is Winslow to us? The Winslows in the bottomland over that way?" He pointed west. His sister Sally Ann had taken visits from a young fellow named Job Winslow from that farm.

"He is an uncle by marriage," she said. There was a helpless look in her eyes that he had never seen before and he turned away.

"Obed Winslow," he said.

"I need you to find him." She leaned forward and hugged him with uncharacteristic fervor. "You're a good boy," she said, which struck him like a blow to the head. "You've always been a good boy, and I know you'll do well." Then she turned away, walked in to her dead husband and shut the door behind her.

14

Going back into the cabin was impossible. Following her was impossible. Peter was confounded. He struggled to hold onto that awareness he had felt beside his father's body. He looked southeast; he glanced over his shoulder, but the gable end of the house obscured the moon. It was a chilly fall night, and his breath formed before him in puffs. The sky was cloudless, and what stars or planets there were, gleaming despite the moon, shone like sharp bits of ice. About twenty or so rods to the southeast lay the shadow of the forest.

Peter had only been to the next settlement, Davistown, half a dozen times in his life, and to Patricktown—further away and more or less directly south—only once. He considered going to the neighbors in the other direction and asking their help to sort things out. Everyone knew his mother was a little mad. Some thought *he* was a little mad, as well, though he wasn't supposed to know that. People, he understood, could only keep a secret so long.

Then who is Obed Winslow? "Uncle Obed," he said, trying out the name. That sharp, almost painful, awareness seemed to call him from the line of trees to his south. He stepped down from the porch and walked into the moonlight. His father's coat was warm.

Out in the stump-strewn field, he stumbled once against an old furrow. Something stirred ahead of him, a small animal, a mouse or a mole, mingling with the remnants of hay, frightened by his unexpected presence. He turned around only once and was urged on by the suspicion of his mother's face in the single window facing east. In a moment he found the old path in the moonlight and vanished into the forest, hardly knowing what he ventured.

He was almost glad to quit the cleared plot of land; even he who had lived all his life among acres of stumpage could imagine, in the dark, limned by the moon, that one out of many of those low-lopped trunks might be instead a figure crouched and watching.

3

Of Peter Loon's First Night in the Forest

THE FOREST WAS THE ENTIRE WORLD; IT WAS ALL THAT PETER KNEW. He might, in his life, have seen a score of cleared acres in one place, but they would have been cleared acres surrounded by trees and wooded hills and populated by stumps and the charred remains of brush piles, and in the midst of any such clearing was at least one building fashioned of trees in next to their natural state.

He knew Sheepscott Great Pond, of course, and the settlement there, but the pond and the settlement were similarly encircled, and the forest, and the tiny patches of hard won ground in the midst of the forest, and the lake in the midst of the forest, and the hardscrabble settlement with its spireless church were all that Peter had ever known, though he had heard tell of deserts and oceans and grassy plains. A neighborhusband two or three farms away—miles away—had once sailed for the British Navy, and he had tales to tell of islands of rock in the South Seas and cities that stretched over hill and valley as far as the eye could see. But forest was all that Peter could reasonably expect to find in his mind's eye when it was all that he had ever known.

He was accustomed to little more than moonlight after dark, and along a moderately well marked trail he was able to move, hardly breaking his stride. Some of the hardwoods had shed their leaves, and the glow of the moon, hanging between nadir and zenith, made the shadows of roots look like holes in the ground, and pale granite and lucid quartz like basking faces.

The wind held a distinct note when the still-clinging leaves had turned and dried, a reeding *hush* that rose and fell like a breath; and where certain groves of oak and sugar maple were losing their foliage, soft dry veterans of summer brushed past his face like bat wings or drifted without noise onto his father's hat. Trees squeaked and grunted in the wind. Now and then the echoes of animal calls drifted among the trunks and aging fern. He walked quietly and naturally, laying his feet down with ease without sacrificing his pace.

After a time, he sensed the large swamp to the west, some distance away—a presence marked by a change of air and sound that filtered through the trees. Beyond the swamp would be Great Pond and one little settlement further still.

When he did not look directly in front of him, the path almost glowed. Above him, the occasional breaks in the trees—a blink of starlight—led the way. The land rose and fell, rose and fell; the path plummeted occasionally and he was warned in time only by the sense of space yawning below him and the wind gathered, as in a great room. Streams trickled across the way, or the way met with one of these rills and followed it to the next little dale. The path widened as it gathered with others like it, or followed an ancient animal run; it wound round the feet of scarpy slopes and followed the course of least resistance between twin hills.

Peter thought of his little brother Amos waking to find him gone, and he felt a stab that was joined to his leaving with nary a goodbye or even a good notion where he was going. Peter was so long and Amos was so small that the little brother could sleep cradled against the big brother like a pea in a pod.

Peter heard the *breent* of a nightjar nearby and thought he caught the glimpse of something wing past a fleeting pool of open sky. He had no idea what he was about, walking the woods in the middle of the night, but he did not find them unpleasant, at first, these immediate sensations.

It was not long, however, before another reality of life, as he understood it, imposed itself—and that was the fact of uncanny things in the forest, the knowledge of curious and perhaps malicious disembodied minds lurking in the darkness between the trees. A moth of panic flickered against his chest and a hymn sprang quietly to his lips. Suddenly the shadows of roots, like holes in the forest floor, looked as if they gaped a little wider, and the pale faces of granite and quartz appeared more aware of him.

One such pale visage brought to mind his father, lying in the dark in their home. He thought of Amos again and what the little boy would do without his big brother to pilot him around the strange still presence in their midst. "Where's Papa?" Amos had asked when their father's body had been laid out in the midst of the room.

Peter stopped and considered what he was doing, what had brought him here, *who* had brought him here. What would the neighbors think when he was not at hand for his own father's burying? What would his mother say if he turned about and went home? She had been so strange, so insistent. Maybe his father *would* have wanted him to find this Uncle Obed. Peter considered the moon, its disc cleft, in his view, by a single bare limb. He looked forward and was conscious of his own dim shadow stretched ahead of him. How many people *were* there in the world? How would he find one Obed Winslow? Would he stop from stoop to stoop asking after the man?

A friend of his, one or two years older, had left Sheepscott Great Pond when he was fourteen, saying he was going to sea. He had not been heard from since. Had the world swallowed him up?

These deliberations drove the better part of his night panic away, though the hymn continued silently on his lips.

Slowly, Peter was insinuating himself forward upon the trail, south and east in the direction his mother had sent him. He would stop and ask after Obed Winslow at Patricktown, and he would be back in time to bury his father, no harm done. Curiosity drew him. He was seventeen and able to take care of himself. There were young women at Sheepscott Great Pond who would listen to him over and again, if he had a story to tell—traveling by night through the woods on his own, visiting strangers in the next settlement. He would have news, other people's stories. The thought of all those people, unknown to him, living their lives, sleeping now in their beds with their different faces and their separate dreams, drew him like curiosity.

He was striding along now at his previous pace, when heavy wings whooshed overhead—an owl, perhaps. "From things that go bump in the night, good Lord protect me," he said; it was a child's prayer, but he stated it with conviction, if not very loudly. He knew that pixies and demons could be confused from their motives if a person turned his coat inside out or wore his hat upside down, and he was about to take one of these precautions when he re-membered that he was wearing his father's coat and his father's hat. *Pa's not even buried or prayed over yet,* Peter thought. His father's spirit was probably abroad, perhaps with him now. He would have guessed before this that the notion of a ghost, even his father's, in the middle of the night in the dark of the woods would have scared him ferociously, but he felt unexpectedly calmed and even comforted that some portion of his father—who had been a brave man—might walk with him.

Peter's eyes had adjusted to the dark, so that he was conscious of ranks of black and umber and able to separate things from their shadows, and to tell near trees from the wall of trees beyond; but even his young eyes were starved for light as the moon westered. Odd flashes of green and red puffed at the periphery of his vision. Startled, he looked away from these images, knowing they would only disappear if he stared after them. He walked for an hour and he walked for two, and the light all but left him and the world became a void clothed in the bark of trees, so he slowed and slowed his progress after tripping once and running his face into a branch, and he searched out the islands of starlight between the trees like a sailor watching for bits of land in an endless sea.

But the light continued to wane and finally died. He had reached a section of ancient wood where the groves overhung the path and thickly leafed oaks and elm and maple hovered their crowns like clouds between Peter and the sky. The sound of the wind in these giants was high and loud and the peep of night creatures and the call of nighthawks and nightjars more constant than in any other part of the forest. Peter's uncertainty crept over him once again. What was he doing, and what would happen to him out here where someone might stumble over his body but never guess his fate?

He thought he would grope around for a tree trunk and sit down against it till light came. His eyes constructed spots of darkness and near darkness in the wall of black about him; then, as if a lamp had been turned up far away, the last of the falling moon found a hole in the forest and drove a single ray of pearly light down a level stretch of path before him. He was halfway down this columned hall when the dim glow began to lessen to a secret. He stood. The moonlight shifted across the path before him, moving like mortal life from left to right. Then he caught the hint of another, strange light on his left again, and heard the slightest beat, like a fat drop of rain.

There was a sudden *huff* behind him that choked any response or reflex, and he stood with muscles stiffened and eyes wide as another patch of moonlight shifted past his gaze. It might have been the trees themselves moving, dark as pines and graceful as birch, antlers for branches, black eyes and hooves for knots and roots. It was a great herd of deer, and he was conscious of them all around him and spread out in vast ranks, as God might be conscious of them without looking; the occasional flash of a white tail or the spot on a fawn's coat had looked like the moonlight moving. He heard them, their hooves scraping the path or turning a twig. The noise of them rose out of the wind like a voice leaving its fellows in unison to harmonize and be heard of itself.

He had not imagined such a tribe of deer; they must be many herds, following a common call to move with the season. Peter hardly dared breathe, and he turned slowly to face the oncoming deer, mouth and eyes wide, fearing his scent would touch off a sudden panic and rush. He might be dead in a minute, cut to ribbons by sharp hoofs and pointed antlers.

And why *hadn't* they scented him? He turned his shoulder as one tall buck walked by, almost brushing the young man's face. It was an uncanny, lengthy wait; he had no idea how long it took, only that scores of animals moved past on either side of him, crossing the road and shifting from deep wood to deep wood. He could smell them, the musk in the air was overpowering, unnerving, and he found himself thinking of those young women, those he would tell his stories to, in ways that made him blush in the dark, and no sooner had he blushed, when it seemed one of the creatures found his presence in the air and let out a curious and half-disgusted cough. Something firm collided with Peter's chin and nearly spun him about. There was another snort and the noise of graceful legs dancing backwards and sideways upon the path and on the surrounding floor of battered twigs and leaves.

Peter took two steps toward the oncoming herd and ran into the trunk of a tree; it seemed hardly large enough to protect him—only a medium-sized sort of oak—but he pressed himself against it. He sensed that the entire herd had stopped in its careful tracks, paused and tested the forest air with ears and nose. He waited, listening to the sniffing and stillness. Then the herd moved forward again, hardly bothered by the tremor of his presence. It was his father's coat that had saved him, he was sure, or perhaps his father himself, standing near.

After some time the sound of the herd passed away, fleeing west toward hillier country. Before the last of them was gone he could almost see their dark shapes moving among the trees, and he *could* sight their tails' white undersides flash as they made the short leap from the path to the embracing woods. He watched with his back to the tree he'd been hugging, wondering if there were the hint of dawnglow in the air. But the moon was gone and the darkness was severe. However, he did not have to wait long for the sky to rise out of blackness, and he had the impression that the single star or planet he could see through the canopy of leaves had intensified its light and turned the surrounding atmosphere to a muted gray.

After the pitch and complete dark, this small shift toward day seemed like noon to the young man; trees stood out opposite him like men stepping forward from a crowd. Peter picked himself up and continued on his way, picking up also the hymn he had been singing in a quiet reassuring whisper to himself.

He had not walked above half an hour before the light briefly waned before blooming into the predawn. He came to the place where the path turned west and met the Sheepscott River in its upwater youth, south of Great Pond. There was a ford where the river and men had conspired together to place large rocks in a neat row, and beyond there was as much cleared land south along the river as he had ever seen in one place.

It was still night in the west; behind the hill across the river the sky was black and strewn with stars, but the scattered rocks upon the slope, a single glacial cast-off, and the hundreds of stumps rose from shadow in the increasing gray light as if they had been hiding. Peter opened the sack his mother had given him and took a hard biscuit. He ate it at the edge of the river before taking a drink there, then he hopped from rock to rock to the other side with the river rushing about him.

At the top of the hill the road began to follow the Sheepscott River south and he walked another half an hour while the night retreated and dawn neared. Birds were noisy along the water's edge and in the bushes and small trees that had grown up in the damp pockets of ground.

Finally he came to a broad slope above the road and a grove of birch in the midst of which stood a single powerful oak; the trees were bare and he broke off a sapling from the edge of the copse and, using its limbs as a broom, drove up a low mound of leaves against the trunk of the oak. He was weary and the wind off the river was cool, so he was encouraged to make quick use of his work. Like a low creature, he burrowed into the russet mound and, with his sack beneath his head, he was soon rewarded with the reflected warmth of his own body and breath; the ground, which he could feel through several layers of dry leaves, seemed welcoming, and he imagined that it beat with its own clement pulse. The river murmured below him. The breeze opened the diurnal events of the surrounding field and the forest across the water, but it only rattled the rough counterpane of his bed and entered his dreams by way of his ears. He was blind and deaf to the balance of the dawn.

4

*How Peter Loon Conjured Himself from a Felled Buck,
and How He Met Two Woodsmen and a Parson*

AN INSISTENT BUTTONHOLE OF LIGHT ROUSED PETER. HIS BED WAS still warm but his young limbs felt antique with stillness and hard ground; an oak root nudged his ribs. He opened his eyes and considered the tiny ray; he attempted to place the position of the sun by it, and concluded that he had not slept more than an hour or so. He was deciding whether to close his eyes again or to rise, press on, and look for Patricktown, when there came the sound of a footstep and something occluded that single spot of thin light.

The furtive nature of the sound touched a nerve and he was reminded of the deer in the forest. It was daylight, of course, outside his bed of leaves, but blind and dark where he lay and several notions ran through him—memories, really, of old stories—the man in the moon walking the night forests, strange creatures that moved among the trees when men dreamed, woodland shapes he had long forgotten or long discounted from tales told to frighten him to sleep.

But he knew it was daylight out, and the sound of a dove also encouraged him; he was about to let out his long held breath, when there was a second footstep and the ray of light returned.

There came a whir and a hard slap, a heavy piglike grunt and the report of a musket.

The weight of something large and dying crashed against his bed of leaves and he might have thought the oak itself had fallen, for something sharp and woody raked his forehead and scalp and there were no other noises save for the thrashing of limbs (of one sort or another) upon the ground.

Shouting equal parts fear and anger, he pushed himself away and stood against the tree. Leaves clung to his father's coat. His head was bleeding and he was missing his hat. Before him, a great buck lay still, and Peter had the wild notion that it was the very stag that had sensed him in the forest the night before. On the road below stood two men, a morning mist about their knees, one with his smoking musket still half raised, and both expressing astonishment across a distance of fifty yards. Peter could hardly imagine the sight he must present, rising up from the ground behind or, presumably, *from* the fallen stag itself, with blood on his head and leaves clinging to his old-fashioned clothes, but even an unloaded weapon, pointed in his direction, gave rise to a sense of threat and he raised a hand and shouted, "Ho, there! I'm Peter Loon from Sheepscott Great Pond!" though the sudden call only startled the two men further.

Amazingly, the hunters appeared ready to give up their kill. They conferred with one another by uncertain looks and short quiet sentences. Something of their perception of the scene reached Peter Loon and he added to his greeting, "I was asleep in these leaves!"

As if this were more than they wanted to know, the two men

grabbed the tackle at their feet, turned away, and began to hike at a swift rate, south, down the road. Peter watched them, and he was open-mouthed and bewildered. They stopped before they were out of sight, however, and considered him again. He could see them conferring with one another.

The man who had fired was loading his musket again, and Peter thought it a good time to find his hat and sack and press on. They were already walking toward him, up the slope, albeit methodically, with soft steps as if other things might be wakened from the immediate earth. They were woodsmen, their kits and axes in a heap by the road. The sun behind them was lifting the dew into steam and their every footfall raised breathlike puffs of mist from the ground.

Suddenly dizzy, Peter slumped against the oak and pressed a hand against the gash on his head. When he raised his head, the men were within ten feet of him and the dead buck. It had been an astonishing sight, for the animal was as large a deer as any of them had seen, and Peter had sprung from nowhere. His face was ashen where it wasn't dark and wet with blood.

"Did the ball crease you?" asked one of the men, suspiciously. He was gray and his teeth were mostly gone.

"No, thank you," said Peter. "It was the buck."

The men frowned, clearly laboring to interpret Peter's statement. The older man held his left arm before him and spit over it, which action was considered among the older folk to be as good a ward against faerie and witch people as could be got at short notice. Peter considered telling the man about turning one's coat inside out, but thought the fellow might not take his word for it just then.

The other younger man was a tall, broad-shouldered, round-faced fellow with straw-colored hair sprouting from beneath his hat. "*What* was the buck?" he asked. They were a little less nervous, having heard Peter speak like a real person, but they were eyeing him carefully, as well as the ground about, *and* their means of quick retreat.

"I was bedded up in those leaves," said Peter, and as evidence of this he reached for his hat, a corner of which he could see in the pile.

"You were asleep there?" said the first man. "On the other side of this buck?"

Peter nodded.

"We didn't know you were there," said the older man, which he may have considered necessary to state, if self-evident under the circumstances. His head made a nodding motion, indicating either the place where Peter had lain, or some expectation of Peter's agreement on the subject.

Peter felt giddy and couldn't understand why they didn't come forward to help him with his wounds; but they only stood by and watched him warily. When he sat down against the tree with a small groan, they did take a step or two in his direction, and the older man carefully prodded the great buck's side.

"Felled him like a hammer," said the bigger fellow, when the creature showed no sign of life. He knelt beside the deer, then glanced up at Peter, as if the young man might demonstrate signs of anger or propriety concerning the animal. They had not yet gotten used to the idea that he hadn't simply sprung from the buck as it drew its last breath.

"What's in the sack?" asked the gray-haired man.

Peter was puzzled by the question. He was more concerned with what was left in his head. He looked at his hand, thinking that he may have stanched the blood. "Biscuits and apples," he said finally.

From his expression, the older man might have doubted it. He was looking at the sack, clearly wondering if it held the answer to Peter's sudden appearance, as if Peter was a witch with potions and spells in his bag. The old man raised the muzzle of his gun in Peter's direction without conscious motive. The younger woods-man caught sight of the movement and looked with wide blue eyes from Peter's face to the musket and back again.

They were then all three startled by a new voice that said, *"He was a mighty hunter before the Lord: wherefore it is said, Even as Nimrod the mighty hunter before the Lord.'"* A rider had come over the slope, his approach hidden by the width of the oak and the de-gree of their distraction; but now he ambled his mount to a point some ten or fifteen paces above them, and as he reined up, he leaned over the animal's withers.

The gray-haired man raised his musket like a bar before him, and the other woodsman stood with his own weapon pointing groundward, but poised with his thumb against the cock.

The rider was long and gaunt, with a large nose and a humor-ous twist to his mouth. He wore no hat and his queue was bound in a ribbon with no attempt at tidiness. The horse was of English stock, as brown as the buck, tall, broad-backed, and massively hooved. The tails of the man's blue wool great-coat spilled past the animal's flanks.

"Genesis ten, nine," said the gray-haired woodsman, who

might have had enough of the old religion to spar verses. Nimrod was a mysterious figure to men of the woods, alluded to but once in scripture and often linked in legend with strange figures that wandered the forests; the old man was not less troubled for the mention of him.

The rider seemed to know this, for he grinned at the old man, then dropped easily from the back of the horse and lifted the hoop of a leather bottle from the pommel of his saddle.

"There are more folk about than I would have credited," said the younger woodsman.

"I wouldn't have credited *this* fellow," agreed the rider, indicating Peter with a nod and almost a laugh. "I was watching the two of you from over in those woods." He pointed south to a line of trees. "As clean a shot as ever I witnessed. But when this fellow sprang up from his bed—!" He found a handkerchief in a pocket and pulled the wooden stopper from the bottle as he walked around the trunk of the oak.

The woodsmen stepped back, though they were not in his way. "You saw him, then?" asked the gray-haired man. "You saw him come out of that pile?"

"Like Adam out of the Earth!" stated the rider. "Did you think he climbed out of the hole you put in that buck?" He doused the linen with water and applied it to Peter's forehead.

"I wasn't too sure," returned the old man, which—from the look on his face—was more straightforward an expression than he had intended.

Peter had been listening to this small conversation as from another room, but the gaunt fellow's touch drew him out of his daze; he flinched a little as the tall man washed the blood from his head. "You weren't any more surprised than I," said Peter. He realized that he had been gazing at the warm coat of the deer, and the hole at the base of the animal's neck, dark with blood. He looked up at the man who had fired the killing shot. Beyond the woodsman, beyond the road and the river, he could see the glistening tops of the trees and a broken column of smoke—rising from someone's house, no doubt—in the distance.

"You've saved yourself the *hire* of a leech, at any rate," said the horseman, and this time he smiled broadly, as from some private humor. "Now hold that tight and see if the bleeding will stop." He pressed the handkerchief to the wound and placed Peter's hand atop it.

The older woodsman had a way of squinting his eyes when someone spoke, as if he could squeeze his concentration of mind into his ears; Peter thought he must be a little deaf. "It was all of an accident," said the gray-haired man. "We didn't know he was there."

"Peter won't hold it against you," said the tall horseman simply.

"You know my name," said Peter, when the man stood.

"You called it out loud enough," said the man.

"I did," agreed Peter. He had forgotten.

"My name is Zachariah Leach," said the horseman, and here the reason for his previous humor was revealed. He reached his hand over the dead buck.

The gray-haired man took the offered hand carefully. "I've heard the name," he said. "Are you the saddle preacher?"

"I testify to the Grace of God and seldom the same place two days in succession. Praise him that made us and the new republic! We can bind up a litter for the deer, and for some sweetbreads and liver," and here Zachariah Leach nodded to his horse, "I'll talk Mars into lugging that buck wherever you want it."

5

How Peter Fell in with Parson Leach

THE GRAY-HAIRED WOODSMAN WAS MANASSEH CUTTS AND THE LARGER,
younger man was Crispin Moss. They retrieved their kits, and one
of them had a rope with which to hang the buck from the oak.
Once they had dressed and strung the carcass, they followed Parson Leach over the hill to his banked coals at the edge of the trees
to the west. The parson might have owned the woods, he was so
like a gracious host—inviting them into a shallow depression where
he had camped the night before. A thick bedroll and two heavy
saddlebags lay as bed and pillow between the fire and the trunk
of an old pine. Leaning against the tree was an old firing piece and
a powder horn.

The woodsmen brought the buck's liver and sweetbread and
soon these were crackling over a lively fire. Still holding the cloth
to his head, Peter produced, with his free hand, the hard biscuits
and apples from his pack. The parson went to a nearby stream to
refresh his bottle, and when he returned, he surprised them with
four brown eggs from one of his bags.

"My hostess of yesterday boiled them hard for travel," he explained, before tossing one each to his companions. "No more
than is called for, as it happens."

Cutts and Moss had waited for Peter to sit down before settling themselves opposite him; they were a little chary of his contribution to the table as well, till Parson Leach broke into a "Northern Spy" with a wet snap. It was a tart apple, with yellow spots where the sun had rarely touched it, but it was firm to the tooth and its skin was tough and handsome. Cutts and Moss watched the clergyman relish its sour qualities and savor its juices as he chewed. Absently, Crispin Moss peeled and ate his egg.

Parson Leach reflected their attention with his own wry amusement. "It's a rare country can make an apple like that," he said.

The woodsmen didn't know how rare the country was, but in October, with the weather still mild and the harvest about the scattered farms and the game on the move through the surrounding wilderness, they did not readily argue with him.

"My grandfather planted the slip those apples grew from," said Peter with some pleasure. "It's almost this broad, now." He held his hands apart.

" *'For thus saith the Lord of hosts'* " quoted the preacher, " *'After the glory hath he sent me unto the nations which spoiled you; for he that toucheth you toucheth the apple of his eye.'* " He did not look directly at Manasseh Cutts, but some share of his study was pointedly fixed upon the man.

Manasseh was thinking hard, but only said, "Zechariah," and there was a smallish sound of defeat in his voice.

"Yes, Zechariah," said the parson. "But I cannot tell you chapter and verse," he admitted happily enough. "Your people were of the old church," he added simply.

"I don't take much from them," admitted Manasseh, "but the memory of old men sparring text."

The tall clergyman nodded. It was the Puritan reputation that no one could better play the contest of *"Chapter and Verse."*

Crispin Moss had finished his egg and was partway through the apple Peter had given him before he stopped and peered at the fruit doubtfully. He looked at Peter with a frown of concentration, then his face lightened into a philosophical smile and he took another bite. Manasseh Cutts watched all this with some interest, but he elected, for the moment, to slip his own apple into a pocket.

The preacher stirred up the coals and raised some flames with wood that he had gathered the evening before; then the victuals were put on sticks and roasted over the fire with a great deal of snapping and appetizing smells.

The day was in full flourish and the sun over the trees across the river had nudged the late crickets into song, soft at first, and few, and never more than a person might imagine he could count. They heard ducks overhead, though they couldn't sight them.

They each, in turn, left this interesting distraction to consider the fire and the meats again, and with some degree of caution, Manasseh said "You're not of the Congregation, preaching on a horse."

"I have ties to no particular creed, these days," said Parson Leach amiably.

"There are a deal too many of them, I dare say," returned the old woodsman.

"The Congregationalists despair of a man who cannot himself *read* chapter and verse," said the preacher, seemingly in agreement, "and the backwoods fellow and the lay-preacher have no use for anyone who hasn't been struck by God like lightning."

This talk was a little beyond Peter's grasp. His mother, who had always displayed little patience with the struggle between proprietors and settlers, and therefore with their respective religions, had kept her family away from church for the most part, though Peter's father had read to them from the Bible on Sundays and taught Peter and his siblings to read some from it themselves.

"You *peddle* books," said the old man, which was not offered as an accusation as much as it was evidence that Zachariah Leach might be more Congregationalist than otherwise.

Peter was surprised that a preacher peddled anything.

"A man might be struck by lightning *and* read a book, as far as I know," said the parson. "A chapter or two of Izaak Walton supplied you those eggs, and more besides."

"I don't know him," said the old man with a frown.

Again the parson quoted, but from another source. *"'Angling is something like poetry, men are to be born so.'* I recently brought some books to George Swain up to Winslow. He has lately taken up angling himself and needed instruction." The name Winslow, though in reference to a settlement, pricked at Peter's ears.

"This George Swain must be a Great Man, or a land agent, if he has leisure to mull over books or fish for sport," said Manasseh Cutts. Parson Leach laughed, which was mysterious to Peter, and Manasseh quickly added, "I take no sides in the matter, and neither does Crispin," but he had perhaps revealed his prejudice.

"Don't you?" said Parson Leach, still with his odd humor. "I dare say I sin in taking sides against whomever I talk to. The Great Men may have the law on their sides and the settlers may have justice, which is what I told George Swain and he scowled at me as neatly as you."

As a matter of principle, Manasseh did not leave off his scowl, but the light of something more agreeable touched the corners of his mouth; indeed, it seemed that he had met a man of similar independence, which surprised him in a preacher. "Ah, well," he said, "I fish, when I do fish, to fill my stomach, but it's not a poor way to pass the morning."

Peter had never met anyone like Parson Leach, unless it were his mother Rosemund Loon herself; there seemed almost an intemperate amount of jest in the man, and Peter could imagine that the parson did take pleasure in battling both sides of a quarrel. "I'm looking for a man named Winslow," said Peter, before he knew he was going to say it. "Obed Winslow," he added when their attention turned to him. "I'm told he's an uncle of mine."

"There *was* an Obed Winslow," said Crispin Moss, which were almost his first words since they gathered near the fire, "up at Bryant's Ridge, near where I was raised." He gathered in the thread of his memory. "But that was back when I was half your age," he finished.

"I don't think my family has seen him for some years," said Peter hopefully, and he told them how his father had died, and how he came to be looking for a man he had never even heard of the day before.

"Ah," said Crispin as something new occurred to him. "It was probably another man. Maybe it wasn't *Obed* Winslow." He made a show of turning the meats in the fire.

"Maybe I should go there," said Peter. "Where's Bryant's Ridge?"

"Northeast," said Manasseh.

"He's dead now, at any rate," said Crispin quickly, but glancing up at Peter, he could see clearly enough that this Winslow's story was called for. "This fellow," he continued, "I don't know that it was *Obed* Winslow, after all—but he took leave of a young girl without her consent, or even her father's, I guess, because they ran him down and I can't remember if he was shot on the chase or caught and hung afterwards. It was a while ago. I was a lad myself, as I say, and I was only told about it."

Peter looked uncertain. "My mother pointed down this way, toward Patricktown, when she showed me where he went."

"She pointed, did she?" said Manasseh Cutts.

"If you came down from Great Pond, you've already passed Patricktown," said Parson Leach.

"Have I?"

"The Balltown line is only half a mile or so down river," said Manasseh.

"I know Patricktown somewhat," said the preacher, "but haven't heard of any Winslows there."

"It seems my mother would have heard of him, if he was just the next settlement over," offered Peter.

"It does seem. Where are you fellows toting that buck?"

"Just across the river, near to Plymouth Gore," said the older man. "Crispin has family there, who'll take us in if we have venison to offer."

"We will have to carry it over the water, but Mars will pull it the rest of the way."

The woodsmen, particular Manasseh, still considered Peter with some wariness, but they had grown used to the preacher. They nodded, though they shot questioning looks toward Peter.

"Peter Loon," said Parson Leach. "You come along with Mars and me. I know as many folk as anyone you're liable to meet in such an accident, and we'll spread inquiries regarding this uncle of yours. I would just as soon discover that he hadn't been hanged, or shot, or hadn't known some poor girl unlawfully—and I can't bare to miss the end of a tale, once it's started."

Again, Peter was aware of that odd humor in the preacher's words. He hadn't any other place to go, however, if there weren't any Winslows to be had in Patricktown. He'd considered turning around and going home for his father's burial, which might have been prudent; but he was troubled a little to face his mother with no more to tell her than a rumor. She had been so very strange. He'd walked further than he would have guessed, too, and the adventurous sense of being so far from home kindled something in him; or perhaps it was the revivifying smell of liver and sweetbread smoking over the fire.

They would be awake now, his family. Amos would ask their mother where Peter had got to. Perhaps he would fear that Peter had died like their father. There came that clutch at Peter's insides again. He looked up from the flames at the parson and realized that the man had seen something dark briefly span his face.

6

Of the March to Plymouth Gore, and
of the Place They Went Instead

"ARE THOSE YOUR WARES?" MANASSEH CUTTS ASKED PARSON LEACH, when the preacher lifted his heavy saddlebags over the horse's back.

"They are. Do you read?"

"Enough," said the old man.

Now that Peter thought of it, there *had* been a tinker, once, who preached when called on; the man had passed through when Peter was nine or ten years old; but Peter had never known a preacher who peddled goods, and besides that, the thought of owning books other than the family Bible or the odd copy of *Pilgrim's Progress* was a strange one to the young man. Apparently Parson Leach had recently sold a book about fishing to someone named George Swain. The notion that someone would write a book about such a simple pursuit was stranger still. Perhaps he had misunderstood. Christ, he knew, had called his disciples "fishers of men," and Peter believed, as they walked back to the river, that this must be the subject of the book in question.

They brought saplings and pine boughs out of the woods and beneath the oak, the carcass of the buck hung, they put together a litter. The preacher was clever at this and Crispin remarked that he learned a knot or two watching him.

"Learned them myself, on shipboard," was all the preacher said in reply.

They tied the litter behind Mars on the way to the river, but took it themselves, one to a corner, as they crossed the stepping stones to the eastern shore in careful measures. Mars forded the river without command from Parson Leach, and shook the water from his sides before trotting friskily before the woods like a colt.

Soon they had the litter hitched to him again, and they entered the road that Peter had come out on; but half a mile or so along this track they turned east onto a path he had not seen in the predawn.

Parson Leach was content to walk; his stride was longer than even Peter's, who was a tall boy, and consequently the clergyman found his gait interrupted frequently as he and Mars paused to wait for their fellow travelers.

A breeze tugged at the bright hardwoods in the little valleys and the thickly needled pines and firs along the stonier ridges, and the fallish chatter of stay-in-winter birds filled the branchy acres. The smaller rills ran quietly or not at all after a thirsty summer, and the low places, where marshy conditions often hindered a traveler's progress, were hardly spongy.

"This Walton who writes about fish," said Crispin Moss, not long after they passed near one of these sun-dried beds, "is he a man you know, that you peddle his book?"

"Not at all," said the preacher. "He lived and loved in England, and died a hundred years ago and more." Parson Leach needed little encouragement, it seemed, regarding his books, and as they walked he fished a copy of the *Compleat Angler* from one of Mars's saddlebags. He produced a pair of spectacles from a pocket in his cloak and he wrapped the ends of these around his ears so that they sat on his prominent nose. Soon he was regaling them with a lively debate upon the relative merits of fishing, hunting, and falconry as defended, in turn, by Piscator, Venator, and Auceps. And he passed the book around when he came to an illustration of one or the other of these fellows at their occupation.

Peter and the woodsmen were, at first, a little puzzled by the discourse, but soon Cutts and Moss were expressing their opinions alongside the dialogue with various grunts and wordless exclamations. When the hunter in the book said (and this in the preacher's rich tones) "And now let us go to an honest ale-house, where we may have a cup of barley-wine, and sing *Old Rose*..." Manasseh actually laughed.

"There's a hunter's head for you!" he said. "The tavern at the end of the chase! I think I like this Venator better than your fisherman, Parson, though I wouldn't know a barley-wine and would be satisfied with hot rum or even brown ale." Then he surprised them by singing several verses of *Old Rose* in a very passable voice.

Parson Leach returned the book to its saddlebag when the prospect of a small pond opened up before them; Traveler's Pond, Manasseh called it. They heard ducks again, and Peter thought, for a time, that the woodsmen would veer from their path and try their luck at more hunting. Parson Leach looked to have thoughts on roast duck, as well. They peered out from a natural blind, over the leaf-littered surface of the water, and Peter caught sight of a muskrat leaving his arrowlike wake across the pond to pierce a crowd of lily-pads.

They did not linger, however; instead, they crossed south of the pond over Brann Brook and skirted this and a smaller pond, as they followed a deer path east and a little south. At a further extremity of the same brook, they crossed again, and at the top of a short, granity knoll they took a bearing on Haskell Hill about a mile away, then continued through a close wood, more or less in that direction. Mars balked once or twice and there was nothing for it but that Cutts and Moss must widen the trail for him.

"He's not a battering ram, after all," concurred Parson Leach, who lent a hand in beating down the underbrush.

Peter had never seen or heard of a *battering* ram, but could easily imagine a large, broad-horned goat. Fortunately, they came to another wood path about halfway to Haskell Hill and such a creature's good office was rendered unnecessary.

About mid-morning they stopped on a hill, where the recent windfall of an old scratch pine had opened a bit of sky and let sunlight onto a patch of ground, which was thick and soft with needles. Mars dragged the litter a few yards away, where some moss took his fancy. They had water and Peter passed around the last of his hard biscuits. He was just tasting one himself, when it occurred to him that his father had cooked them and that he would never taste anything from his father's hand in this life again. His heart was suddenly leaden and his breath came with difficulty.

The woodsmen had relaxed their guard against Peter by this time; Manasseh Cutts had wavered first of all, but Crispin Moss, when he dropped his wariness, did so wholeheartedly. The bigger fellow had found his voice and was telling them about a bobcat he once met while stepping out of a privy. Peter hardly heard the tale. The biscuit seemed dry and without flavor.

Parson Leach leaned forward with his leather water bottle and offered it to him, saying, "That'll do you good."

Peter wondered what the preacher could know about his thoughts, but thanked the man.

"He was chasing a bird," said Crispin Moss, "like a kitten, and I promise you, that bird was having fun with him."

The mention of the bird made Peter oddly conscious of the chirps and chatter in the woods about them. The first sip of water did more than slake his thirst; it lent savor to the bit of biscuit in his mouth. He took another sip, then another morsel and the weight in his chest seemed to lift just a little.

Something else was said about birds, and Crispin Moss asked them "Have you ever seen this?" then cupping one hand in the other, he put them to his lips and made an odd sound, as if he were kissing the back of his fist. His eyes shone like a child's as he flashed his gaze along the tops of the surrounding trees.

Almost immediately there was a change in the quality of bird-sound; the birds nearabouts grew excited, then louder, as they approached Crispin Moss and increased in number. Chickadees and sparrows and redpoles flitted in from the surrounding hills and groves.

A trio of chickadees behind and above the woodsman's big head looked so humanly curious that Peter almost laughed aloud. Crispin continued to make the kissing noise at the back of his hand and the birds were further emboldened. Several dropped onto the ground and hopped among the men, cocking their heads from side to side, flicking their tails in the pools of sunlight. When Crispin did leave off the noise the creatures stayed for a moment or two, looking startled to find themselves there before retreating to the nearby trees. From these safe heights, they set up a chorus of scolds and slowly dispersed into the forest and returned to their previous concerns.

"I've seen an Indian do that," said Manasseh Cutts, who was the first to stand.

"I learned it from an Indian," returned Crispin Moss. He seemed pleased with the trick. "Just a little fellow; hardly came to my belt."

"He wouldn't have to be very little," said the parson.

The conversation was continued on foot, with Crispin Moss leading the way. Peter hardly felt rested; accustomed as he was to long hours tending field or cutting wood, he was not used to walking such distances and though he was a hard muscled lad, his feet and shanks were beginning to flag beneath him. But Parson Leach asked Peter to tell them about his father, and the young man forgot his sore muscles and his fatigue as he recalled Silas Loon to his companions.

They rounded Haskell Hill to the east, and from another height found a plain view over the northeastern settlement of Balltown and the lake known as Great Bay.

"*There's* a place we should ask after your uncle," suggested Parson Leach.

The woodsmen loathed to lose the horse's helpful labor, but it was not much further to Crispin's relatives, so the two men released the animal of Parson Leach's promise. Parson Leach was thankful for his horse's sake, and the older woodsman allowed, in a wry manner, that the creature had worked enough for his master's word.

Manasseh and Crispin had reconciled themselves to Peter and shook his hand; they considered that he had proven himself mortal enough, after all, having had the good sense not to grow fins and disappear into a stream, or wings and leap from a hill.

" 'Good company and good discourse are the very sinews of virtue,' " said the parson before Manasseh Cutts and Crispin Moss turned east again. "Those are more words from Mr. Walton."

"He was a wise man," said Manasseh Cutts, perhaps wryly, before leaving, "even *did* he write books." He insisted that the parson and Peter Loon take a cut of the buck's thigh. "It'll make you more than welcome at the tavern down yonder," he said, and though he was glad enough to be shaken of the young man who had appeared to spring full grown from the fallen creature, he inquired of Peter's wounds before he left and wished him well. The preacher hung the deer thigh at his saddle and climbed onto Mars with a small groan.

And so Peter Loon did not go to Patricktown, or even Plymouth Gore, that day, but accompanied Parson Leach and Mars around and down a series of small hills to the settlement on the shores of Great Bay in the part of the district known as Balltown. They flushed a partridge on one of these slopes and Peter was startled from a weary daze by the creature's sudden noisy flight.

There were about ten or twelve sizable buildings in the settlement, and as many small outbuildings and privies. Peter could see no church, or at least no building attempting to look like a church—no spire or high windowed nave. The street took a dog-leg to the right and there were two or three more buildings nearer the shore of the wide lake.

It was not Parson Leach's first visit to the hamlet, as was made evident when they approached the single dirt street and he re-marked that there were more people about than he had seen there before. He had, in fact, preached there on several occasions, which was evidenced by the greetings hailed to him by passersby, or more accurately lingerers round about the tavern in the midst of the little hamlet.

"Souls or sovereigns will it be, Reverend Leach?" wondered one wag, who may have seen a book or two, even if he had never read one.

As they neared the center of the settlement, Peter could sense the giddy air of important business that riles people who lurk along the periphery of understanding to foolish behavior. Two or three young men approached the parson to inquire if he had come into town because of the rumors flying about. "I don't seek after rumor, as a general thing," was his reply.

"Do you think we'll be to war again?" wondered another.

"What, have the British come up river?" returned the parson, but Peter could see the man's interest was up. "The last I heard, peace was signed, eighteen years hence, but I've been in the woods a fair bit." There were enough horses and carts about that the few hitching posts in town were occupied and the parson tied Mars to the railing of the little porch outside the village tavern.

"It's our own Great Men come up the river, you might say," said the first young fellow. Two or three older, more sober-faced gentlemen came up to the tavern stoop to see what the ruckus was.

"You surprise me," said the parson simply, indicating something opposite by his expression. "But Peter, here, and I would share out some of this thigh," he informed the congregants outside the tavern, indicating the portion over Peter's shoulder, "if there were a man with the price of the beer and victuals to go with it. And that man would have the doubled pleasure of telling us all the fox-talk and rumor hereabouts and why you're all gathered here, if not to hear me preach."

7

*How Peter Loon and Parson Leach Were Received
at the Ale Wife's Tavern, Who They Met,
and What They Learned There*

THE ESTABLISHMENT BEFORE THEM WAS KNOWN AS THE ALE WIFE'S
tavern, though some simply called it the Fish Wife. Above the
door there hung a sign, painted with the image of an alewife, a
common enough fish thereabouts in the spring and early summer,
though this one was dressed as an old woman, with a bonnet and
rolling pin besides. Peter gaped at the sign while he approached
the door, but was soon taken by the sight of Parson Leach's long,
gaunt frame entering the premises before him. He was then more
conscious of the preacher's height and his broad shoulders as the
man followed three respectable looking fellows inside, and Peter
marked the unexpected ease with which the parson moved his
lanky form.

The young man thought then to take the deer thigh with him,
since it appeared to be the expense for their meal; he trudged up
the tavern steps and into the dark interior.

There was a single broad room in front, with immense beams
crowding low over the rough tables. Stools and a few chairs
ranked these trencher-boards, and nothing was very far in con-
struction from the raw wood as it had come from the sawmill.

There was a broad fireplace at the other end of the room, but the fire was left small during an October day like this, and Peter could see a puff of steam when he let out a deep breath. He smelled something cooking, however, and guessed that the hearth taking up the backside of the chimney would be livelier as the evening meal was prepared.

A man appeared in the doorway to the rear of the tavern and acknowledged the new patrons with a wave. "Knock this fire up," he said to someone behind him, then he stepped forward and spoke cordially to his guests. "How be you, Mr. Leach."

"Hungry, Mr. Tillage. We've some venison we'd trouble you to cook, and those that share it with us will throw in for the dinner to go round it, if you please."

Tillage met them halfway across the tavern floor and shook the parson's hand before taking the leg from Peter. "I've some pies and a thick soup cooking, and should I carve this up fine enough, it'll all be ready before you're much more hungry." He hardly glanced at Peter, but took in the other men accompanying them. "Take the table by the hearth," he suggested. "It's cold as church in here, now, but Nora will stoke the fire and we'll have it sociable before you know it."

Peter then noticed a girl kneeling before the fireplace. She was a thin creature with straight russet hair falling carelessly from beneath her cap. Her pale dress—more of a shift, with an old cloth belt around the middle—was a little large for her and more of a summer garment than something to wear when winter was on so close an approach. She stirred the coals and stacked kindling wood over them, then took a crude pair of bellows and blew up the flames, leaning close to the fire as if she were glad for a warm task.

The girl looked over her shoulder for a moment, not regarding anyone in particular, but Peter saw that she was older than he had thought—a young woman, really, rather than a girl—and closer to his own age, perhaps. Peter was used to the look of hunger in the faces of children. Life in the backcountry was backbreaking and more often than not hand-to-mouth; it was a common enough practice, though by no means universal in those parts, to feed the parents and older children first, as they were the workers who kept the farm neck-above failure. Younger children learned quickly the art of scouring the dinner table once their elders retired, and scoured the countryside as well for the odd rabbit they might snare, for berries, and even birch bark when there was nothing else.

But Peter had lived with the notion that a tavern keeper's household was fat and jolly, and he was moved by the small, serious features, the high forehead and the large blue eyes before the young woman returned to her chore. She had not looked behind her above a moment or two.

A few more things were said between the taverner and his guests before Tillage turned back and disappeared into the kitchen with the leg of venison. Peter lifted his hands and he had blood from the venison on them.

"Follow him and there'll be a tub to wash your hands in," suggested the parson.

Peter felt awkward and out of place, not knowing anyone, and never having been inside a tavern before. He did follow Mr. Tillage, however, and was directed to a bucket and a rain barrel just outside the back door. When he returned, chilled by the cold ablution, Mr. Tillage inquired where Peter hailed from.

"Sheepscott Great Pond," said Peter. Nora, the young woman at the fire, came in then and went out past him for an armload of wood. She gave Peter only a glance, and he looked after her for a moment before volunteering "Should I help bring in some wood?"

Mr. Tillage glanced into the corner to Peter's right, as quickly as a stone skips on water. Then he turned back to the venison, which he was cutting up, and said "If you like."

Peter followed Tillage's quick look and was surprised to see a dark-haired and bearded man sitting in the corner by himself.

"This is Nathan Barrow," said the taverner. "Mr. Barrow, this is . . ."

"Peter Loon." The young man was half out the door, but he looked back at the man in the corner and nodded. Nathan Barrow only stared back, but like a man who is not sure he sees well. He was a medium sort of fellow with an unpleasant expression on his hairy face, such as one might wear if he smelled something bad, or was bound up in the privy.

Peter stepped out into the sun, drying his hands against his breeches. Beyond another building and a narrow field, he could see the lake. To his left there was a crude lean-to and a neat pile of wood. The young woman was just finishing the stack in one arm. She looked strong enough, despite her thin carriage, as she hefted the load in both arms. When she turned, Peter found himself nodding to her, almost as an extension of the nod he had given to Nathan Barrow, but he averted his gaze and stepped aside for her. He looked back at Nora as he approached the woodpile, wondering what was so obviously feminine about her narrow bones in that shapeless shift. When she passed him this second

53

time, he caught a glance of her wrist and thought he could span it with his thumb and forefinger.

"There are a great lot of sinful men up to Sheepscott Great Pond," said Nathan Barrow to Peter when the young man nudged open the door with his shoulder. He had taken a stick or two too many and was in fear of losing the balance of his load and looking a fool.

"There are?" he said, for lack of any other response. "When were you there?" he asked.

"I've never been," said Barrow, but with an odd degree of indifference in his voice. "That's why I know."

Peter could hardly make sense of this statement as he hurried back into the tavern room.

"Put you to work, did they," said Parson Leach.

Peter lay the wood upon the small stack beside the hearth as carefully and quietly as possible. He straightened a tipping length or two, then brushed the dirt and loose bark from his shirtfront. Nora, who was feeding the lengthening flames, turned her face up hardly an inch, and without looking at Peter, said, "thank you," so quietly that he almost didn't hear her.

He nodded some more, then retreated to the nearest table, where the preacher and three other men sat and several others gathered round. Once she had the fire snapping, Nora returned to the kitchen.

"I heard they stripped him clean," one of these bystanders was saying, "and strapped his arse with branch bundles till he brayed like an ass himself."

"I heard they left him a sock and a sleeve," said one of the men at the table. "And Isaac Prince told him, 'Never let it be said we left a man naked, like some we know have done.'"

The first man laughed at this, and there were any number of reactions round the long table. Parson Leach made a face that a parent might make at a child who behaves foolishly.

"How do you think it will fall out down there?" wondered another man aloud.

"I always thought the Barrows had more claim than Knox and those among them. It's not old Tory land, but Indian deeds, though mixed up with one another, one deed contradicting the next, to keep the courts busy for years."

"But they do lay claim, and Prince was served a formal writ, though he tore it up and says he's never seen it."

"Do they know down in Wiscasset that it was Prince?" wondered Parson Leach.

"They all blackened their faces," said the first man sitting at the table, "but Jemmy Bligh came in this morning and said that Trueman recognized Isaac's voice and could place a dozen others."

Peter listened to this conversation and it was not long before he was able to piece together the story that these men were so anxious to tell Parson Leach, and the reason for such a crowd hanging about the tavern.

First of all, he understood that *White Indians* had been abroad in the settlement of New Milford; *White Indians* was the epithet given to any group of settlers ganging together to raise each other's ire against the Proprietors who claimed great tracts and miles of land based on the grants of King George and his antecedents, or in the light of Indian deeds. The latter, it had been argued, might be considered null with every other agreement with the Indians, and to be reneged upon; the former declared void since King George and all his rule and law had been driven out of the country these eighteen years past.

The White Indians were not always content to fan each other's anger with talk and rum, however, and if any of the proprietors or their agents were more active than usual in pursuit of their suits, violence was almost sure to erupt. One John Trueman, as the story was told, had discovered this truth the hard way, and upon serving a writ of summons to Isaac Prince in New Milford, he was stripped, beaten, and sent home for his troubles.

All about the surrounding countryside—miles beyond the limits of New Milford—in tavern and meeting house, church and den, there would be men and women gathered to discuss the meaning of this new instance of revolt.

More details of the incident were laid out, till Parson Leach leaned back and said, "You know a lot about the whole business. There weren't some of you boys among them were there?"

"No, no," said one, clearly troubled by the notion.

"Upon my word!" said another.

"There ain't none of us been to New Milford for a thing, Mr. Leach, and that's the God's honest truth. But Nathan Barrow came last night and told us all about it."

"Barrow!" said Parson Leach. "What's Barrow to do with it all?"

"He drove them to it, if you believe the man," said someone.

"Do you think?" said the preacher dryly, for obviously *he* could easily imagine it. "Is he still hereabouts?"

"He's in the kitchen," said Peter.

Parson Leach looked surprised. "Do you know the man, Peter?"

"Not at all," said Peter, and glad to deny it. He recalled what Barrow had said about sinners in Sheepscott Great Pond. "Mr. Tillage just introduced him to me."

"Did he?" said the parson.

And then, as if having heard his name—and perhaps he had—Nathan Barrow opened the door from the kitchen and stepped into the tavern room. Peter was surprised to see the young woman Nora standing behind Barrow, watching his back soberly. She put a hand up to pull aside a lock of red-brown hair. She had a spray of freckles across her nose.

Barrow was dressed well enough, though nothing seemed quite put together on him. One leg of his breeches was torn at the thigh, and his stockings were dirty. He was of medium height and broadly built at the shoulders. He had a sure way of moving that had nothing to do with Parson Leach's easy manner; he stepped up to the occupied table without expression on his face, and regarded the preacher for a moment before speaking. "Mr. Leach," said Barrow. "Have you come to preach to these people? They are quite beyond it, I promise you."

Some in the room looked discomforted as Barrow spoke.

"They're good indeed, if a sermon is of no use to them," said Parson Leach wryly.

"Sinners learn nothing from a sinner," said Barrow with conviction.

The rest of the room was silent, and men at the periphery of conversation were looking to see if they could drift away.

Parson Leach did not blink at this, but said simply, "I have heard your creed, Mr. Barrow."

"It is the creed of Christ, Mr. Leach," said Barrow with slightly more heat.

"I have but your word for it, sir," said Parson Leach. He barely shifted in his seat, but suddenly Barrow seemed at a disadvantage, as if he had been deigned an audience with the preacher.

Peter would quickly understand that Nathan Barrow was himself a self-styled preacher, and more besides, if he were to be believed, for he claimed a terrific vision of Heaven and Hell and that his guide had been none other the Lord himself. "It is *the* creed, I promise you," said Barrow.

"It is a creed the apostles did without," added Parson Leach.

"I care nothing about the apostles," said Barrow, losing his previous mein to a sneer.

"Nor the Word of God itself, if I am to understand you. *'If any man shall add unto these things, God shall add unto him the plagues that are written in this book.'*"

"Nor *your* Word of God."

Parson Leach hardly stirred. "Well, the *written* Word is of little use to a man with no letters," he pronounced.

"You sound like a good Congregationalist," answered Barrow, and his sneer deepened. If the insinuation that he could not read bothered him, he hid his feelings well.

"I say it with no shame that the Congregation and I share the same word," said Parson Leach, "though we may quibble over its details, now and again."

"You'll have time enough to quibble, Mr. Leach, in Hell."

The men surrounding the table had grown increasingly distressed as this conversation progressed, and two or three men gasped to hear Parson Leach spoken to in this manner—all the more so since several of them had taken Nathan Barrow's vision and his continued revelations to heart.

Then Zachariah Leach said, with renewed humor, "I would rather think that you and I both, Mr. Barrow, will have opportunity to quibble in paradise." This was said with such real good feeling, and it was such a surprise, that several at the table chuckled softly. "The Lord is a powerful deity, Mr. Barrow," said Parson Leach with the sound of summing up, "and I warrant his plans are big enough for you and me and a great deal more."

Mr. Tillage made an appearance, then, with a tray full of mugs and tankards and his feet hurrying beneath him; and he appeared to have ambivalent feelings about such a debate in his tavern, between Nathan Barrow and a paying customer. It was an opportune moment for Barrow, however, and he left the table for his own against the wall, where it must have been a good deal cooler. Nora went with him and Peter and Parson Leach were each startled, not to say alarmed, to see her sit close beside the man with the sort of attention toward him that a wife might display if she were very young—which Nora was—and very reticent.

The tavern keeper followed Barrow to his table and laid down a tankard before the man.

"That is your daughter, Mr. Tillage?" said Parson Leach, when the taverner had returned.

"Nora? Yes, Mr. Leach, she is." Tillage was serving the clergyman without looking at him very directly.

"Are she and Mr. Barrow married?" asked the preacher.

"Not a bit, sir," said Tillage.

"Intended, then?"

"No, Mr. Leach, she's only under his wing, so to speak. His tutelage in God, as he calls it."

"I'm sure he does," said the parson quietly. All eyes glanced toward the other table. Barrow was watching them. Nora was staring into the middle distances. She looked, to Peter, resigned, and perhaps even content.

Tillage looked determined about something, of a sudden, but only about not answering further questions it seemed, for when he had finished serving the other men he turned and left the room without another word.

8

*Concerning a Conversation on the Beach, and the
Consequences of Mr. Tillage's Peep of Heaven*

PETER'S HEAD FAILED HIM FOR A WHILE AND HE DOZED WITH HIS
wounded scalp throbbing from the exertions of the day.

The conversation had steered from the White Indians and
events down in New Milford. With Barrow in the room no one
seemed comfortable with the subject, and other matters came to
roost which proved convivial because of Parson Leach's determination that it should not be otherwise and despite Barrow's occasional stare.

Peter roused himself easily enough, however, when an early
supper was served. He had rarely eaten so well, and the ale made
his head swim. More men had come into the tavern by that time
and, amidst the noise, a carefully modulated conversation could
return to previous concerns. The business of John Trueman, the
harried land agent, was gone over again and further opinions expounded whether the business would serve to incite one side or
the other, and who would most regret it.

Parson Leach was circumspect with his opinions, though he
did not look happy whenever the tale of the unfortunate John
Trueman was related, and he even winced when some new detail
concerning the man's brutal treatment was recalled.

"You went to war yourself, once, Mr. Leach," said one older gentleman.

"Yes, I did, Mr. Flint," agreed the preacher. "And that was soldier to soldier, as a rule. But I was a young man then, and it would be strange indeed if my views did not change—not to say moderate—with age and experience."

"Then you regret your part," suggested Mr. Flint.

"I believe I would do the same today as I did at twenty, and certainly I have no regrets about our new republic, God bless it. But I might also wish that particular ends could be achieved with less blood and more charity."

"There was little charity at the end of a British musket," said another respectable fellow.

"I know it for a fact myself, sir," said the preacher. "But a hungry man may dream of a table such as this. And a lonely man may dream of his wife or his sweetheart. And a man who has known war—and do you disagree?—might dream of settling his disputes in peace."

Mr. Flint and the other older fellow did not find fault with these speculations.

Peter began to drift again, his head on his arms, and then suddenly he was conscious that Parson Leach was not at the table, and that those sitting about, smoking their pipes and drinking their ale had allowed him to sleep peacefully by dint of ignoring him.

Peter rose unsteadily, looked to Barrow's table and saw that he and Nora were gone as well. Outside the tavern, in the light of late afternoon, Peter breathed the sharp October air, and tried to rouse his clouded brain. Mars was not at his post by the porch, and Peter was concerned that Parson Leach had pressed on without him.

"Under his wing," he heard someone say, from around the corner of the tavern. "She's under something of his, to be sure."

"He is, to be sure, a *lay* preacher," said another amid the chuckles.

Peter moved a little further into the tavern yard and found the younger men that he and Parson Leach had met when they first arrived; they were standing in a group at the side of the tavern, watching something down by the lake, he thought, but they turned when he hove into view and hailed him brightly enough.

"The parson went to visit friends, he said to tell you," called one of the young men.

"Thank you."

"He said, you should wait around here, if you like, and you could share his room tonight."

Peter nodded. "Have any of you heard of Obed Winslow?" he asked, without hardly thinking about it first.

The young men looked to one another, each with his own frown of concentration.

"Is he the fellow down to Newcastle," said one of the young men, "tried to swim his horse across the river last spring and drowned?"

"I don't know," said Peter, a little shocked.

"That was Winthrop, was his name," said another. "He didn't drown."

"The horse got away from him," said a third, and still another young buck declared that the whole business had turned on a wager. Two or three of the fellows continued to look every now and then toward the water, as if something of interest might come in to view. Peter thought on what they had been saying before they saw him, and some barely conscious mix of curiosity and longing drew him along the dirt street, past the young men and around the dogleg to the northern border of the lake.

There was a clear path to the shore, past someone's garden and a small, mowed field. A boat was pulled up on the grassy slope above the water, and another two little skiffs stood on a narrow wedge of sand, their moorings beside them in full sight. The summer had been dry, and the lake was low; it was a pebbly stretch, no more than thirty or forty feet long, and Peter seemed to have it all to himself.

He half clambered down the short section of steep bank and crunched with his moccasins on the gravel beach. There was a breeze, with enough room to play over Great Bay and drive up the hint of whitecaps. Peter heard a crow laugh harshly to his right and watched as the bird swooped down to the beach and bounced stiff legs across the pebbles to a broken clamshell which it turned over and studied.

From the black of the crow, the corner of his eye was taken by a white presence against the bank. Nora Tillage sat with her back to the grass and her shoes on the gravel. She wore the same white shift, but had a throw of some sort over her shoulders. Her bonnet was pulled further down the sides of her head, but her hair, careless as before, moved in the breeze. If he had wondered before what it was about her slight frame that bespoke so strongly of the feminine, he wondered now how the haphazard movement of her hair in the breeze could affect him so.

He was a little speechless, surprised to see her and affected by the sense of fragility about her. She looked back at him, at least as surprised, and perhaps a little concerned that he had purposely sought her out.

"I didn't see you there," said Peter, without otherwise greeting her.

She was hunched a little against the breeze, though the sun was on her. It was a sharp-sighted day when the dry fall air carried a view to the eye in perfect articulation. Peter was somehow amazed by the white of her dress, which had only seemed pale and even drab in the dimness of the tavern, as he was taken by the grass and the sky and the reflective water. Nora Tillage's narrow hands were folded on her knees. She appeared to sway back and forth just slightly, almost as if she were in a rocking chair. Her face showed concern and even interest, but she said, though almost more to herself than to Peter, "I'm not supposed to talk with you," and when these words had died in the air she quickly said, "I think."

"I'm sorry," he said, which might have meant—and probably did mean—several things. He gathered himself to return the way he had come, when she spoke again.

"Are you with Parson Leach?"

Peter considered this. "I am, yes, I think."

"I like him," she said. "I heard him preach once. It was about a man who climbed a tree to see Jesus."

Peter didn't know the story, but he stood half-turned toward her, his head turned the rest of the way, cocked slightly—not un-like one of those birds that Crispin Moss had called on the road, or the crow that was watching them. Peter nodded, indicating his interest in what she said.

"He was a tax-collector, I think," said Nora. She was looking past him, out over the surface of the lake. Peter had some moments to look at her directly and began to see the imperfections— that is the humanness—in her face, none of which diminished her attractiveness to him. "We went to hear Mr. Barrow preach three weeks ago," she said. "Papa was *struck*. He fell right down and hit his head on the floor of Mr. Buelly's front room. And when he told us what he'd seen, Mr. Barrow said he been touched by Christ, for Jesus took Mr. Barrow to see Heaven and so Mr. Barrow knows what it looks like. He said Papa'd seen just a peep of it. He said Papa would never have to trouble about doing wrong again."

Peter took this in slowly. "Did you see anything?" he asked.

"No."

Anyone watching from another shore would hardly know they were talking, they looked so separate, but the young men outside the tavern, if they could see Peter standing, could never see Nora hunched low against the bank.

"He told Papa that I'd never have to trouble about doing wrong, even if I wasn't struck, if he took me under his wing. He said Papa would have lots of things in Heaven, because you're supposed to give up your sons and daughters."

Peter squinted one eye and looked down at a speckled rock at his feet.

"But Mr. Barrow said Parson Leach was a Congregationalist and a devil," she added in sudden haste. "I'm not supposed to talk with you." Nora rose from her little niche in the bankside like an animal poking its head from a hole. She did not try to reach the worn path, which would have meant passing by Peter, but scrambled instead up the little bluff of slope, grabbing hanks of grass and roots to pull herself up. Her bonnet bobbed above the crest of the bank.

"I don't think he's a Congregationalist," Peter called after her, but his voice was so weak, the wind must have carried it away.

9

Concerning Antinomianism and Other Matters

PARSON LEACH WAS STANDING ON THE SMALL PORCH BEFORE THE ALE Wife when Peter came up from the shore; the young man had the feeling that he was being looked for.

"I thought you had pressed on," said the clergyman.

Peter told Parson Leach where he'd been and the man nodded, glancing back at the tavern door, then at Peter again, as if he were connecting Peter's explanation with something else. Peter wondered if the parson had seen Nora Tillage come up from the lake before him, and *What would he make of that?* "There's another supper inside, if you can tolerate it," said the preacher with half a smile.

Peter was sure he could. The shank of the evening came hard on the heels of this meal, which lasted through a thicket of conversation and debate over the recent events in New Milford. Nathan Barrow and Nora Tillage were not on view, but Mr. Tillage—a widower, as it happened—put his younger children to work serving the crowd.

Peter was not used to eating so royally, and though he had slept in the middle of the day, he felt himself growing drowsy again. The glimmer of firelight conquered the room as the sun set and the few windows dimmed, and pipe smoke filled the air till there was a blue haze tumbling against the low beams. Parson Leach himself smoked and with his lanky legs stretched out before him, he drew on his long clay pipe whether he remembered to keep it lit or not.

The room grew crowded as evening drew on; Peter didn't know when he'd seen so many people; many of them were from outlying farms, come in to get the truth of recent events in New Milford. Land agents had been in the vicinity, some said, and while news was bandied about and rumor spread thickly, the ale and the sharp cider and rum flowed, and the warlike opinions of many in the assemblage grew apparent. Peter heard the name of Nathan Barrow on several lips, as if that man might appear at any moment to lead them against their oppressors.

As the belligerence of the crowd increased, Parson Leach became quiet and even watchful from behind the smoke of his long pipe. Others tended to listen more than talk, and one of these—Mr. Flint—turned to Zachariah Leach, during a lull in the general discourse, and asked if the parson had any words to inspire them. There was a chorus of assent and several slurred exhortations to the clergyman to stand and speak.

Parson Leach looked at his pipe and he looked at the tankard before him. The latter he pushed to one side and the former he lay down upon the table before he rose. Peter, sitting next to the parson, craned his head back to watch him.

Through those clear gray eyes and over that large nose, Parson Leach regarded the gathering before him. "*Let your moderation be known unto all men,*'" he said quietly.

Several men peered skeptically into their tankards, one or two croaked their disregard for such wisdom, and one in particular fired a hard gaze at the parson. There was only the briefest lapse, however, before several voices called out "Philippians," and "Philippians, four, five."

The preacher raised his head a little higher, as if enlargened by these remembrances. "And I say," he continued, "Moderation in all things save these: Love for God, love for your neighbor, and love for yourself. This last may sound strange to you, when so often we are counseled to accept discomfort and denial as the hallmarks of religious increase; but the human heart is the temple of God, and you would not invite such a Guest into an unkempt house. Therefore you must care for yourself as you would your Master's quarters.

"So, moderation in all things save these; and the love for God is love for the father, and the love for your neighbor is love for Christ, and the love for yourself is love for the Holy Ghost. In all other things, let even your enemy understand your temperance."

This last statement generated a fairly particular silence. Peter had never heard Parson Leach preach, and this taste of it and this sight of the man standing before the tavern crowd moved him to wonder if he had, until this moment, been looking at the wrong person.

Parson Leach did not fill the room as might an overwhelming personality, but drew all eyes and ears, and even hearts in his direction with a force of magnetism that had hitherto in Peter's experience lain not entirely dormant, but had rested beneath a deceiving and amiable surface. Peter could never look at his new friend so simply again.

"How shall we prove moderate," said someone nearby, "when

men of force covet so *im*moderately the very land we have labored into small success?"

Some gave wordless agreement to this, but others were a little shocked that anyone would argue with the clergyman. For his
part, Parson Leach showed no vexation; this was not a church, after all, and he had not delivered of a formal sermon.

"It is easy enough," said another man by the door, perhaps emboldened by the first man's words, "easy enough for you to preach
moderation, sir, traveling from place to place on your horse, gain-
ing your suppers by sermons and the clothes on your back by your
books; but what of we who live in hovels while we clear the land
and watch our children half starve for all the rocky ground can
flourish and be half eaten by swarms of bugs and gnats in the
fields and burned in the summer and chilled in the winter for lack
of clothes? And we who bring down the wilderness with our bare
hands are supposed to approach moderately the enemy who wields
unjust power in the courts, and with his wealth, raised perhaps in
the service of King George himself with whom so many of us have
fought, and with this wealth buys what friends he needs and purposes he desires?"

The man by the door was standing before he was finished,
and those around him cheered when he sat down again. He may
have been unused to speaking up among so many, however, for he
appeared embarrassed and exhausted by the effort.

All eyes turned back to Parson Leach, and he said, "I am not
in great sympathy with the so-called Great Proprietors of Maine,
but as long as the law, by whatever influence, takes their part,
I would not see any of you become outlaws. I hear men beside

me advising that Henry Knox's mansion be burned, or that land agents and surveyors be hung at the crossroads; and I ask: What reply will Boston send but the State Militia in an attitude of war?"

The parson now leaned, with his fingertips upon the table before him. "My friends, I believe that a man who carves the wilderness of his own main strength has greater claim than does a grant countenanced by a king who never set foot upon it or rightly understood the size and weight of the gift, or yet had the moral right to give it at all; but since England was expelled, revolutions in other parts of the land have been duly crushed, and it is only the distance between yourselves and the seats of power that keeps your cause balanced with that of your adversaries."

Another man spoke up, then. "Preacher Barrow says it is our duty to rid the nation of evil men."

"I know what *Mr.* Barrow says," said Parson Leach. "And he will drive you up to desperate acts, but will he lead you?" Some low pools of discussion were raised by this question, but Parson Leach added, "This will be a hard fought war, won by time and generation as much as by design and plan. I warrant, some action is justified, but for the love of God, your neighbors, and yourselves, it is enough to take the land agent's and the surveyor's labor and not their lives. Rather stake your claim by good work, than destroy another man's by fire and ruin. This is the moderation I argue, my friends."

It was not a speech to quell anyone's spirit but to make a man think, and by the faces before Parson Leach, it was, in this office, successful. He was himself, it seemed, a man of moderation, which in this instance meant knowing when he had said enough on one subject. He picked up his pipe and before sitting down he turned to Peter and indicating him with a nod, said, "This young fellow, by the way, is looking for his uncle."

Peter's head came up. It was a moment, however, before the crowd could take in this sudden digression. Some were amused by the parson's new tack, some relieved, but some were for the moment nettled that their own thoughts on the matter had not been expressed.

"What's his name, young fellow?" asked one of the men at the parson's table.

"Winslow," said Peter. "Obed Winslow, I'm told, though I've never met the man, and know almost nothing of him."

"And what is that?" asked Mr. Flint.

"What?" Peter gaped.

"What is it you know of him? If it's little, it should be quick to tell."

There was a long moment, during which the snap of the fire-place and the drawing on pipes took precedence. "I guess I *do* know nothing of him," said Peter, turning red. There were some smiles and a few quiet chuckles.

"Obed Winslow," said Mr. Flint. He shook his head.

"I seem to remember a Winslow," said a man far enough away as to be hard to make out in the dark, smoke-filled room. "Not sure if he was Obed, though. Came through at harvest time, years ago, when I was still at my folks place. Worked there for a few days, before moving on. Don't know where to."

Another fellow spoke up. "There's the Winslow, over the other side of Balltown, who talks to his hens." This did raise a good laugh. "Claims he gets two eggs a day from them. Gathers eggs in the morning, then goes back in the afternoon and talks his hens into believing they haven't laid a thing since the day before."

"Perhaps he could come by tonight and have a talk with my wife," called out someone from the far end of the room, and a great roar of laughter filled the tavern. "Begging your pardon, Mr. Leach," came the voice.

"If he's such a fine talker," said the clergyman, "you had better be careful what he says to her," and this was spoken so off-handedly past the stem of his pipe that the laughter redoubled, and the man at the other end of the room half-choked on his ale he was so delighted. But when the hilarity subsided, the preacher took the pipe from his mouth and pointed to the back of the room with the stem. "Now you've gone and made me speak disrespect-fully of a good woman, George Clary." Peter thought that the preacher's concern was not entirely feigned.

"I'll ask her pardon for the both of us, Mr. Leach."

"That's the spirit!" Parson Leach stood. "Gentlemen, good night to you. Peter, you look ready to drop." Peter nodded. "Come along. Then I shan't embarrass them, and they won't corrupt you." There was laughter again, but Peter gratefully took the lantern handed him and followed the parson outside and up the stairs. His head ached again.

The rooms upstairs were small and without fires, but each shared a portion of chimney and something like warmth emanated from the bricks next to the pinebox bed, which was covered with a thin down mattress and some wool blankets. There was a single window of nine tiny panes. Simple as it all was, it was more than Peter was accustomed to, and he stood by the door while Parson

Leach sat down and hauled off his own boots. "Are we sleeping here?" asked the young man.

"It puts a heap of oak leaves to shame, doesn't it, lad. I'll wake up and think I've a church and a congregation."

The jest put Peter in mind of an earlier conversation. "This morning," he said, "Mr. Cutts said you couldn't be a Congregationalist, because you preach from the saddle."

"Yes," said Parson Leach.

"But Mr. Barrow called you a Congregationalist, and Miss Tillage, this afternoon, said something like it and more."

"So you *were* down by the lake with the girl," said the parson.

"I didn't know she was there," said Peter, which was more or less the truth.

"There's no harm, in my experience, talking to a young woman. Yours is more seemly companionship than what she keeps, I'd guess."

"She said her father gave her up."

Parson Leach put his stockinged feet on the floor, lowered his head and rubbed his brow. "Lord preserve us!" he said under his breath. As he drew his hand down over his face, he looked up at Peter, wondering perhaps what the young man understood. "We take more note of difference than similarity, Peter," he said, choosing to answer the original problem.

Peter frowned and shook his head.

"We most of us walk on two legs, lad, and speak with our mouths, and breathe with our lungs, but ever since Cain and Abel, we ask each other, Which are you? Are you the hunter or the farmer? Are you Catholic or Greek? Are you Reform or Catholic? Are you Church of England or Puritan? Are you Puritan or anything *but* Puritan?" The clergyman leaned his sharp elbows on his bony knees and gazed, almost with longing, toward the wall. "And here we've asked, are you Patriot or Loyalist? Federalist or Jeffersonian? And now, are you Congregationalist or Evangelical? The words get longer, is all."

"Are you?"

"What?" Parson Leach's tone was sharp. Peter did not respond, and the preacher's expression softened. "I read the Bible and distrust sudden conversions of bitter men, and that view, lad, would suspicion a backcountry evangelist. But I ride a horse and preach where I may, without benefit of established church or diocese, which makes me unwelcome among the Congregationalists. Neither worship claims me, yet I preach in similarity to both. We all claim Christ!"

"But is there such difference between them?" asked Peter.

"Twins will argue whose mother was prettiest," said Parson Leach, almost with a laugh, and when Peter frowned again, the gaunt fellow said, "Men often fight most fiercely over the smallest differences." The clergyman threw off his coat and crossed around to the other side of the bed. "Though I fear *this* difference in land and claim is not so slight."

"It seems strange, Mr. Tillage's daughter with Mr. Barrow," said Peter, proving that he was himself capable of digression.

"I dare say it is," said the parson, without having to think very long on the subject.

"I thought they might be married, too."

"I thought they *should* be, perhaps."

Peter felt something tighten inside of him, and he had to clear his throat before he spoke. "They say Mr. Barrow is a preacher."

Parson Leach lay back on his side of the bed with a sigh. "He is an Antinomianist," and he hardly gave Peter the chance to show his nescience before he let out a short laugh and explained, "He believes that once he has been covered by God's Grace, he is no longer bound by moral law. His sins past *and* future are wiped clean, so since he *has* salvation, it matters not how he sins."

"But that would include murder!"

"Well," said the parson, one arm over his eyes, "he must still consider the law of the land, I suppose. But, yes, that would include any outrage."

"I can see how such a belief might draw folks," said Peter, innocent of humor. The *tap tap* of rain at the window startled him.

Parson Leach peeked from beneath his arm to see just how innocent a person could be, and the sight of Peter's honest astonishment made him smile again.

"I thought she was frightened of him," said Peter, unnoticing. His head still throbbed.

The preacher let out a wordless sound; the smile left his face and he covered his eyes once more. "He frightens *me*," said Parson Leach.

Peter lay down and tried to imagine what it would take to frighten Parson Leach, which was about as much as it would take to frighten his mother, he guessed.

When Peter was only nine or ten, a wild-haired self-proclaimed prophet had come to Sheepscott Great Pond, but Rosemund Loon had kept her family from the fiery meetings the man held in the settlement. The man appeared, one afternoon, at Loon Farm, and standing before the front door he threatened the entire family with damnation and hellfire if they did not attend his next gathering. "Get him away, Silas," said Rosemund Loon evenly to her husband, "or I will brain him with a kettle," and she disappeared into the cabin.

Peter's father had done his best to reason with the man, but to no avail, and soon Rosemund flew out of the cabin with the promised article of cookery. She had very nearly proved as good as her word, and the prophet of Sheepscott Great Pond scurried off in the direction of Beaver Hill, jumping stumps and dodging brushpiles like a deer.

Having only run about half a mile or so, Rosemund Loon had returned, calm as ever. Peter's father had smiled just a little when she went back inside and he allowed how the matter had been "good for all involved." Half asleep, Peter smiled just a little to recall his father's face as he said this.

Sometime in the night, Peter woke to find the shadows strange in the room. He peered out from beneath his half closed eyes and eventually located the parson, who was sitting on the floor with a single candle beside him, his spectacles on his nose and a book in his hands.

10

*Of the Road to New Milford, Unexpected Meetings, and
How a Peaceful Man Might Be Driven to Anger*

"ARE YOU COMING WITH ME?"

Peter Loon came awake with Parson Leach shaking him by the
shoulder.

"With you?"

"Are you coming with me, lad? You've time for some breakfast
before we leave."

The quality of light through the single window was not en-
couraging; the sun, which would not be seen today, had hardly
raised its head above the curve of the earth. Peter could hear rain
rattling the isinglass panes.

"Are you coming with me?" asked the parson again.

"Yes," said Peter, and the clergyman seemed satisfied. He
tossed Peter's coat at him, gathered his own kit and left the room.

A few minutes later, Peter hurried down the outer staircase
and into the tavern. He was surprised to find Manasseh Cutts and
Crispin Moss sitting at the table nearest the fire. Peter greeted
them and looked around for Parson Leach.

"He's gone for his horse," said Manasseh. "He said, ask for
some breakfast in the kitchen."

Peter stumbled at the threshold as he stepped into the room

at the rear of the tavern. Something had been left to burn in the fireplace and Mr. Tillage was berating one of his children for the transgression. The taverner stood straight and looked at Peter.

"Parson Leach said to get some breakfast," said Peter.

Mr. Tillage took a sausage out of a pot and wrapped some bread around it. He placed this in Peter's one hand and pressed an apple into the other. The back door opened and Nora Tillage, damp from the rain and looking like a sleepless night, stepped inside with an armload of wood. She paused just long enough, at the sight of Peter, for her father to take note. "Leave it there," he said, hooking a thumb at the kitchen fireplace. "Go see to the hogs."

The young woman tossed the wood on the pile by the hearth, then scooped up a bucket of slops and hurried out with only a quick glance at those behind her.

"Can I help with the firewood?" asked Peter.

"Lad," said Mr. Tillage, "I want nothing disagreeable with Mr. Leach or any of his friends, but you're not to be talking with Nora."

Peter just blinked. He wondered how many people had noticed him down on the shore the day before.

"You're leaving with Mr. Leach?" asked the taverner.

Peter nodded.

"Well, God speed, then," said Mr. Tillage and he turned his back on the young man.

"Mr. Cutts and Mr. Moss have elected to join us," said Parson Leach, when Peter stepped out the front door. The clergyman had on a hooded cape against the rain and he was tying off his saddlebags and checking his gear and musket, which was wrapped now in a fringed leather sheath.

"Where are we going?" asked Peter. He tugged on his father's hat and joined the three men in the wet yard.

"New Milford." Parson Leach made no wasted motions, and in fact seemed to be in a hurry to leave, despite the weather, though nothing he did in particular could be called rushing.

Peter went over to the trough, which was dancing with rain, and drank a handful or two of water to help down the sausage and bread. He was surprised when he looked up and discovered Nora Tillage standing a few feet away with the empty slop bucket. Peter hesitated between retreat and greeting. She hardly acknowledged his presence, at first, and only looked at him glancingly; but she said, before she turned and hurried off, "Are you with Parson Leach, then?"

"Yes," he answered, and would have said more, but she was gone.

"What was that?" asked Parson Leach over Mars's back, and when Peter told him, he said, "Your questions last night convicted me, lad. I spoke to her father this morning, first thing, but he is adamant that his own salvation rests on doing as Nathan Barrow deems fit. So Lot would give up his daughters to Sodom." He tightened a strap with rather more firmness than he had intended, and needed to let it out. "But I did speak to him," he added. "Sometimes a word does not have a straightforward effect."

Manasseh Cutts had a horse himself, this morning, and he was mounted and ready to go, hunching in the rain with the water dripping from his battered three-cornered hat. Again Peter looked curious, squinting up at the old woodsman. Manasseh said, "Crispin's family was cleared out, and not a one of them left behind. A land agent came with the sheriff and demanded they pay or abandon their farm, so they packed up and headed for the backcountry to start again. Two or three weeks ago, this was. We doled most of the buck out to the neighbors."

"There's been more news from New Milford since last night," said Parson Leach to Peter. "Throw this over your shoulders," he said, tossing a blanket at the young man. "It'll keep the rain off you—for a bit."

"Is there going to be a fight?" asked Peter, hardly stirring. He held the blanket before him, as if he had not yet discerned its use.

"Well, son, let's hope not," said Manasseh Cutts.

Crispin Moss seemed less ready to speak on the matter.

Parson Leach swung himself up on Mars and gave a little nudge and a *click* of the tongue. Without ceremony, he led the way.

Peter wondered where all the men at the tavern last night were this morning. Had they trudged home already, slogging to their backcountry farms through the rain? Or were they watching the parson and his companions leaving the hamlet? Had the angry men gone to New Milford before them? He stood in the muddy road and watched as the parson and the woodsmen went ahead. He was trying to number the days. Would they be burying his father today? Would they be burying him in this rain? The children shouldn't be out in it, Peter thought. He looked over his shoulder in the direction he and the parson had come from the day before. He wanted to go back and see his little brother Amos and his sisters Hannah and Sally Ann. It felt like he had been gone a month.

He had left in the night and slept part of yesterday morning, so it was difficult, strange as things were, and befuddled as he was, to figure just how long he *had* been gone.

"Are you coming to find your uncle, Peter Loon?" called Parson Leach from down the road. The woodsmen, too, had stopped to look back at him.

Peter gave them a nod, and hurried after. He shook open the blanket, as he ran, and wrapped it over his head and shoulders. His moccasins were filled with water before he reached the end of the street, and had he not felt so suddenly lost, and otherwise so friendless in this foreign hamlet, he might have changed his mind and turned around. He looked back at the settlement and the Ale Wife's Tavern when they reached the field where he had crossed to the lake shore the day before.

A pale figure stood at the back of the tavern, watching them, seemingly unheeding of the weather. She still carried the bucket in one hand, looking small and finally indeterminate through the rain. Peter tired his neck looking back as they moved parallel to the northern extremity of Great Bay.

The track south along the western shore of the lake was well worn and at times the parson elected to ride the grassy bank above the road and avoid the mud. It was Manasseh Cutts, perhaps inspired by the harvested fields along the lakeside, who sang up a hymn.

Fields of corn, give up your ears,
  Now your stalks are heavy,
Wheat and oats and barley-spears,
  All your harvest levy.

It was not long before Parson Leach joined him, singing in a rumbling baritone.

Where your sheaves of plenty lean,
Men once more the grain shall glean
Of the Ever-Living,
God the Lord will bless the field,
Bringing in its Autumn yield
Gladly to Thanksgiving.

And on they sang, growing a little bolder with their voices as they went— *"Vines, send in your bunch of grapes,"* and *"Gardens, give your gayest flowers."* On the second verse, Crispin took up counterpoint. Peter did not know the words, but he quickly caught up the tune and hummed it. When they were finished, Mars let out a snort, spraying rain from his muzzle. A distant rumble in the west caught their interest, but it was not repeated.

They followed a ridge above the water for a mile or so, the horses walking slowly for the sake of the men on foot. It was not frigid, for a rainy day in October, and Peter got rather used to being wet, as if he were bathing in the lake. Their exertions kept them warm. The water to their left was brown and roughened by the rain and runoff, and crows were the only birds with voices in the broad gray expanse of the morning. Some distance away, a treefull of black-winged wags bawled and laughed at one another, or—as Parson Leach suggested—at the foolishness of men who didn't know enough to take shelter from the downpour.

Manasseh began to sing "The Ladle Song," which Peter did know. Halfway through the first verse, however, Peter found himself falling off the tune. The subject of the song, which concerned the marriage between an old man and a young girl, saddened him. Then he worried that Parson Leach might notice his reticence and make something of it, and Peter picked up the next verse with more enthusiasm, however feigned. His scalp ached.

They passed the narrows, where Great Bay gave over to Damariscotta Pond, and after the second mile or so, they began to climb away from the water, toward the height that had lately been called Bunker Hill, after the more famous eminence in Charlestown. The banks became steeper and the way forced them to walk the muddy road and soon enough they were covered, foot to fardel, with sprays of wet earth. Peter and Crispin in particular wore the road as the horses had a tendency to kick up clods of mud and splash in every puddle.

Once they climbed the hill, they rested, though there was little comfort, hunkering in the weather. It had been raining all the night before, so even the trees were adrip and offered little refuge. Some large gray and white birds lit down upon a stretch of field below them and Peter watched them with interest, shielding his eyes from the immediate rain.

"This weather came from the opposite quarter," said Parson Leach, and when Peter asked how he knew, the man said, "Seagulls. They've been driven inland. The storm came in from the sea. That thunder we heard was it rubbing shoulder with the hills west."

Peter had never seen seagulls. They were extraordinary to him—graceful in flight, ungainly on their broad feet; they were bright figures in the dismal air, arguing noisily over something that one of them had discovered in the field.

The four men sat and watched the gulls for such a long time that their bones creaked a little when they finally stood. Parson Leach, in particular, hobbled around for a bit, warming his joints with some movement, and he elected to walk for a while "to keep," as he said, "from rusting up like an old hinge."

A little further on, the trail fell alongside the tree-lined perimeter of a cleared field. Walking through the wet heavy grass was the next thing to wading in water and they left a dark line behind them at the edge of the forest. Some of the ground had grown up in recent years and Manasseh wasn't sure how far they were from the path that would take them west. Once they reached the shore of Damariscotta Pond, they considered the way before them. Through a narrow gut, south upon the water, they could see a small island near the opposite shore, though it wavered in and out of view with the shifting persistence of the weather.

"There's another island, but we can't see it from here," said Manasseh, "just off this shore. The path we're looking for is near to it."

They moved south, toward the narrows, and crossed a brook, which was wide and rushing from the accumulating rainfall. Peter slipped on a mossy rock and Parson Leach somehow caught him before he fell in. At the narrows, it was natural to step out on the little point of land and consider where they had been, and where they were going. They could see the second island now, and Peter looked for some sign of the path.

They had not gone very much further, when they heard a sound that Peter thought was the bark of an animal. Manasseh lifted his head and looked behind them.

"There's your path," Crispin Moss was saying, pointing south to a dark cut in the forest; then a second sound reached them which was most definitely the shout of a man.

Manasseh stepped out on the little swell of bank to look back through the foliage and over the low point of land that formed one side of the narrows. The others crowded round him, and indeterminate noises reached their ears, screened by the sound of rain shushing the pond and rattling on the brims of their hats. Parson Leach did, in fact, throw his hood back and cock his head to one side.

"Look," said Crispin, pointing. Several figures, two or three of them mounted, were suddenly visible at the point where the parson and his companions had first reached the pond. They heard more shouting, which was distinctly angry, and Peter had the brief and unpleasant sensation that they were being pursued.

Parson Leach felt around beneath his cloak and produced a spyglass on the end of a leather braid. He put the instrument to his eye and telescoped the lens till he could see the group of men. "Barrow!" he said, with a note of question in his voice.

"What?" said Manasseh.

The distant figures halted at the edge of the water and appeared to be taking stock of their situation. More shouts followed and Peter thought he saw some of the men pointing at something.

The clergyman fiddled with the length of the glass, and said "Barrow!" again.

"What does *he* want?" said Crispin Moss, and quite unconsciously, he swung his covered musket off his shoulder.

"They're pursuing something, or someone," said Parson Leach, still peering through the glass. "But I dare say, it can't be us."

Just beyond the point of land between the two parties, Peter caught the glimpse of something pale that flashed between the scrubby pines. "It's Nora Tillage!" he exclaimed with instant conviction.

"What?" Parson Leach shot a perturbed expression at Peter.

"It's Mr. Tillage's daughter!" said Peter again, and the parson let out a snort of disgust.

"What's that?" said Manasseh.

Parson Leach had no more than put the glass to his eye again, when the others were just able to discern a person's head and shoulders over the next point of land. Someone was hurrying along the shore, but disappeared, perhaps in a stumble, then returned to view and continued more slowly. The men, further on, scrambled after, closing the gap between themselves and the bit of pale figure.

"Heaven preserve!" said Parson Leach. He swung the glass beneath his cape and hurried to Mars. "Peter!" he called as he swung onto the great horse, and Peter was quick to be pulled up behind. "Hold tight!" declared the preacher, and then he shouted *"Heeyaa!"* whereupon Mars leapt forward at a near gallop through thickety cover. The animal lowered its head, Parson Leach put his own face against the creature's neck, and Peter was almost swept off the horse's back by a swatting branch. Then they broke into an open glade and Mars mounted a broad shelf of granite where the preacher skittered him to a short halt, sparks flying from the animal's shoes. Peter all but fell off with the clergyman's sudden vault from the saddle, and he slid without ceremony down Mars's hindquarters.

They were still some yards away from the person scrambling

toward them, however; Peter saw the unmistakable figure and face of Nora Tillage, and he shouted, almost angrily, "Parson Leach! We must get her!"

But the parson had pulled his musket from its sheath and he was loading and priming it, leaning over the firing mechanism to protect it from the rain. "She'll reach us before they reach her, lad!" he shouted back. "And I need a moment to ready this!" It was true, had he gone the entire distance to the young woman, he might not have had time to load and prime.

Peter ran across the granite projection and tumbled down the side of the rock, using his sudden momentum to propel himself toward the girl. He heard an angry bellow and perhaps the snap of flint against steel. No explosion followed, however, and he barely slowed himself in time to avoid knocking the young woman over when he reached her. Other angry shouts and curses raised a panic in Peter's heart. He was aware of two horsemen closing the distance with them, but he turned about and half led, half carried Nora Tillage to the stand of granite.

Parson Leach had his musket raised. He shouted a warning, waited several beats, which kept time with the sound of hooves, then pulled the trigger. The powder in the pan had fouled with the rain, however, and there was no resultant kick or flashing bang.

But directly behind him Manasseh Cutts pulled his own musket to his shoulder and the gun roared with an alarming blast of flame. He was aiming at the muddy flat just before the oncoming horses and the ball kicked up a shower of mud and stone, which proved more impressive than harmful. The horsemen drew up;

one animal slipped and fell back on its rear legs, and the other slued to a halt.

Crispin Moss passed Manasseh his own loaded musket, then held out his arms and Peter lifted the slight young woman up to him, before scrambling after. Parson Leach had blown out his pan and was repriming, leaning over the firingpiece. Nora Tillage collapsed in a heap at their feet, shivering from fright and exertion as much as from her thin soaked garments. In a moment, Crispin had Manasseh's musket loaded and primed; he nudged Peter behind him. Mars let out an angry sounding snort and shifted his shod feet loudly on the granite porch.

"Leach!" came a shout from beyond the first horsemen.

Nora let out a single sob at the sound of Barrow's voice, and she clutched at Peter's leg, almost like an animal that has ceased to know friend from foe, but scrambles at any cover near.

Nathan Barrow glared from the back of his horse. "You give her over right now!" he declared, his face behind his bristling beard purple and puffy with rage. His mount danced nervously beneath him, as if sensing the danger in the man. Barrow seemed to be spitting when he bellowed, but it was the rain running down his mustache and into his beard, spraying out as he shook. He pushed his horse forward and broke past the two riders before him, but stopped short of the halfway point between the narrows and the granite shelf.

There were almost a dozen men with Nathan Barrow, hunkering against the rain. Most were on horseback, but some stragglers bringing up the rear were on foot. Parson Leach was speechless for a moment; he and Peter recognized several faces from the tavern the night before. He looked behind him at the young woman, collapsed upon the gray rock, and glanced, as he turned back, at his companions.

"Give her back!" roared Barrow again.

"I would say she's not overfond of you, Mr. Barrow." Parson Leach had lowered his gun so that the pan might possibly remain dry beneath his arm, but the expression on his face was near to warlike.

"She's been given over by her father himself!" shouted Barrow. He nudged his horse a little closer. One of the other riders came up along side of him, though with less certainty.

"He wouldn't be the first father do wrong by his child," said the parson, hardly audible to Barrow over the rain.

"It's the letter of the law," growled Barrow.

"You've declared the law your enemy," replied Parson Leach, his voice rising again. "And there's no law leads a man to ruin his own."

"Give her over, Leach! She's under my wing!"

"Your wings are under the sites of two bores, which is a good deal more to the point."

The man behind Barrow squinted up at the rain with almost a smile, as if he thought those two bores would prove of little use. "Her father said to get her back, Mr. Leach," he called as he edged his horse forward a pace or two.

"I didn't take anything," said Nora, almost conquering the wail in her voice. "I never took so much as a coat, so they wouldn't say I stole."

Peter shook himself from his daze and pulled her onto her feet where she tottered against him.

"Her father wants her back, Mr. Leach," said the other horseman again.

"Her father *doesn't* want her back, as far as I can tell," said the preacher, "or he would've come for her himself."

This new spokesman looked to Barrow, then said, "We'll see she comes to no harm."

"Not like you chased her down, then," said Parson Leach evenly, "like dogs on a deer."

There was no answer to this, and in fact some of the men hung their heads.

The rain increased between them, and Barrow stiffened on his horse as he stood in his stirrups. "There are only four of you and but three armed!" he bellowed. "We'll storm over you like perdition!"

"No gun out here," said Manasseh, squinting into the rain, "will be good for anything but a club," though he held his own firing piece as if he might get one more shot from it.

"I can't believe," called out Parson Leach, and he nodded to Barrow's mob, "that any of these men care to be a party to murder, and that's what I promise it will fall to, before you wrest this woman from my protection. On the other hand, *I* may *just* be angry enough to pick you off that horse, Mr. Barrow; and looking at you, at this juncture, is not pacifying me in the least."

"You heard the threat!" declared Barrow, but the rider beside him leaned close to the man, rain dripping from his hat brim, and quietly reminded Mr. Barrow that he had threatened first. Barrow shot an angry glance at his cohort, and the man straightened in his saddle, giving Barrow as good a look in return.

"What's it to be then, Mr. Leach," said this second in command. He seemed a reasonable enough fellow, now that everyone but Barrow had calmed somewhat.

"I don't want you following us, sir," said Parson Leach. "It might be too tempting for Mr. Barrow to try and take her from us, and it will end in tragedy, I promise you. You may be no happier than ourselves if one of us were to be killed in such circumstances, for the law would surely hunt you down."

"*His* law!" snarled Barrow. "*His* Great Men and *his* Congregational . . ." but the other man gave him such a look, that Barrow fell to muttering.

"I am no kidnapper, you know that," continued the parson, and when the man beside Barrow nodded, the parson said. "She fled her situation of her own accord, and it's the law will determine things now. I am a law-abiding man, on the whole, and I will deliver her to decisive powers when we reach the next settlement."

"How are we to know, if we can't follow you," said the rider.

"Word will be sent, but I am not sure Mr. Tillage will want to appear for his daughter, at any rate, Lot and Sodom notwithstanding."

This reference was so keen and so final, that several gasps rose from the mob of men. Some looked a little horrified, suddenly, to be a part of such a business. It was amazing to Peter, how one sentence from Parson Leach could reverse the view these men took of their own behavior. Without much further hesitation, the pursuers turned about and headed for the point along the shore where Manasseh first detected them. By association, Barrow was tugged along with his mob, but he craned his head back and looked over his shoulder at the parson and his companions, till his horse mounted the far bank and carried him into the field beyond the forest and out of sight.

11

*Concerning a Change in Plans, a Parting of the Ways, as
Well as an Introduction to the Busy Abode of Captain
Clayden as Governed by Mrs. Magnamous*

"THIS DOESN'T LOOK TO BE STOPPING VERY SOON," SAID MANASSEH
Cutts, as he considered the rain. He might have thought the storm's
intentions immaterial if not for the shivering young woman among
them. Her pale shift was flimsy enough, and her undergarments
were in such short supply, that the severe soaking she had under-
gone rendered her appearance slighter still, adhering her clothes
to her in such a manner as to be considered indecent. She seemed
unaware of her pitiable state beyond the obvious fear for the consequences of her recent flight, and it was yet difficult to know the
division of physical and emotional effects that caused her to shake
so. She clung to Peter without motive, besides the desire to stay
upright. Peter himself held her with less motive than he might
have credited; he was greatly unnerved by the confrontation with
Barlow and his followers.

"God bless you for standing with us," said Parson Leach to
Manasseh Cutts and Crispin Moss. The rain ran off the tip of the
preacher's long nose like water off an eaves. "Peter," he said,
brushing the slick from his face before raising his hood again,

"you acted admirably. And Nora Tillage, I could have wished it happened under more clement circumstances and with less distress to yourself, but it was a brave deed coming after us and fleeing that man." He considered Peter with an interested expression, as if the young man might have known something about her flight beforehand.

The parson went to a large leather sack that hung behind one of Mars's saddlebags, and from this he eventually wrestled his blue greatcoat. Nora seemed hardly big enough to carry it on her shoulders, and when he wrapped her in it, she all but disappeared with her small face and bedraggled russet hair peering out from between the collars; but she clasped it around herself thankfully and seemed almost to leave off her shivering.

Then the preacher found a beautiful red apple in one of his bags and gave it to Mars, apologizing to the animal for using him so dangerously and stroking the horse's nose as he held the soft brown muzzle to his cheek. Mars appeared to forgive him, and he nudged the parson's head with his own while he made quick work of the offering. The preacher walked Mars off the granite shelf and called to Nora. "Now, Miss, let me help you up and Mars will warm you as well as rest your feet." In her shift, Nora could sit none too gracefully upon Mars's back, but the parson's great coat covered her like a quilt, and she was so exhausted that it was an obvious pleasure for her to lie forward and hug the horse's neck.

"We'll be heading south," said Parson Leach, who had already made his decisions. All his motions and words had the same innate sense of deliberate haste that Peter had perceive when they left the tavern. "I won't bring this young woman to New Milford, where trouble brews," the preacher was saying, "and I know of someone in Newcastle who will take her in for a time. Peter, you will come with us?" he asked, though the force of the sentence gave it the sound of a statement.

"Yes, Parson."

"We'll go with you, if you like," said the older woodsman, and Crispin agreed.

"I think it unnecessary," said the clergyman. "The sooner cool heads arrive in New Milford, the better. Certainly you're welcome, but . . ."

"We'll head west, then," said Manasseh Cutts. "And if someone *does* follow, it'll be less clear which direction you went. They don't know who *we* are, but you made it pretty plain, it seems, that your interests lay west of here."

They followed the shore road, which rose up to a bank above the lake where it was bordered by a thickening forest and here they found the track west, which was hardly more than a deer path.

"We'll wait here some," said the old woodsman, "and be sure Barrow doesn't change his mind."

"If he does," said Crispin Moss, "I'd wager he does so alone."

"They didn't seem too happy with themselves, his fellows," agreed Manasseh.

"I'm none too happy with land agents and proprietors, just now," pronounced Crispin, "but if Barrow's the sort of man I'm siding with, I'll not need to be so particular *which* direction I point and fire."

"Come," said Parson Leach to Nora and Peter. "We have only

half as far to go now as we have already traveled, and you, Miss, need not walk a step. Peter?"

"Yes, Parson."

"Are you fit to go?"

Peter nodded. He hardly looked fit, drenched to the bone and as pale as Nora. Parson Leach may have been conscious that he looked little better himself. He took Mars's reins and led him off; they left the woodsmen by the trail west to New Milford, where the forest crowded the traveler with fern and root and sagging wet limbs; and so parted company with little ceremony beyond "God speed." Peter was glad to know that Manasseh Cutts and Crispin Moss lingered behind them.

Parson Leach, for his part, was not lingering. For all his manner, they might have been on a walk from church on Sunday, but his pace was quick and his stride was long, and Peter caught the parson stealing more than one glimpse over his shoulder at the road behind them. Sometimes the gaunt man turned about-face and walked backwards for a moment, concealing his true motives by speaking to Peter, and always in the most genial tone, but he never slacked off the sharp pace he set for them at the start, and Peter, who was long-legged himself, half-ran to keep up.

The road south followed the length of Damariscotta Pond; and as the water narrowed, the further shore grew clearer through the wet atmosphere. The forest to their right hovered close by, a dour presence on the slopes of the river valley. They heard crows jarring under cover of the trees.

Peter trudged along, to one side of the horse, glancing occasionally at Nora, whose face was turned away from him. She had pulled the collars of the parson's greatcoat over her head, but her wet tangle of hair fell from beneath the cover and he was mesmerized by the color of it; that dark red brown *belonged* to fall, it seemed, and shared something melancholy with the oak leaves and maple and elm that fell, stripped from the trees in the rain. And yet again her hair was almost the color of Mars's coat, which was strong and supple and glad. One thin hand reached from beneath the blue coat and pressed against the horse's neck, looking as white as bone.

Above, the caps of the forest surged in the rain, and that broken foliage, consonant with Nora's wet darkened hair, fell about the road and their muddy feet and hooves in an eddy of wind.

Peter stumbled in the mud and recovered himself by clutching at the tail of Parson Leach's coat. It seemed to him that the man on the other side of the horse said, "Watch where you walk, now," but Peter had heard nothing. He glanced over the horse's back and Parson Leach was facing forward and had not broken his stride. Nora readjusted the great coat and turned, her head still resting upon the neck of the horse; she watched Peter with the candid stare of a child. Soon her eyes closed and Peter wondered if she had fallen asleep.

Peter himself imagined the remainder of their journey through the rain as in a dream. They had not walked so very far, and the weather was not what it would be in another month or so, but he was not used to walking distances at all, and less used to the knowledge of new places and new people and dangerous men. It occurred to him, as it had now and again these last two days, that his father was gone, and his heart plunged a little and his head spun to consider what it meant that someone, anyone was no longer in the world. *Are they burying him today?* he wondered, and *What has my mother sent me to?*

At some point the parson began to sing softly.

Oh, my Lord God, young Jesus dear,
Prepare Thy gracious cradle near,
And I shall rock Thee in my heart,
And never more from Thee depart.

After a while, Peter thought he heard Nora humming along with the clergyman, and how much more potent her small contribution seemed than all the broad tones of his male companions, who sang in the shank of the morning.

Several other songs, each with several verses, brought them around the southern extremity of Damariscotta Pond, where they reached the Mills and the lengthy spillway that emptied into Great Salt Bay and the Damariscotta River. Here the houses came more frequently and Parson Leach was recognized by one or two individuals braving the weather. One invited him and his companions to dry by their fire, but he graciously declined with the excuse of pressing matters.

Peter could have done with a fire; even the exertion of walking seemed to have lost its warming effect, and a chill had soaked through his skin to his bones so that he hardly believed he would ever be rid of it. Nora sat atop Mars in relative comfort, not so much soaked with rain anymore as damp with steam.

Parson Leach's cape and hood had long since ceased to ward off the rain. "It's not much further," he insisted. "Were we to stop and dry off, the last leg through this rain would seem twice as cruel."

So they trudged on, and it was not more than half a mile further on before they were atop a low hill and Parson Leach pointed south and east to a head of land jutting into the river. Perhaps a quarter of a mile away stood a magnificent house and several barns and outbuildings. Smoke rose from the chimneys and in the dim atmosphere and through the rain they could see cheerful lights at the windows.

"There is Clayden farm," explained Parson Leach. "And as snug and satisfactory a hearth as exists from here to General Knox's, not to mention as lively and gracious a family as you are likely to bear in your time. You will not regret our refusing previous offers." He looked to his young companions, but could not extract any enthusiasm from them. He smiled, though he must have been weary and chilled himself. "Let's leave the road, and cut through the fields," he suggested. "We can't be any wetter than we are now."

So he turned them off the road, and led them through ankle high grass that squirted and squelched as wetly as Peter's moccasins. They descended a small knoll, crossed a busy rill and came up level with the cluster of buildings. The rain seemed to increase, as if to add drama to their arrival. A dog barked, then two. There was the sound of a horse neighing in the barn as they passed it and Mars answered with an impatient snort. A small face peered from one of the rear windows of the house and disappeared again.

They were rounding the broad back of the estate, and coming into view of the yard when a kitchen door was thrown open and a large woman in bonnet and apron leaned out to take stock of the travelers. Some exclamation rose from her and she swatted at the air as if she would drive the rain away like gnats. "Lands and living!" she declared. "It's unfit to be about. Who is it and what could drive them out on a day like this?"

Three faces peered out from behind the woman's wide hips, clinging to her apron and skirts. She swatted at one of these, but without conviction. A young man ran out with a coat thrown over his head and met the three wayfarers in the muddy yard. He peered into the parson's hood and knew him immediately. "Mr. Leach!" he cried, as much to identify the man to those in the doorway as to address him.

"Ebulon," returned Parson Leach. "How are you, lad."

"My mother has made apple pandowdy!" declared the boy, who was not more than nine or ten and didn't seem to mind sharing such a treat with new arrivals.

"I'm half-filled just hearing about it!" declared the parson.

"Is that Mr. Leach?" called the woman at the door. "What ever brings you out on a day like this?"

"Surely to see you, Mrs. Magnamous, and to taste your apple pandowdy."

"Ebulon, take his horse," called the woman. "Get under cover and by a fire, Mr. Leach—you and your friends."

Ebulon was already in the process of taking Mars from his master, but happily shouted his agreement to the woman, who was his mother. Parson Leach lifted Nora down from Mars's back and caught her when she stumbled on her own legs. Peter hesitated beside them, but the parson nodded to the door and told him to hurry inside.

Peter wondered what greater pleasures heaven could supply than that kitchen, for he stepped in from the driving rain and en-

countered warmth and dryness and the snap and light of a crackling fire and the smells of cooking and herb brooms hanging from
the beams and the faces of three young people, peering from the
pantry door.

One girl in a beautiful dress, her dark hair done up in curls
and bows, stepped up to Peter boldly and said, "I saw you first,
you know. I saw you through the window in the nursery." She was
only fourteen or fifteen years old, but regarded Peter as if she
were accustomed to being heard. Peter was not sure of a response,
nor did his confusion lessen when she looked at him and said,
"Were you in a fight?"

After a moment, Peter touched the fresh scar on his forehead.
"No," he said.

The girl's frown indicated that more information was needed,
but when he added nothing to the simple denial, she looked him
up and down and exclaimed, "What happened to your shoes?"

"They got wet," was all he could think to say, but he realized
that she was amazed by the slits he had made to accommodate his
feet.

"Father's things will fit you," she pronounced. "Father is at
sea."

By this time, Parson Leach had half carried Nora to the hearthside, and thrown off his cape and hood with a splash. Mrs. Magnamous began to lift the blue greatcoat from Nora's shoulders,
when she realized the state of the young woman's dress. The
woman let out a cry of dismay and pulled the coat around Nora
again. "However can she be traveling like this?" said the woman to
no certain person. "Shoo! Shoo!" she said to two young boys who

attempted to gape past her substantial midsection. She swatted at them and drove them back a yard or so. "She must have dry things!" declared the woman.

"She has none, I fear," said the parson.

"What is it? What is it?" came an elderly, if commanding, voice and a large gray-haired gentleman shuffled into view at the pantry door. He had spectacles lifted unto his brow and he squinted into the kitchen till he laid eyes on Parson Leach. "Zachariah!" he said, with evident pleasure in the discovery.

"Captain Clayden!" returned the parson. He strode dripping across the kitchen to shake hands with the old man.

"What commotion!" said Captain Clayden. "What have you brought me today? I asked for Robert Burton when I saw you last."

"He's brought you half-drowned children!" asserted Mrs. Magnamous.

"What? You look half-drowned yourself," said the Captain to Parson Leach. "Get out of those things! Have you dry clothes to wear? I don't know that any of us are tall enough to supply you."

"I see Ebulon charging from the barn now," said Parson Leach, peering through one of the kitchen windows, "and the good fellow is bringing my bags and kit."

One of the younger boys rushed to let Ebulon in, and the sound of the rain was, for the moment, a loud and chilling presence in the warm kitchen.

"Emily, Sussanah!" said Mrs. Maganamous, unable to abide dawdling any longer. "Take this poor child and change her clothes! No, don't take her to your rooms, she's soaking to the bone! Set her by the fire in the nursery and drive the children out. Then bring her something decent and warm. Sussanah, something of yours will answer." Mrs. Magnamous hugged Nora Tillage to her all this time, as if she were her own daughter. "Lands and living!" she said again. "Mr. Leach, what are you about, hauling these children through storm and water? Are you trying to kill them?"

"It is, as they say, Mrs. Magnamous, a long story." Parson Leach smiled, though he looked a little wary, lest she swat at him as she had the little boys.

The young woman who must have been Sussanah, since she was more of a height with Nora, came up and took Nora's arm. There was great sympathy in her dark blue eyes, and curiosity as well. The other young woman, Emily, left Peter less readily, and watched Nora with something next to suspicion. Her eyes were pale and striking against the dark frame of hair that hung past her shoulders.

Mrs. Magnamous took stock of Peter then and similar cries of maternal anguish and concern filed the air. "And I suppose he is without wardrobe, as well!" she said, and upon the parson's affirmative, she answered, "Captain James's things will fit him—"

"I'll get them," said Emily, already bustling away from Nora to this office.

"You'll do nothing of the kind! James!" she shouted. "James!"

A fellow of about ten or eleven years showed himself in the pantry door.

"Take this young man—up the back stairs, you had better—and fetch him some of your father's things."

James never said a word, but nodded once, and went to a closeted stairway on the other end of the kitchen. Peter threw a worried look at the parson, but that man only smiled and shrugged; this was no more than he had expected. James opened the door to the back steps and waited for Peter, who dripped across the kitchen floor and up the steep stairwell behind him. Peter looked over his shoulder, before he disappeared, and saw Mrs. Magnamous press Nora's face with both her hands and kiss the young woman fiercely on the top of the head.

12

Concerning an Interview with Captain Clayden

PETER LOON HAD NEVER SEEN SUCH A HOUSE AS CAPTAIN CLAYDEN'S before this day, and certainly he had never seen the inside of such a magnificent home. The back stairs, leading to the humblest quarters, might have been marble steps, and the unfinished chamber above—filled with chests and old furniture—a palace room. The chamber was colder and darker than the kitchen, but enough light came through the gable window, and enough heat rose from the hearth below, that Peter could look about him and not quite see his breath. Rain pounded noisily on the roof above and streaked the small panes of the single window; the weather was almost pleasant, seen and heard from inside. Peter sneezed.

"Devil behind," invoked James, then considering Peter's dripping state, he said, "Perhaps you had better stay here. I'll bring you some of my father's things."

While James was gone, Peter listened to the sounds of conversation and laughter belowstairs, muffled beneath the rain. He tried to recall the welter of circumstance that had led him from the little cabin his grandfather had built—a splendid enough affair by their neighbors' standards—to this extraordinary manse with its lively people and handsome children. He had been particularly taken—puzzled really—by Emily's insistent stare, and quite glad that Mrs. Magnamous had not let the girl retrieve clothes for him.

"Is Mrs. Magnamous your mother?" asked Peter when James returned with an armload of clothes and a pair of boots.

"Good heavens, no," said James. "She's our cook." But the boy took no offense. "Captain Clayden is my grandfather," he added. "My father and mother are at sea, and Mr. Magnamous, too, who's third mate aboard the *Duration*. My father is Captain James Clayden," finished the younger James with evident and (to Peter) merited pride.

"I'm Peter Loon," was the simple reply, which almost seemed presumptuous, speaking to the offspring of such grand folk.

James put his hand out and shook Peter's firmly. "James Clayden," he said, though that was now clear to Peter. "You are traveling with Parson Leach, then," said the younger boy, with the indication in his voice that this sounded exciting.

"Yes," said Peter, but without conviction.

"Emily thinks you've been in dire circumstances, I can tell. She came into the den, shouting 'Pilgrims! Pilgrims are coming!' and didn't Grandfather laugh."

Peter gaped, not quite understanding the jest.

"The girl with you . . ." began James.

Peter shivered in his wet clothes. "Nora," he answered.

"She did seem distressed."

"She was being chased when she found us," said Peter. He heard the door below opening and footsteps on the treads.

"Chased? By whom? And you and Mr. Leach found her?"

"And Mr. Cutts and Mr. Moss," added Peter; when James frowned, he added, "They're woodsmen."

This was beginning to sound as good as anything Emily could imagine, and James was zealous with curiosity. The presence of two woodsmen in a tale of chase and rescue only deepened the story's promise.

But Parson Leach appeared at the head of the stairs and perceived the tenor of the conversation immediately. "James," he said evenly, "perhaps you would allow Peter and me to change into some warm clothes."

James nodded his way out of the room and closed the door behind him, but it was obviously a torture to him. They could hear his footsteps hurrying down the hall beyond.

"I should have told you, Peter—the less said, right now, about our recent adventures, the better. I will tell Captain Clayden what has happened, of course, since I believe he will be of help to us. But we don't want rumor bandied about before we've had a chance to take our first breath. I fret what might be said of Nora if the wrong notions took wing. Don't concern yourself," added the preacher before Peter had the opportunity to ask the parson's pardon. "Now, let's get dressed."

Peter looked at the heap of clothes that James had transferred to his arms and the parson indicated a chest where he could lay them. Parson Leach slung his own gear into a corner and pulled dry clothes from one of his bags. He gave out some instructions to Peter, who was a little mystified by some of the buttons and loops and ties. The young man wasn't accustomed to so many pieces to his wardrobe.

"You're a canny young man, Peter," the parson said, as he adjusted the collar of his young companion's coat here and tugged at a sleeve of his shirt there. "You ask questions when you don't know, which is the first sign of thought, my father used to say. Never trust a man who doesn't question you, he told me. But there is a thing or two you *couldn't* know to ask about. The first thing is that these are very good and gracious people, and they will be pleased if you compliment their house and their circumstances, but they will think you a bit of a bumpkin if you act as if you've never seen such things before—so don't gape, when you're not speaking, even if you haven't."

"Yes, sir."

"The next thing is that the women here, I believe, are going to see you as something of a champion, before long." Parson Leach laughed at Peter's wide eyes. "I don't think the girls will get *very* much from Nora, but they'll surmise enough to carry their opinion of you. Remember, a little modesty is an admirable thing, but let them think highly of you, if they want, for you behaved very bravely out there this morning." The parson nodded gravely.

Peter only blinked. He was still shivering, in fits and starts, and longed to linger by the fire downstairs.

"Stand there," ordered the clergyman, and he retrieved a brush from his kit. With this he combed back Peter's long wet hair and stood back. "You had a bath today, at any rate. I haven't given you a good stare till now, Peter Loon, but you are a stalwart-looking fellow." And it was true, Peter had taken after his mother's handsome features. The parson chuckled, "Captain Clayden is liable to give you a place on one of his brigs, just to hie you away from his granddaughters. Here, we'll hang these wet things on the beams."

"One of his brigs? But I'm looking for my Uncle Obed."

"Yes," drawled Parson Leach. "We'll ask after him." He considered Peter, as a painter might his nearly finished canvas, and seemed satisfied with the work. "Just remember, keep your compliments short. If it's masculine, it's grand; if it's feminine, it's lovely."

Silently, Peter tried out these adjectives.

"Now, pull on those boots. I'm throwing these moccasins of yours in the midden." They made a wet slap in the corner of the room. When Peter was ready and had gone to the head of the stairwell, the parson motioned him to the other end of the chamber, saying, "Come this way, down the front stairs like any guest."

Peter now got his first view of the palatial end of the house, and it was suddenly difficult to put the parson's advice into use. He did close his mouth, after a bit, and tried not to stare at the paintings along the broad staircase, or touch the flocked wallpaper. The parson led him to the room that young James had dubbed the *den*. A happy fire roared at the hearth in argument to the rain at the windows, and Captain Clayden—wearing an old-fashioned wig now—was perusing his book-lined shelves, as if hunting for a place to put whatever volume Parson Leach may have brought him.

"Zachariah," said the Captain, greeting his guests as if he had not seen them half an hour before. He shook the preacher's hand and then took Peter's. "Mr. Loon, welcome to Clayden Point."

"Thank you, sir."

"I have ordered supper early," said the Captain, "so we will gather in an hour or so and you shall be introduced properly, young man. Zachariah, what is James telling me of this poor young girl having to be rescued? What is happening to the District? Sit down, sit down!"

The guests did as they were told. Peter sat by the fire in a wide, hardwood chair with dark broad arms. He'd never sat in anything like it, but did his best to appear complacent. Above the mantle was a semicircle of wood on which had been painted the scene of a house that might have been the Clayden estate from the opposite shore of the Damariscotta.

"The young woman's name is Nora Tillage, Captain," said the parson, when he and the elderly fellow had settled themselves.

"It's an old name," said Captain Clayden. "There were Tillages in my mother's genealogy."

"Perhaps she is related, sir."

The Captain's eyes flashed with knowing humor. "Where did you come by her?" he asked.

"She's from Balltown, in the northeastern hamlet there. Her father has a tavern known as the Ale Wife."

The Captain grunted. A connection to Balltown was not promising to his mind. The Ale Wife he had never heard of.

"Lately, Mr. Tillage has come under the preaching of a man named Barrow."

"Barrow."

"Nathan Barrow," said the parson and he could not keep some level of his prejudice against the man from affecting his pronunciation of the name.

The Captain grunted again, less happy still. "I know the man, by reputation. Wasn't he one of the chief agitators in New Milford the other night? Or perhaps you haven't heard."

"Yes, I have. There was some unfortunate business, there, I know."

"Unfortunate! They stripped an honest man to a sock and a sleeve and beat him with sticks! I dare say *he* thinks it unfortunate!"

Peter was alarmed by this outburst, but the Captain's temper quickly cooled, if only in time for a further explosion.

"Mr. Barrow, as it happens, has some power over Mr. Tillage," explained Parson Leach.

"Is it debt, then?"

"No, worse, it's religion."

The Captain, it would soon be revealed to Peter, had known Zachariah Leach for years, and it was only because of this that he was not shocked or surprised by this strange pronouncement. "And the young woman is meant as some devotion to this Barrow?"

"She is considered part of his due, yes."

"Well, then, this Barrow is a *bastard!*" shouted Captain Clayden, and he leapt to his feet and seized a poker from the hearthside, as if he would fight the man then and there. "And her father is a more bastard *still!*"

Peter's eyes went wide and he stiffened in his chair. Parson Leach was unperturbed, however, and he did not stir an inch; a twinkle of humor glanced from his eyes to Peter to reassure the young man.

The old man showed no embarrassment for his sudden fit of temper, but sat down again, growling all the while.

"I have met the girl, once or twice before," continued Parson Leach. "She and her father came to a sermon I gave a year or so ago. Peter spoke with her briefly, just yesterday, under no guise but cordiality, but he understood her situation quickly enough and advised me of it." Some of this was news to Peter, or the clergyman credited him with more understanding than he owned.

"And you whisked her away!" declared the Captain. "As was the thing to do!"

"I did not," said the clergyman, perhaps a little abashed. "I spoke to her father about this arrangement with Barrow, but it was her father, after all, who had agreed to it in the first place, and I had wider concerns at the time. I had to think of Peter, who was with me, and we were not among long-standing friends in Balltown, though the folk there are as decent as any."

The Captain made a noise that left room for doubt on this position.

"But, soon after we left the village, she ran away, it seems, with only the clothes on her back; and some miles outside of the settlement—on our way to New Milford, actually—she caught us up with Barrow and a dozen or so men in full chase."

Peter half expected Captain Clayden to leap up and call for his horses, but he had wrested control of himself, and merely let out a fuming sigh and glowered at the fire. The poker he held, like a weapon, across his lap.

"There were two good men with us—two woodsmen—Manasseh Cutts and Crispin Moss, and thank God for it, for we were able to dissuade a stronger force and their fairly persuasive leader from pursuing her further."

"You turned them about."

"The *cloth* has some mortal advantages," said Parson Leach wryly. "They were not bad men, the most of them, and as taking Nora from us would have necessitated some violence, they were loathe to press the point."

"Still, you stood your ground and gave her protection from those scoundrels." Captain Clayden prodded a footstool under his heels and scowled at his boots. "But you will continue to defend these people, Zachariah," he said more thoughtfully.

"I will speak for men, though not always of necessity, for their actions."

"A man *is* his actions."

"A rich man who steals is more guilty than a poor man who steals to feed his children."

"So you say," grumbled the old man, though he mounted no argument against the parson's opinion. "I have wealthy friends, Zachariah, who are among the Great Men in our district. Do you intimate they are thieves?"

"They believe they are sole proprietors of Maine, of that I am certain, and therefore incapable of stealing what is rightfully their own."

"Rightly so!" said the Captain, as if finding a correct opinion in the parson for the first time.

"And I believe their claim ends with the wilderness, where the labor of common men must tell for possession."

"It is the proprietors' by *Right of Grant*, Zachariah!"

"Grants from a king whose will and power we have deposed. Grants to landed men who, in some instances, fought *against* our revolution."

"And by deed," continued Captain Clayden.

"From Indian contracts that contradict one another. Are the great men of this district not wealthy enough?"

"It is not simply wealth, Zachariah, and you know it. The commoner does well to have Great Men watch over them. It's not just the land, but what is best for the district and the nation, affairs about which your backlanders can know nothing."

"They would say the same of you, who do not struggle as they do."

Captain Clayden laughed then, which Peter would not have predicted. "Ah, well," said the elderly fellow, who may have only been testing the clergyman's continued resolve upon the matter. Strangely, to Peter, they seemed to think the better of one another, though they disagreed so particularly on this subject. "Ah, well," said the Captain again, then, "you've rescued the girl from terrible circumstances, is all that matters."

Parson Leach waved his hand, as if his part in the affair was unremarkable. "It was Peter who charged forward, when I stopped to load my musket, and rescued her truly, and it was only the rain, that we might otherwise have cursed, that fouled the gun fired in his direction."

This was more news to Peter, but he recalled the nasty snap he had heard behind him when he first reached Nora.

"Let me shake your hand, young man," said the Captain, and he leaned forward to do this.

Peter awkwardly put his own hand forward, reddening as the elderly fellow pumped his arm rigorously.

"Well," said Captain Clayden, when this was done. "Will the girl's father be coming for her?"

"Of that I can't be sure," said the parson carefully.

"Not that she wants a thing to do with him, anymore," said the old man. "She's not of her majority, it's clear. What is she, sixteen, seventeen years? It's a legal matter, to be sure, but I don't know a judge who would take up her father's case, did he hear the whole business. I'd throw him in jail, and there are those who would cherish *any* justification to put this Barrow behind a lock. How a preacher, even a self-proclaimed unordained wanderer—begging your pardon, Zachariah—could behave in such a fashion! Why, he sounds like one of these Antinomianists!" Peter caught another smile from Parson Leach, but Captain Clayden was growling into the fire. "She will stay here, till further arrangements are made," said the old fellow with sudden decision.

"I believe she's a fine young woman," said Parson Leach.

"She knew enough to quit *that* rabble." The Captain considered the poker in his lap as if he could not remember how it got there. Then he looked up at the parson. "This situation between the girl and Barrow . . ." he began, but hesitated to finish the thought.

"It was a recent arrangement," said the parson carefully, "which she fled in a timely fashion." Peter wondered how the man could know this; he had himself thought otherwise.

Captain Clayden nodded slowly. "Yes."

"Not that it is of any matter," said the parson offhandedly. "It was an involuntary business for her, at best, that much is clear."

Captain Clayden raised his head and considered something, came to a new decision and nodded again. "She will stay here," he said again.

13

How Peter Spent His First Night on Clayden Point, and How He Was Perceived by Young Women There

PETER DID NOT CONSIDER HOW HUNGRY HE WAS—HOW HUNGRY HE had been, perhaps, his entire life—until he came into the dining hall of the Clayden house. It was a long room, lit with candles and an elegant flickering chandelier. There was a shallow fireplace, and the fire there added to the dancing aspect of the light and threw a cozy warmth into the room. The table itself was half as long as the room, and piled with every imaginable victual and some Peter could not name; meats and vegetables and fruits, pies and puddings and a basket of boiled eggs, bread and cheese and ale and wine and a pitcher of milk, cooled in the larder. It seemed to him more like a table laid for a village fair than a meal set for a single family. He glanced at Parson Leach, who brushed his own chin in such a way that Peter remembered to close his mouth.

Sussanah and Emily had already entered, with Nora in tow, and a fourth young woman as well, whom Peter had not seen before; they stood across the table from him, having entered from another room, and gave the appearance of certainty and elegance—Nora Tillage being the only exception. She had, it was true, every advantage of fashion that could be provided by Captain Clayden's granddaughters, and though a fragile sort of beauty was yet evident through her angular features, any pretense to real poise was lost in the confusion and apprehension those features expressed. She seemed to feel strange and unnatural in her borrowed finery and her stately surroundings. There was not one person in the room, beside Parson Leach, that she had known before yesterday.

The light of the candles shone like bronze in her russet hair, which had been tended with great energy and success. She was dressed in a shade of blue that was perhaps a hue too cold to compliment the blue-veined pallor of her skin, but all in all, Emily and Sussanah had performed admirably in the time allotted and derived no little satisfaction from their labor. Sussanah's clothes were too *filled out* for Nora, but tucks and pins, and a ribbon in the right place had done wonders.

Peter saw Nora's hand tremble slightly, however, on the back of the chair before her, and she seemed more intent on Parson Leach and himself, than upon her appearance or demeanor. From Emily's expression it might be intimated that she considered Nora a challenge and perhaps a bit of a bad pupil.

The sisters had not neglected themselves during their efforts on Nora's behalf, for they were flounced out as prettily as could be imagined. Their cousin, Martha Flemming, the fourth young woman, who had light chestnut hair and shared their blue eyes— somewhere between Emily's pale blue and Sussanah's dark—had been informed, it seemed, about the young man who would be at dinner, and had also prepared accordingly.

Dressed in Captain James Clayden's fine clothes, combed and adjusted by Parson Leach, Peter was his mother's son in the realm of natural gravity as well as in his dark good looks; and all that separated him from his hosts was the roughness of his hands and the weatherburn to his face. Captain Clayden, the grandfather, approved of the young man the more for his diffidence, which he imagined, for the time being, to be the product of a cultured reserve. The young women were pleased to have him to look at (the scar on Peter's forehead only gave him the look of an adventurer) and young James also admired Peter as they gathered at the table.

"Sit, sit!" commanded the Captain. "Please, you must vary yourselves," he added, and he proceeded to direct the seating arrangements, so that male and female were mostly alternated about the table. Mrs. Magnamous made a cooing sound when she brought the roast beef into the dining hall and saw the gathering.

Peter hesitated to reach for anything, more from awe at the abundance before him than from refinement or courtesy, but very quickly he was aware of a fashion to the proceedings to which his mother might have hinted, at odd times in his childhood. *What would she think of this?* wondered Peter. *What would Amos, and Hannah, and Sally Ann think?* He felt almost charged with guilt to be sitting before such abundance.

After Parson Leach said grace, Captain Clayden asked for Nora's plate, which surprised Peter, and Nora too; Martha, opposite Peter, smiled though not unkindly at the look of mystification on Nora's face. It reminded Peter to close his mouth again and he glanced at Parson Leach, who nodded.

"What do you think of our ladies, Mr. Loon?" asked Captain Clayden. He had returned Nora's plate with a piece of beef and was holding his hand out toward Peter.

From the corner of his eye, Peter caught Parson Leach tapping his own plate. Peter said, "Oh!" and handed his plate, not very gracefully, past Nora's face. "The ladies are *lovely*," he said, remembering the parson's instructions.

The ladies in question—except Nora—shifted almost imperceptibly in their seats or looked aside. Nora had taken up her knife but remained undecided as to the fate of the beef in her plate.

Emily very sensibly began to send other things around the table. "Mr. Loon," she said, with a bowl of mashed squash extended.

Peter took a moment to respond, the address was so solemn and the pale blue of the girl's eyes was so extraordinary. "Thank you," he said.

If Emily's expression was one of serious regard and perhaps practical curiosity, Sussanah's dark eyes were filled with something more obviously tender. Her voice sounded breathless, and her ardent attention like that of a person in great suspense. "I hope you find our home comfortable, Mr. Loon," said Sussanah.

Peter was not sure how someone's home fell on the masculine-to-feminine scale of things, and any number of solutions ran through his mind in a panic. Captain Clayden, he suspected, had built the house, and it did have a certain masculine robustness; but on the other hand, Peter's mind attached domestic matters to feminine concerns. Before he had made a proper decision, an answer seemed required. "It's grovely," he professed solemnly.

Sussanah's look of wonder told him that something extraordinary had happened, even if his own ear did not. He closed his eyes, shook his head once and, looking back at the lovely young woman, corrected himself with "It's grand."

She smiled prettily. Emily frowned at her sister and said, "Turnip, Mr. Loon?"

"Lovely," he said, almost in a whisper.

Either the young people of the Clayden family were extraordinarily versed in the proprieties or else the Captain had leveled a directive about conversation at the table; if curiosity were evident in the brother and sisters and in the cousin, no question was posited regarding Nora or her immediate circumstances. They did, however, hang upon the words of Parson Leach and Peter Loon, as if some unexpected tidbit might get past them if they were not paying strict attention.

Martha inquired of Peter his origins, and he seemed so very ill at ease admitting he was from Sheepscott Great Pond that she blushed and turned to ask Emily for news concerning her cat, which lived in the barn and purportedly terrorized the mice there. Emily was aware of Martha's miscalculation, but also very proud of her cat, so she allowed the subject and related a tale regarding "Henry" (her cat) and one of the Captain's dogs. The story was not flattering of "Duke's" courage, and the Captain huffed noisily through the final portion of the piece, but it was clear to all that he was amused.

"I will tell Duke he has leave to *chase* Henry from the chicken coop in future," said the elderly fellow, with as much sally as significance.

"I'd guess the rooster will do it for him," suggested James, which was exactly what had happened, though Emily would not admit it.

"The rooster must presume," thought the parson aloud, "that possession of the coop *is eleven points in the law*."

Peter wondered if the parson was throwing a jocose barb in the Captain's direction, but the old man was up to it if this was the case.

"At any rate," he said, "cat, dog, or rooster, it is *I* who own the coop."

The parson thought this very good and smiled.

Peter, in the meanwhile, would have done well to pay attention to the limits of his plate—for at first, he realized that he was allowing himself miserly helpings of the meal, and that the puny dollops of squash and turnip looked ridiculous next to the slab of meat on his plate. In compensating for this daintiness, he applied great portions before him till he quickly ran out of room. Everyone else helped themselves as the servings passed, as if it were the most natural thing. He was in near agony, not understanding the manners of his hosts and certain that his awkwardness was visible, even conspicuous, to those about him and that they would share a good laugh at his expense when he was gone.

Nora, meanwhile, though she might have had more sense of eating among strangers than Peter, allowed hunger to overcome nicety, and set upon her portions as they reached her plate. The Clayden sisters were quick to raise interesting subjects for the attention of the table.

"I hope it doesn't continue to rain," said Sussanah, looking sweetly at no one in particular. "If the fields have dried enough tomorrow we might *pique-nique*," which last phrase she pronounced in her best French.

A general cry ran up among the young people, and James declared, "Yes! The last of the season! The last of the year!"

Peter was taken by their enthusiasm, though he had no idea what it meant to *pique-nique*.

"You are not to take these young people out on one of your expeditions if tomorrow isn't proper," said the Captain firmly.

"They've experienced enough weather now, and could do with their feet by the fire. You go on one of your outings and, pounds to pennies, Sussanah will let Miss Tillage's bonnet blow away, and James will pull Mr. Loon into the river, trying to guddle a minnow. Emily will chase Henry into a briar and have to be rescued."

Just these sorts of things might have happened before, since the pronouncement garnered laughter rather than indignation.

"I don't suppose *Martha* has ever done anything wrong," said Sussanah with feigned vexedness.

"Martha has not yet revealed the degree of her mischief to me, but I don't doubt she has some." This was all said with great affection, and Martha was delighted, the more so—Peter suspected—because she hadn't a degree of mischief in her, though she may have hoped she did.

Even Nora seemed to appreciate the jocular mood of the gathering and Peter was conscious that her rigid bearing had calmed somewhat. He turned to the pale young woman and flashed a small smile, but she could not return his gaze with anything like it and he was moved to reflection again.

The meal continued in much the same manner for Peter—there was his amazement with the gracious plenty before him, and pleasure in the generally light company; it was not disagreeable to note admiring looks from the young women at the table, nor troublesome to know that he incited their interest; but his pleasure was mixed with wonder. He could not be other than sensible of his differences from these people, most of all because of their unhaunted ease and cheerfulness. Peter hardly knew what it meant to be careless, and was a little frightened by its display.

Throughout the meal, Parson Leach was like a bit of familiar country to Peter, just as he must have been to Nora, who watched him with barely concealed anxiety. The Captain was cordial and gentle with Nora and plainly approving of Peter, and it was an example of a vast separation between them that the cordiality of the hosts could not entirely win over the apprehensions of their young guests.

Peter flagged in his appetite long before his plate was cleared; he was not used to such abundance and his stomach felt fit to burst before he was done. Wine was served at the meal as well, and Peter, who was only used to small beer and the occasional corner of rum, felt a little heady from it. Nora, as the daughter of a tavern keeper, was used to more food and tended to her meal with some vigor despite her narrow carriage and whatever doubts that plagued her.

After dinner they retired to a parlor which was more elegant than anything Peter and Nora had yet seen. It was expected that everyone would sit and continue conversation and perhaps play a game or two, but Peter and Nora were beyond imbibing any further novelties. Their present surroundings were so remote from the circumstances they had left only that morning, and indeed so foreign to anything in their experience, that strangeness alone would have worn them out even had they not known the chill and sapping power of the rain and fright and nervous exhaustion.

Parson Leach took command of Peter and Nora and ordered them to bed, and the others took pity on them. The young women escorted Nora, amid a chorus of goodnights, to the room and bed she would share with Sussanah, and the parson allowed James to lead himself and Peter to guest quarters on the other side of the house.

On the stairs, however, Nora had a moment—or was given a moment—beside Peter, when she said beneath her breath, "I am with you, now," which sounded part question and part vow. He recalled her question of him the day before and this morning—"You're with Parson Leach," which again was difficult to separate as query or statement. Peter was not afforded the opportunity to reply, if reply was warranted, but was whisked off by James to the room he would share with Parson Leach.

"Well, Peter," said the parson, when they shut the door and considered the two beds in the room. "We'll be spared each other's kicks in the night, if not the snores. See, they've laid out nightclothes for you."

Peter picked up the long nightdress and fingered the soft-worked cloth. The goosedown pillow and mattress were an amazement to him, and the sheets felt cool and crisp beneath his hand; he almost forgot Nora, considering them. When she did surface in his thoughts, a series of associated ideas led him to Captain Clayden's kindness toward the young woman.

"It is difficult not to be fond of Captain Clayden," said Peter quietly, almost speaking to himself.

"As it should be," replied the parson. "He is a fond gentleman. Certainly it is difficult to dislike a gracious host, otherwise we should flee hypocrisy, scavenge supper, and sleep out of doors."

"But he is against my father," said Peter, who did fear hypocrisy, "for my father would have been in disagreement with him about our land and the claims of Proprietors." He stood at the window with the curtain pulled aside—he had never known curtains—and looked out at the last graying portion of the day. He thought the rain had fallen off, and that the wind had come around to another quarter.

"He does not disagree as completely as the Proprietors themselves," answered the clergyman, "nor as much as many a satellite, who is the more vehement for wanting to please his master. Each man will turn with the wind that favors his course."

"My father said something like," Peter half-whispered.

"From what you tell me of your father, Peter, and from your conduct, I guess that he was a wise and prudent man."

"But it seems as if I am accepting comfort from an enemy, from a man who would strip the people I know best of what they've worked hardest for."

"I don't think, in the end, that Captain Clayden would." Parson Leach had been extracting his feet from his boots and sat on the edge of his bed wiggling his toes in his socks and relishing the relief this brought to the soles of his feet. He may have appeared to be answering Peter without feeling, but the young man had learned to suspect deeper things in the parson's complaisant surface.

"They buried him today, no doubt," said Peter.

"Yes," said Parson Leach. "I will say a prayer."

Peter looked over his shoulder to see the man seriously considering his word. The parson looked a little sad, in fact, and Peter had another dizzying sensation as he wondered what he was doing there.

How many people can there be in the world? he wondered. "But from what I understood of his opinion," said Peter, "Captain Clayden would put down my claim to the acres I have cleared and anything I accomplished there."

"He would have his own account of justice. He may have attempted to survey those acres himself, years ago."

"What's that you say?"

"He is a Captain of men by necessity, and was a brave and cunning leader in the war, but he is by training a surveyor, and worked for the Plymouth Patent when he was a young man."

Peter considered this, feeling no less dizzy for the knowledge. "And yet, I like him," he repeated finally.

"I should think less of you if you didn't; for you see, if we only love those who *agree* with us, then our society has no future. The old world has kings and queens to fall back upon, to blame as well as praise, but we have only ourselves, and it is a measure of this civilization, this strange nation of ours and its particular refinements, how willingly we live beside each other in peace when our opinions, and even cherished beliefs are *not* in harmony. Reasonable men *can* disagree, Peter, and there will be every imaginable permutation of opinion and thought—and some that you or I could *not* imagine—no man's lights reflecting any other's completely, not Captain Clayden's and mine, not mine and yours. Captain Clayden might not be in accord with you or me on the necessity of opening the wilderness, or at least not in absolute accord, but I know that he would not willingly see harm come to any man or his children."

"He *is* taking Nora in."

"Yes, he is indeed."

"Each man will turn to the wind that favors his cause," quoted Peter.

"Reasonable men can disagree," said the parson, as if repeating a catechism. "All else is war and a blasphemy to God."

"At any rate, Captain Clayden—with whom I *do* disagree—seems more reasonable to me than Barrow, who would support my claim."

"And it is Barrow you must shake off," said the parson with sudden energy, as if he were suddenly in the midst of a sermon. "For any cause of men must hold their own to the highest standards of good will and decency." He rose and hung his coat behind the door, saying, "You must be the first to call out the man in your own camp who fails in principles and exact yourself to constant watch, demanding of you and yours the behavior you would hope for in your adversary."

Peter smiled in such a knowing way that the parson might have mistaken him for a Seminarian. The young man said, "Some would not admit that those were the tactics to win a war."

"They are the tactics to *avoid* war," said the clergyman.

Peter understood this, though perhaps only at that very instant.

Briefly, as Parson Leach turned away, he gripped Peter's shoulder.

14

Of What It Meant to Pique-Nique *and
the Inevitability of Certain Failures*

WHEN PETER WOKE, WITH SUNLIGHT BRIGHT IN THE ROOM, PARSON Leach and his boots were up and gone. Peter took some moments, blinking at the ceiling and the play of light there, to appraise the events that led him to this chamber and the house surrounding it, none of which he would have had the experience to envision two days ago.

He could sense as much as hear life in the house about him, below him. He heard a shout in the yard, the *chip-chip* of a chickadee, then the disorderly laugh of a crow. Someone was running in the house, but the building was so much larger than anything Peter had ever known that he couldn't place the sounds or estimate their distance from him.

He sat up and swung his feet out of the bed and onto the floor, and from this position he contemplated a new outfit of clothes draped on the chair by the window. Where were his things? he wondered.

At the window he considered the day, which might be just what the young Claydens had hoped for. The sun was bright and warming, the wind had retraced itself to the west and must be drying the fields as it ran past; the trees about the house had lost many of their leaves, and were losing more still as they tottered to the breeze. Peter heard the crow again, then an unfamiliar cry, and he leaned down to peer at the sky through the window and caught sight of broad white wings angling over the river.

There was a small mirror on a table in the room and Peter looked at himself when he had dressed, hoping that he had fastened all the buttons and loops correctly. Without the parson to direct him, he couldn't be sure, but nothing looked as if it were ready to fall down so he gathered his courage and went quietly down the stairs.

Captain Clayden stepped out of the den and met him in the front hall. "Good morning, Mr. Loon. The young people have great plans for you and Nora, but if you are not sufficiently rested you must beg them off and firmly." The elderly man had a book in his hand, keeping his place with one finger. "Zachariah has gone out and may not be back till evening, so he exhorts you to enjoy the day, which I hope you may."

Peter did not know how to answer any of this, except to say, "Thank you."

"The man has not seen fit to discover what he's brought for me," said the Captain, who was on to other things. He lifted the volume in his hand to indicate what were his real concerns. "But I will corner him tonight, with luck, and add something to my shelves. You are welcome, by the way, to avail yourself of anything here." Captain Clayden led Peter into the den and swept the book-lined room with a single gesture.

Peter did not have a large command of the printed word and the idea of abiding within a book for a pastime was strange to him, though curiously appealing. He considered the leathery backs of

Captain Clayden's books and thought that no other subject of conversation could have so demanded the parson's presence. "What are they about?" he asked.

The Captain looked sharply at Peter, but only for the briefest moment; his expression softened as he studied the boy. "All creation," he said, with a fondness in his tone that Peter could not completely understand. "Here is a geography of the known continent," he told the young man, pointing to one tall binding, "and here are the creatures that inhabit it depicted in engravings from life," he continued, pointing to the next volume. "There is an astronomy, and here is 'Roderick Random' and 'Joseph Andrews.'" The elderly man walked the perimeter of his den, pointing out favored books as he would friends standing by to be introduced. "Mr. Johnson's Dictionary, Mr. Boswell's life of Mr. Johnson, Tristram Shandy, Thomas Paine, Izaak Walton—"

"The fisherman!" said Peter, pleased to recognize a single name, if only a name he had learned the day before yesterday.

"Do you know Izaak then, my lad?" said Captain Clayden with surprise and sudden interest.

"Parson Leach does," said Peter. This seemed meek enough reason to invoke Izaak Walton's name, but Captain Clayden only nodded, as if he approved of Peter knowing someone who knew the famous angler's writing. "Yes," said the elderly gentleman, "Zachariah supplied me with this edition."

They could hear a dog barking, and Peter hoped it meant that the parson had come back early, but instead young James Clayden bounded into the den with the hound happily in tow. "You're awake!" he declared as if this were news and also long in coming.

"You'll be wanting breakfast," said the Captain to Peter. "Mrs. Magnamous will have saved something out for you."

"We're going to *pique-nique*," said James, as if he had had to tell his grandfather this more times than was necessary. "He can eat with us!"

There were more footsteps in the hall and while the Captain and James escorted Peter toward the kitchen, they met Sussanah and Martha. The young women were, if anything, prettier than the night before; they had been out in the day, and the wind and the sun had put apples in their cheeks and brightened their eyes. They were nearly more vision than Peter could graciously receive and he feared, afterwards, that he had disobeyed Parson Leach's instructions to keep his mouth shut when he wasn't speaking.

"We are going for an outing, Mr. Loon," said Sussanah, a little breathlessly. "Mrs. Magnamous is packing things for us."

"Nora has agreed to go," said Martha, with a kindness implied in the statement, she was that quick to let Peter know he would be with someone she believed he knew well.

Peter was amazed by their enthusiasm, it seemed so childlike to him, who had known the sober pursuits of subsistence farming his entire life, and the duties of an older brother and a laborer for the most of that. He understood the nature of an *outing*, he thought, though he hadn't the slightest notion what to expect from a *pique-nique*. He hardly knew how to answer their question, but said "Certainly," and as this seemed to please these lovely young women—which, just then, was his soul's entire purpose—he added nothing to it.

James let out a shout of joy and charged toward the kitchen.

"Emily and Nora are getting ready," said Sussanah. She watched Peter carefully whenever Nora's name arose, as if to see what affect it had upon him.

He looked very *braw* in their father's clothes, with an old pair of riding boots serving for lack of anything else appropriate, and a brown waistcoat and jacket over a white shirt, and dark wool trousers. He had pulled his hair back, and in the kitchen found the nerve to ask Mrs. Magnamous for a bit of twine with which to tie it back. She did him better by producing a dark bit of ribbon from an apron pocket, and the effect of this behind his head along with his rugged outfit was the appearance of true gallantry, though he hardly suspected it.

Not only was Peter in strange waters, but he had lost his mooring in the absence of Parson Leach; he was a little perturbed with the clergyman for leaving him in a situation for which he was not equipped.

"You'll have some breakfast," said the cook, and "Of course he will," declared the Captain, but James insisted that Peter would eat soon enough outside. "Nonsense!" said Mrs. Magnamous and she shooed the boy away while Captain Clayden chuckled; nothing would do but Peter had at least a bit of sausage on a piece of toast, a hard-boiled egg, and a bowl of milk, and she managed this in between loading a basket with victuals for the youngsters' outing.

Emily appeared in the kitchen with an air of authority and briskness about her; Nora came behind with a good deal less energy, and she graced Peter with an expression that was a little more than relieved and not quite as much as a smile. "Parson Leach left this morning," she said, as if he might not have known or, if he did, did not realize the gravity of this circumstance.

Peter was perplexed how Nora's anxious presence could make him feel more comfortable in such strange surroundings, but intuition told him straightaway that, if he were without a mooring— in the form of Parson Leach, Nora had her own in the form of himself, and a mooring must be a steady thing. "He'll be back this evening," he said, with a certainty he had not felt when he first heard the news.

Nora had benefited from the Claydens already; there was a sense of security among them, they were so secure themselves and in themselves; and little can be said against a bold dinner and breakfast and a good night's sleep in a comfortable bed. Peter, when he thought about it, felt revived, but thought his state was nothing compared to Nora's, whose color was higher and whose eyes shone with more curiosity and less fear. She might have put on a pound of flesh over night, she looked that much prettier.

Peter was not the only one to notice this, for Captain Clayden complemented her on her bright appearance, and Mrs. Magnamous was very pleased to have helped the cause by feeding the young woman what was good for her. Emily seemed to think *she* had manifested this transformation, and promised that Nora would do better still, given time.

Peter was famished, but he put the minimum amount into him that Mrs. Magnamous demanded, as the Clayden brother and sisters and Martha were chafing to go and since they promised him food at the end of their exertions.

The sun was out, but it was an October day after all, and coats were found for everyone, and bonnets and hats. Nora and Peter, all the while, watched the goings on with interest and concern. Sussanah and Martha and James talked incessantly, and Emily went about frowning at all the preparations till Mrs. Magnamous handed her a quilt and James the basket and drove them out. Captain Clayden laughed as they tumbled through the kitchen door and Mrs. Magnamous gave out orders to be cautious that were scarcely heard.

One of the dogs set up a bark and the chickens scattered in the yard as they stepped into the day. James was having difficulty with the basket and Peter offered to take one handle. Sussanah came forward hurriedly, then, and explained, in a whirl of words, that James was too small for such a chore and she was his big sister, and how it was proper that she help him, which meant of course that she was helping Peter to carry the basket before anyone else knew what was about. Peter caught an anxious look from Nora and Emily shot Sussanah a look of disapproval that was not easy to mistake.

They were quickly past the yard and walking in a cluster toward the river and the extremity of the point about a quarter of a mile away. They walked in rolling fields and there was a grove of hardwood alongside the beaten track, and the river pulling itself in and out. The shore was a series of irregular features, waning and waxing into the water with rooty mounds of soil, granitic outcroppings, and long mounds of white debris, which the sisters insisted were crushed oyster shells, left by ancient Indians who feasted at these river shores.

Peter didn't know an oyster from an octopus and wondered if he were being told a tale, or if Sussanah and Emily had been told one before him. Who was being led astray? Courtesy dictated that he accept the idea with a straight face, but wariness lit his eye with something that must have looked to the young women like wise humor.

The mowed fields had grown little since late summer, and there was a wistful aspect to the waving calf-high grasses as they passed. The young women's dresses shushed as they walked, and the breeze tugged at the locks of hair outside their bonnets. Peter was conscious of the necessity of keeping his stride moderate—that he didn't hurry Sussanah—and also that Sussanah, herself, was not walking as fast as he imagined she could. The result was that they fell behind several times, and Sussanah seemed to slow the more when everyone else noticed and came back for them. It happened only once, however, before Nora placed herself a step or so behind Peter, if some paces to one side, and stayed there. Emily made noises at her sister to hurry along.

Peter understood that they were taking a basket of food to some remoter portion of the Claydens' property to spread it out and eat it there, and this seemed a curious business to him; he was not used to making extra work out of such a fundamental matter as eating. The out-of-doors, the trees and grass, the wind and water were elements of his daily life, his work life, and often the agents against which his small increase, and that of his family, must struggle. The young Claydens hurried into the open-air as to a "town day."

He had known gatherings of people, of course—days in which people of Sheepscott Great Pond and, on occasion, one or another of the nearby hamlets, came together; but they were always times of renewed labor, when a neighboring farm was raising a building or a nearby settler had grown sick or had died and his family needed help plowing their rock-strewn fields or bringing in the plain harvest at the last of the season. The numbers of people would divide the labor, and bring about a sense of respite toward the end of the day; rum and beer were in large supply at such gatherings from the start, and though the work would get done, there were also carousings and brawls and sometimes something like leisure as folks sat about a stump-riddled yard and told stories or shared complaints. Evening might bring song. Peter had known such gatherings, but they had been few and far between, and always born of necessity.

He felt a little mortified by the enthusiasm of the Claydens and their cousin, it was so unhidden. He looked at the Clayden women and thought of his sister Sally Ann. She would shine in dresses such as these, he thought, but she could not have looked so careless and happy. Nora, who must have seen many a spontaneous celebration at her father's tavern, looked surprised, as if she had not seen such glad behavior from anyone but the smallest child. But James and Emily, Sussanah and Martha were unaware of the curiosity they aroused, or unheedful of it.

They came, finally, to a place where birches stood in tall white ranks, their yellow foliage like bright hills glowing in the sun. The trees stood on a brief knoll, where the sun and wind had dried the grass and below which boulders and courses of stone riled the river narrows. On the opposite shore, a cow grazed placidly.

Peter was struck by something he had not known before, and that was the smell of salt water, which intoxicated him as had the wine at supper. The day itself was beyond anything he had experienced when he saw it over the river, and he looked with fascination toward the town where the masts of several vessels swung gently against the sky.

The quilt was spread over the grass before the birches, and the basket laid beside it. Peter stood awkwardly at the edge of the quilt, while the women sat and kneeled and James clambered down the bank. Nora had followed her guests' lead, but could not recline so carelessly, nor look so natural, nor drape her limbs so gracefully. Emily actually reached out and, with a quick motion, tugged the hem of Nora's skirts over her ankles.

"Oh!" cried Martha. "Everything is so sweet after it rains!" and she took such a breath that her whole form seemed filled with it. Peter watched, fascinated, as she drew this luxurious breath, and every line and curve of her seemed to pulse with a feminine energy that made his ears turn red; and yet it was wholly innocent and without motive. Sussanah was less unfettered in her joy of the day, but Emily sprawled like a cat on the quilt so that even Nora smiled softly.

Peter went to the edge of the knoll to look out over the river and James's activity among the rocks of the shore, and all the feminine eyes were upon him. He was a tall, straight young man, made lean and muscular by the life in which he was raised, and the uncultivated figure in the refined attire made a contrast that pleased his observers.

The chatter died some, while the wind moved in the trees and the sound of the water reached them on the knoll. James shouted something they couldn't understand; exclaiming over some discovery. Peter was conscious of the sudden quiet and began to feel more unwieldy, standing there with his back to the others. When

Sussanah spoke, the anxiousness in her voice made her sound almost like Nora.

"Have you been to Newcastle before, Mr. Loon?" she asked.

Peter was not used to being addressed so formally and he had to wade through this before he could consider his answer. "No, I haven't," he said, after some toil.

"Oh."

In all his life, he had never been so far from his birthplace, and he was attempting to conjure a way of saying this without sounding exceedingly cloddish, when he said instead, "Have you been very far from here yourself?"

"Father took us to Boston, when we were young," said Sussanah.

"*I* don't remember," said Emily, as if that were more to the point of his question.

This small exchange served as an excuse to look at the young women, but this in turn made further conversation more necessary still. He'd heard of Boston from the old sailor who lived, now, in Sheepscott Great Pond, but nothing the man had told him seemed proper to convey to such refined people.

"Is it very different where you live?" asked Martha. She watched him with such a soft expression, and her features were so mild, that his heart went out to her in an entirely unexpected manner. He thought again of his sisters, and in such a tender light that he wished he'd been alone for a time to ponder this sudden emotion. He had the vision of his sisters toiling in a manner these young women would probably never know or understand, and he was touched by an unaccustomed sadness. It seemed strange that he must come to this place, so foreign to the circumstances of his own life, before some verity regarding his own people came home to him. "Yes," he said, in the midst of this confusion.

The young Clayden women were beginning to think their conversational efforts were unsuccessful, when Emily said, "How did you meet Mr. Leach?"

"I was looking for my uncle," he said, and began to tell them of his father's death and his mother's peculiarities and how he had been sent to find a man whose existence he had never suspected, and whose present circumstances were unknown to him. He told of his walk through the forests at night and his experience in the midst of the deer herd; then he explained how he had made a bed of leaves at the foot of an oak and how the woodsmen Manasseh Cutts and Crispin Moss had mistaken him for some singular manifestation of a felled deer.

The tale sounded poor and hardscrabble to Peter as he told it, and he considered his own roughened hands, as if they were emblems to prove it; but the story was myth and legend to the young women, Nora included, and when James clambered back up the bank with an eagle feather in hand and news of his venture along the shore, he was shushed to silence, and soon he too was enthralled by Peter's account.

By the time he was done, and they had extracted (by question and comment) all they could from the tale, they had all but forgotten the purpose of their outing and gazed down at the quilt with dreamlike gazes. Emily was the first to rouse herself and consider practical matters; with sudden resolve, she delved into the basket that Mrs. Magnamous had packed for them, laying plates and jars out on the quilt. Martha and Sussanah asked Peter who his uncle was and they speculated, with James's assistance, about the man—somewhat fancifully, as can be supposed. Peter was amazed at their notions, at the wealth and attainments they conjured for the unknown uncle; Nora did not appear to be as charmed by the story, or by its implications, as if she were uncertain what it meant that Peter had such a task to accomplish. She had said almost nothing since speaking to Peter in the Claydens' kitchen.

"You won't be sick after a while," stated James categorically, when it was decided that Peter would need to sail somewhere foreign and strange to find his uncle. "Momma said she hardly feels ill at all, anymore, when she sails with Poppa."

Peter was amazed again by the abundance laid out before them, and also by the affable manner in which it was shared. The Claydens laughed and referenced private jests among themselves and praised the day and asked him more questions. Emily thought to draw Nora into the eddy of conversation, but this proved a difficult undertaking, for Nora grew quieter still when she was questioned or spoken to.

The day was rare, as only the fall can offer, and Peter began to understand the young Claydens' responses to it, though it continued to open a melancholy sort of hole within him. The Claydens prompted a game they called "I Spy" while they ate, and Sussanah at one point, fell to tickling her brother as a forfeit for his having failed an impossible challenge—"I spy the corner of my eye."

Even Nora feasted—though she only watched and listened to the game—and she did seem to grow less troubled, if not absolutely glad of her circumstances; it was difficult not to be pulled along by laughter and good feeling. There were meats and a peach pie and apples and cranberries and cider, and they made good on the most of what was pulled from the basket till they must fall asleep or work off their meal. James called out for a game and Martha declared hide-and-seek. Peter continued to be astonished, for his companions were more like children than ever and they leaped up with shouts and laughter.

Someone would hide and everyone else would look for them, each joining the missing person in his hiding place when they found him. There were certainly places to conceal oneself, for the immediate countryside was dotted with hills and gullies, and the shore was rife with pocks and tree shaded inlets. The boundaries of the sport were laid out and James declared that he would be the first to hide. Everyone else must bury their faces and count to one hundred together. Peter felt silly, but complied with the rules and when the count was done, he looked up, his sight dazzled pale by the brilliant sunlight.

Emily and Sussanah and Martha sprang to their feet and scattered in separate directions, leaving Peter and Nora standing by the quilt looking bewildered.

"I've played this, a long time ago," he said, as much to himself as to the young woman.

"I am with you," Nora said to him.

Peter felt a mounting frustration with her, as if she were simple and had only a small measure of thoughts at her command. Already, when he looked about them, Emily and Martha had disappeared. Only Sussanah lingered in sight, and then Emily's figure rose up from beneath the next knoll to the west and pulled her sister along. Soon they were both gone and Peter and Nora were alone in the landscape.

"We should search for him, I guess," said Peter simply.

Nora had an odd look about her. She glanced around for signs of their companions, then stepped past Peter, catching his hand as she went. He was surprised, and not displeased with her touch, and he allowed himself to be jerked into movement and led along the shoreline. The young woman appeared to be looking for something below them, tugging him along in a walking, cautious hurry. Peter was reminded of their meeting on the shore of Great Bay.

She was trembling, the vibration translating to Peter's arm like the wing-beat of a small bird. Her breathing was short and shallow, perhaps frightened by her own purpose. Her red-brown hair fell untidily beneath her bonnet, as if disarrayed by emotion alone, and her slight figure proved uncommonly strong and compelling as she pulled him with her.

They came to a broad pine overlooking the water, where nature had hollowed a place between the roots and a separate sort of nature had feathered the hollow with grass and fern. She made a sound, as if she had discovered what she knew would be there. She tugged at his arm and pulled him to the other side of the tree. He could read nothing in her expression, and even less in her words than before when she said again, "Parson Leach went away."

"Yes," said Peter, fascinated by the sight of her shaking before him.

She shouldered herself out of the coat she had been given and laid it in the hollow beneath the tree as carefully as Emily had laid the quilt. "I am with you," she said, when she confronted him again with that plain expression. The breeze blew a lock of hair over her eyes and she brushed it aside.

Peter's heart pounded with blind anticipation, and he thought it would burst from his chest when she leaned forward and kissed him. At first the mark of affection grazed his cheek, but then it pressed his own lips and lingered.

Nora pulled away then and considered the effect of this, her small features sweet and ethereal. She took handfuls of his coat and drew him toward her and kissed him again with an urgency that even Peter's inexperience could consider odd. He gasped a little when she pulled away this time. She seemed as real and as potent as anything in his entire life, and her small hands and her narrow shoulders, the serious set of her mouth, were like the essence of something he had not recognized before that moment. His entire surroundings fell into the emotions she had provoked in him—the air rushing in the trees, the call of a river bird, and the sound of the river itself, the sun on his back.

When she leaned forward a third time, he was prepared and he thought he might draw her inside of him, his heart felt so ready to be filled. His hands went up to the back of her neck and touched her hair, then swept down to hold her shoulders to him. Her knees buckled—not with weakness, but with design—and he was suddenly kneeling beside her. She continued to shake and as a result of some sympathetic energy, a cleaving together of motive and response, he found himself shaking as well. All the while, she never lost touch of him, and pulled him down atop of herself. She kissed him fervently, insinuating her hands beneath his coat, and twisting beneath him so that one knee rose up alongside his thigh.

There was a scent to her skin and her hair, and a mysterious softness to her hard, gaunt body. Peter felt he must touch everything about her and press her entirely to him and calm her trembling with his closeness.

Then her trembling became something else, and a strange sound rose in her throat, like a muted expression of fear. Her shivering increased beneath him, and his first instinct was to press her closer, to speak in a low hush, but she only shivered more violently. Another, strangled sound rose out of Nora, and her shaking might have seemed like an attempt to throw him off if, at that moment, she had appeared at all capable of motive.

Frightened, Peter pushed himself away from her, and kneeling at her side he watched with helpless horror till her quaking was like a fit he had once seen taken by a rum-soaked neighbor. Her arms and legs twitched horribly. Her eyes creased shut. She let out another low cry or two, then rolled on to her side and fell into a paroxysm of grief. Her hands gripped at the roots of the broad pine and her legs convulsed, kicking without purpose at dirt and stones.

Peter looked up the bank, suddenly aware of where he was and what the scene might seem to someone stumbling upon them. He felt guilt and fear, and then an extraordinary, tender sort of sympathy that all but overwhelmed his ability to move or speak. His eyes were filled with tears and his throat raw with emotion. His initial fear of being found in such straits was pushed aside by the belief that Nora was in a terrible danger which had nothing to do with her physical being, and that she needed immediate care that he was incompetent to offer.

Nora's sobs altered into something more human and answerable; she covered her mouth with one hand to quiet herself and curled her legs close to her body. Peter approached her carefully, but when he kneeled beside her and she showed no extra-violent reaction, he dared to prop her up and drape her coat over her shoulders. Then he took her into his arms, with one hand beneath her knees and the other behind her back, and stood with her. He had never been so conscious of the stark angularity of her body, not three minutes before when he was pressing her close to him, nor the day before when she appeared along the shore of the lake, drenched in her insufficient clothes.

She actually clung to him and put her face against his shoulder. She was quivering still, but it was as a secondary reaction to what had occurred between them and not the initial tremor of fear and grief, and he had the impression that this time his physical presence had soaked up her distress rather than increased it.

"I must get you back," he said, wondering if he could safely carry her up the steep bank.

"Please, don't let them see me!" she said in a hoarse whisper.

"No," he said, then, "But . . ." She was trembling less and he could imagine that whatever had happened had not stricken her in a permanent way. He thought he heard voices from over the bank and he let her down onto her own feet. She shivered slightly now, but as if from a chill and she pulled the borrowed coat around her shoulders.

There was another shout from one of the Claydens.

"I'll be fine," said Nora, which seemed an astonishing pronouncement to Peter. She did not look at him, but stared at her feet. A secondary sort of sob occasionally choked her voice, but she seemed to have regained herself.

Peter wanted to reassure her that the parson would be back, that she was with the Claydens now, for a time, which was to be preferred to being with a young man who couldn't even find his own uncle, who had never been to Newcastle before, and who hadn't the smallest notion how many people there were in the world. An apology died in his throat.

"Mr. Loon?" came the voice again, and he caught sight of Martha looking off in another direction. Before she could see where he sprang from, he leaped up the bank and walked several paces to his left. Then he shouted back and waved.

Martha was startled to see him there. "My goodness, Mr. Loon, we thought you had gone hiding yourself. We've all found James, but you and Nora." This last thought was followed by a small look of embarrassment, as if something unintended had been implied.

With a simple gesture, Peter gave a surprisingly expert indication that he needed to speak quietly. "Miss Tillage was feeling weary and is resting down by the shore," he said, when he approached her, a little dismayed at how easily he contorted the truth.

"Oh, the poor dear!" said Martha. "Have we exhausted her so?" and she would have gone looking for Nora, but Peter impressed upon her that Miss Tillage was sensitive about her fragile condition, and while he spoke, a renewed sense of guilt and confusion swept over him. "Ah, well," said Martha sweetly. "We'll let her rest, then, away from Emily and James. You're kind to continue helping her."

Peter never looked at Martha, but took a sudden, if not heart-felt interest in knowing where James had hidden. He glanced back to the shore before he followed her over the knoll.

They did not play hide-and-seek anymore, but returned to the place where they had eaten and spoke quietly about unimportant things till Nora reappeared without explanation or apology. Her expression may have been difficult for the others to read, but Peter saw in it the mirror of his own humiliation and regret.

They were a decidedly quieter group on their way back to the Clayden house. Peter caught only a single glance from Nora, and he suffered for what she thought *he* thought about her.

15

Concerning New Visitors to Captain Clayden and Their Opinions

SOME EXCITEMENT GREETED THE YOUNG CLAYDENS AND THEIR guests upon their return, for as they neared the house, half a dozen horsemen entered the yard at a near gallop, to the accompaniment of the family's dogs, which bayed and barked. The riders were all well-dressed men in fine clothes and broad capes and polished boots, and one wore a sword at his side. Four of them wore wigs beneath their hats, and the others—younger men—wore their hair pulled back in a simple queue.

One of these younger men—a tall, broad shouldered *Hector*—broke away from his fellows to greet the Clayden ladies and James. He bowed over the young women's hands as they received him, and even the practical Emily appeared pleased by his attention. Martha, however, he saved for last, and he lingered with her, and affected such a degree of tenderness over this particular greeting that it could not be missed if a man had only his ears to serve him. Her round pretty face blushed to see him, and she fairly glowed to have him lean close to her as he asked after her health and that of her family in Falmouth.

"We're all quite well, thank you for asking, Mr. Kavanagh," she beamed. She was not a short woman, but she appeared dainty beside him.

Mr. Kavanagh flashed a look of slight interest in the direction of Peter, and another of slightly more interest toward the slender figure of Nora Tillage.

"Sir," said Martha, with smooth formality, "may I introduce Mr. Peter Loon. Mr. Loon, may I introduce Mr. Edward Kavanagh."

"I am pleased to know any friend of the Claydens, Mr. Loon," said Mr. Kavanagh. He put his broad hand out and gripped Peter's firmly.

Peter felt great physical power in the grip. "Yes," he said, daunted by the man's presence and energy, and still shaken by his recent experience with Nora by the shore. "Thank you. I too."

When Nora was introduced to the man, he greeted her with more formality, though with all his charm and gallantry at full tilt; the result was that she could hardly speak to him. Charm or no charm, Emily must have thought this enough, for she stepped up to rescue Nora, asking Mr. Kavanagh when she could expect to ride his horse Malborough. The man laughed and declared it would be worth his life if the Captain caught him letting her ride such an animal. Emily pretended a comic disgust with him, but the thing was neatly done and Kavanagh turned his bright light from Nora back to Martha, who was quite prepared for it.

During all this courtliness, the gentlemen with whom Kavanagh arrived were instructing Ebulon Magnamous how to tend their animals, and Ebulon, who may have known more about horses than all of them put together, dutifully nodded his head and accepted these mandates with grace.

"Edward," called one of these men—an older fellow, whose florid complexion contrasted unflatteringly with the snow white of his wig.

"I will see you before we leave," said Mr. Kavanagh in the direction of the younger Claydens, but he was plainly speaking to Martha.

"You might escort a lady to the door," suggested Emily, and she gestured in such a way that Mr. Kavanagh was constrained to take her arm and obey. The effect of this was that both groups tromped into the kitchen together. The wigged gentlemen did not balk at this entrance as, even then, it had been a long-standing tradition in the district, taken from old Anglia, that strangers and peddlers come to the front door, and that besides these, only the ostentatious and the crude insist on greeting people at the main entrance.

The kitchen was a madhouse, with the younger Claydens shouting for their grandfather and the gentlemen greeting Mrs. Magnamous in loud voices to be heard over the young folk and Mrs. Magnamous complaining more loudly still that the bread would fall with all the noise. A dog had got in with the crowd and was racing about, his tail whipping things from the kitchen table, till the door was opened and one of the older men booted him down the steps.

"What! are the British returned?" came a new voice above the rabble, and Captain Clayden stood in the doorway, shouting half in delight, half in astonishment. "Good gracious! What actions!"

One of the wigged gentlemen stepped through the press and greeted the Captain with a handshake and a "Pleased to see you again, sir."

"Come in, come in!" declared the elderly fellow. "Get out of Mrs. Magnamous's kitchen before she puts you in a pie!"

"The bread will fall!" she said again.

As the group of men followed Captain Clayden from the kitchen to his den, Mr. Kavanagh turned to Peter and said, cordially, "Come with us, Mr. Loon. This may interest you." The handsome man glanced from Peter to Martha, and it was clear that Mr. Kavanagh himself was interested in finding more about this young man who was spending time in the company of the Clayden cousin.

"What?" said the older ruddy-faced newcomer, and he looked Peter up and down as he would a horse for sale. "I dare say," he ventured, though he sounded unconvinced.

They continued to empty from the kitchen, when one wigged fellow tripped suddenly and fell face forward. James, whose foot had been in the wrong place, helped the man up and apologized profusely, but he told Peter later that he felt avenged upon the fellow for kicking his dog.

There were not chairs enough for everyone in the den, but the Captain and the two eldest (or at least the *grandest* fellows) took seats and a fourth chair was brought in from the hall. The others stood about the hearth, which barely glowed, or before the book-lined shelves. Mr. Kavanagh pulled a volume from one of these and thumbed it with the look of serious curiosity, but before the conversation had very much gotten under way, he closed the book and put it back in its place. Peter, standing next to Mr. Kavanagh, envied the man his ease and carelessness.

The den was a sanctuary of immaculate comfort. Elm trees shaded the house, and the sun touched the windows with a fitful radiance. Lamplight set a golden tone to the dark furniture, and ensconced in his lair of books, Captain Clayden was the gracious host. "I would offer you wine, gentlemen," he said, "but a tumbler of ale would seem fit for an afternoon visit and a spirited ride."

"That would answer the humors, splendidly," said one of the seated men.

"James!" called the Captain, but his grandson was at the doorway and he simply shouted, "I'll get them," and was gone.

The old man noticed Peter, then, and twisted up his mouth in an expression of inner debate. Peter felt out of place, and thought it perhaps impolitic for him to be there, however boldly Mr. Kavanagh had invited him. But Captain Clayden simply nodded seriously and said, "Have you met Mr. Loon, gentlemen," as courteously as could be, and indicated the young man with a respectful gesture.

The five pairs of eyes that had not yet had the pleasure turned to Peter with varying degrees of doubt and inquisitiveness. Mr. Kavanagh nodded and made a sound to signify that he had already observed the niceties.

"Mr. Loon," said Captain Clayden, and he indicated the other gentlemen in a counterclockwise manner. "Mr. Ethan Flye, Mr. Benjamin Shortwell, Mr. Harold Whitehouse, Mr. Morrison Marston, and Captain Elihu McQuigg. Gentlemen, Mr. Peter Loon. He is looking for a lost uncle, it seems, so if any of you know of an Obed Winslow, you could do the lad a favor."

The men nearest Peter offered their hands, and two of those seated half-rose and nodded. Someone mumbled that the name Obed Winslow had a familiar ring to it, but the others shook their heads. Captain McQuigg—he with the florid expression and the sword at his side—simply grunted and waved a negligent hand.

"My pleasure," said Peter, after hearing this nicety from several of the men.

"*Mine* will be the pleasure, which is more to the point, boy," said Captain McQuigg, "if you are prepared to ride with us to New Milford."

Peter could see that Captain Clayden had expected something like this, and that he was none too pleased to have his expectations so completely and immediately realized. "Is there hunting in New Milford, these days, Captain?" he asked dryly.

"There will be, yes, Captain," pronounced Captain McQuigg.

"There are those who've run their game, that'll be run themselves," said Mr. Whitehouse darkly.

"Yes," drawled the host. "I've heard what happened in New Milford."

"Then you know why we are here, Captain!" declared Captain McQuigg.

"I understand the spur, but you must make clear the purpose."

"To chastise these scoundrels!" exclaimed Captain McQuigg.

"To quieten the district," said Mr. Marston with a little less fire.

"It will be loud enough when I'm through!" continued to declaim Captain McQuigg. "We must rout these rebels!"

There was such a note of repugnance in Captain McQuigg's use of this last term, that Captain Clayden stiffened a little. "Never forget our own rebellious days, Captain McQuigg," said the elderly fellow mildly, and Peter guessed from this that the two captains had perhaps fought together against the British. There was a degree of tolerance in this counsel that rung hollow among these men, and if Peter had struggled to understand Captain Clayden before, it was all the elderly gentleman needed to say to exact the young man's admiration.

Captain McQuigg's ruddy complexion darkened further and he scowled into the glowing coals before him, his eyes themselves like hard embers. "That was a war among equals, where squire fought squire and commoner fell upon commoner, but these miscreants must know either their betters or the heels of our boots!" There was general agreement to this, though Captain Clayden said nothing and Mr. Kavanagh chortled softly so that only Peter, standing near, could hear him.

"If we allow the backcountry its lawlessness," said Mr. Flye, with a little more circumspection, "and give these rioters rein to harass our agents in the conduct of their duty, then we will soon be dealing with emboldened rogues in our own midst."

"It's enough that we have sailors to the one hand," added Mr. Marston, "and wandering foresters, who call no man master, to the other. Let us not encourage the simple farmer and mill man to illegality with permissive means. The servant who speaks familiarly to his master will soon despise him."

She might have been listening in the hall, Mrs. Magnamous was so timely in her entrance and topical in her directness. "Captain Clayden," she demanded. "Are these gentlemen breaking bread, I should like to know! And if they be, I'll arrange matters after I sweep out the dirt they've tracked through the house!"

Captain Clayden smiled to be so addressed by his cook after the speech from Mr. Marston. "Gentlemen," he interpreted. "Mrs.

Magnamous is inviting you to dinner, and if you dare eat her provender after raising her ire, I extend the offer."

"We have other places to go," said Mr. Marston.

"We must raise the countryside of patriots," rumbled Captain McQuigg.

"Thank you, Captain Clayden," said Mr. Flye, "but we have other houses to visit."

"It's Mrs. Magnamous needs our thanks," said the Captain pleasantly. Then he called, "Thank you, Mrs. Magnamous. We will do with ale, it seems." James then came up behind the woman with several tankards of the stuff on a tray, and Mrs. Magnamous turned away with a low exclamation. "Yes, Mr. Marston," said Captain Clayden, still with his puckish humor. "We must keep the servants in fear of us."

Mr. Kavanagh thought this very good, but the other men were not so amused. Peter thought he heard hoofbeats near the house, but his attention was quickly taken by the words of the ruddy-faced Captain McQuigg.

"It is very well to jest," he was saying, while James served out the drink, "but we are dealing with men who must be taught the letter of the law, since they cannot read it themselves!"

At this, Mr. Kavanagh laughed aloud and slapped his thigh. Peter thought the words insulting and shot an angry glance at the tall young man. Captain Clayden gave James, who was lingering as inconspicuously as possible, the sign that he should leave, and the boy unhappily complied.

"You may make sport, Captain Clayden," Mr. Marston was saying, though with more caution than Captain McQuigg, "but it is a serious thing for an honest man to return from the back country, stripped and beaten."

"I believe it is, sir," agreed the Captain. "And I fear giving the mob that is responsible its justification after the fact, were we to ride into their farms like a standing army and do harm to man or property. If we pretend to represent the law, then we must practice it without hypocrisy, and present it by its most liberal face."

"Hypocrisy?" exclaimed Mr. Whitehouse.

"Captain Clayden!" declared Captain McQuigg. "It is liberality that got us to this place!"

"It is liberality we demanded from the King, Captain Mc-Quigg!" said the elderly host. "It was a *great* liberality signed into law nearly ten years ago!"

"And so we may live to regret it!" countered Captain McQuigg. "It was a mistake, ever to read the Constitution to a rabble of illiterate clods. It raises them in their own minds and plants seditious notions in them, based on a lack of understanding. A man who can't read the document itself has no right to its merit, I say!"

Again Mr. Kavanagh let out a burst of laughter, which was not appreciated from the more earnest corners of the room. Captain Clayden threw Mr. Kavanagh an indulgent glance, however, though Peter stepped away from him, his heart darkened with each of these jocular outbursts.

"I wonder, Captain Clayden," said Mr. Whitehouse, gesturing to the library about them, "that you can surround yourself with so much knowledge and yet defend men who would contemn your tomes and volumes."

"The reading of books is itself the signal of a rebellious mind," came a new voice, as the door to the hall darkened with the long form of Parson Leach. Peter could have embraced the man, he was so relieved to see him. There was a shadow behind the preacher, and Peter had the impression that Nora had followed the parson down the hall.

The parson entered the room alone, however, radiating good will and his own manner of carelessness. "The British broke many a printing press," he continued, "if you will remember, *and* the heads of some printers, I think. No, it is a suspicious thing to put oneself in a corner and peruse words no other can hear. *Sedition* may be written as *well* as the law, and many a scurrilous notion has been given legitimacy for having been bound in leather. *'Of making many books there is no end; and much study is a weariness of the flesh.'"*

Captain McQuigg sputtered wordlessly.

"Twelve, twelve, Ecclesiastes," cited Mr. Shortwell.

"Well," said Captain McQuigg, finding his voice again, "You will be the saddle preacher Mr. Leach."

"Zachariah," said Captain Clayden, making his familiarity and friendship with the parson immediately plain, "it is good to see you so soon again." And here he introduced the roomful of men, though the clergyman knew Mr. Flye already.

"A purveyor of books, as well, if I am to understand," said Mr. Marston, when he shook the newcomer's hand.

"I am that humble peddlar," said Parson Leach.

"Then surely *you* have no sympathy with this ignorant class that squats upon other men's estates."

"I have sympathy with suffering, sir," replied the parson. "I have respect for hard labor. It is a paradox, of course, that the price for land the proprietors demand from these people inflates even as the debtors improve upon the wilderness. I am a great believer in debate, sir, and relish a true disputation over the *propriety* of land grants from an ousted king and Indian deeds that oppose one another."

There was general outrage expressed over these sentiments. Mr. Kavanagh himself grew serious for the first time during the conversation.

"You are *not* a Congregationalist, sir!" said Captain McQuigg, shaking a finger.

"I do not share that distinction, Captain, no. Nor am I a Methodist, nor would the Baptists of Freewill lay claim to me."

"Are you such a heretic to have no church, Mr. Leach?" wondered Mr. Marston, though not with some underlying touch of humor.

"Do tell, then!" said Captain McQuigg, hardly breaking from his previous declaration. "You are a similar wiggler with that Nathan Barrow! You are an Anti- an Anti*mummerist* or some such thing!"

The parson glanced once toward the hall, before he answered, but Nora's shadow was gone. "An Antinomianist, is very much what I am *not*, sir," he said, and Peter was astounded how he could return such a charge so mildly and with a smile upon his face.

"The *devil* you say! You are his supporter or his enemy, sir! This Barrow is a villain, and the men who follow him prove, by association, their wrongdoing in these matters discussed!"

"A man might be wrong about the tide, and right about the weather, Captain McQuigg."

"He may be wrong about the both!"

"And a man may know the word and misperceive the sentence."

"And what do you mean by that, sir?"

"I mean that there are men who *can* read—that is, they have the *function*—but it is no promise they can *interpret*. Ignorance might come in as many guises as wisdom."

Captain Clayden appeared ready to interrupt this discourse, but Captain McQuigg had heated himself to the boiling point, and was ready for the slightest provocation or imagined insult to explode in a hiss of steam. "If you would speak that again, but plainly," he said, "I would strike you on the nose, sir!"

"You would do well to make it land, I warrant," said Mr. Kavanagh and without warning, he slid one of Captain Clayden's books from its place and spun it across the room toward the parson with a snap of his wrist.

Peter drew in a gasp, but though the parson was hardly looking in Mr. Kavanagh's direction, his hand came up with the speed of a snake and snatched the book from the air, demonstrating indeed that Captain McQuigg would have been lucky to land a blow on the nose in question. The parson laughed once and peered at the spine of the book.

"Perhaps you would read some of that to me, Parson," said Mr. Kavanagh, "as I am without letters, myself."

Captain McQuigg sat straight in his chair and the other men gasped a little to think of the insults thrown so recently upon illiterates. With this unexpected intelligence, Peter struggled to reimagine Mr. Kavanagh and his laughter. Mr. Marston absolutely looked ready to bolt and run, and Mr. White gazed down at his feet and said, "I do beg your pardon, Edward!"

Mr. Kavanagh laughed again, however, and Captain McQuigg stood, saying, "Well, Captain Clayden, we had hoped to add you to our muster, but I trust we will not lose your good will."

"I think not, Captain McQuigg," said Captain Clayden graciously.

"If something changes your predilection, we hie to Wiscasset." Captain McQuigg left the room, sword swinging at his side, and as he had to pass close by the parson, he gave him an eye for good measure, though he said nothing else. Others in the group muttered, "Mr. Leach," or "Pleasure to meet you, sir," as they left.

Mr. Kavanagh stopped, however, and said, "You came upon a highwayman at his work, down Freeport way, two or three years ago."

"I do remember something like it," said the parson.

"I heard you walked up to him and, before he knew what you were about, you snatched the pistol right from his hand." Kavanagh made a gesture to imitate this deed.

"Someone must be misremembering," replied the parson.

"That was my brother he was robbing," said Mr. Kavanagh with a smile, and he was gone.

"He was not a very experienced robber, I think," said the clergyman, and there was a roar of laughter from down the hall.

"I am sorry for that unpleasantness, Zachariah," said Captain Clayden, who was standing now with his back to the hearth.

"Not at all, sir. Aren't I 'a great believer in debate?'" he said, quoting himself. From the kitchen they could hear Mr. Kavanagh saying goodbye to Mrs. Magnamous, and something else that raised a laugh from the woman.

"I can so testify," said the Captain dryly. "And you, Peter—I am sorry to expose you to such harsh opinions. There *are* men, I promise you, who are not in full support of the settlers in the backcountry, who would yet deal with them with a tolerant hand."

"You are proof of that, sir," said Peter.

"You are gracious to say so. Zachariah?"

"Yes, Captain." He laid the book that had been tossed at him on a high table by the door. Outside, the small thunder of hooves passed by the house as Captain McQuigg and his men went in search of further allies.

"Are you hungry?"

"I am, but I must be off before dusk."

"Away again, so soon?"

"I'm going to New Milford."

"I thought as much. You must be careful, my friend. I fear you put yourself between two armed camps."

Parson Leach turned to Peter and noticed the look of some trouble in the young man's face. "What is it, Peter?"

"Perhaps I could go with you."

"I thought you might like to stay with Captain Clayden till I get back. I spoke with him about it just this morning."

"You are more than welcome, my boy," said Captain Clayden.

"I should be looking for my uncle, sir," said Peter.

The Captain nodded. Parson Leach considered Peter for a moment, then said, "You'll need your clothes."

"He'll take what he's wearing," said Captain Clayden, and the old fellow held his hand up to stem any disagreement or even thanks. "Yes, yes," he said. "We'll make him a proper kit."

"Then you're coming with me, Peter," said the parson. "But you'll do everything I tell you, and leave me or stay behind, if I so say."

"Yes, Parson."

"Nora will be fine with you," the clergyman said to Captain Clayden.

"She and the girls are getting along like otters."

"Then it's a swift supper and the road, Peter Loon."

"Where are the ladies?" said the elderly man as he led the way out of the den. "Find the ladies, Mr. Loon, would you please?"

Peter took a breath. It had been a day of shocks and surprises. At the mention of Nora, the business on the riverbank returned to him and his heart fell. On his way from the room, he glanced at the binding of the book that Mr. Kavanagh had thrown at Parson Leach; after some work, he could read, on the binding, the words *The Tenth Muse Lately Sprung Up in America.*

There was a voice from across the hall, and he approached the parlor on the other side of the house, hoping to find the sisters, or Martha perhaps. James stood outside the parlor door, which was shut, and the young man appeared as if there were something on the toe of his boot that fascinated him. Peter realized that the boy was in an attitude of concentration, and that the voice of one of the sisters was coming from behind the door.

James looked up at Peter with a sly smile, and said in a whisper, "Emily says Sussanah should leave you be."

Peter was astonished. "She does?"

"They drove me out," hushed James, not at all ashamed to be caught eavesdropping, "and I pretended to walk down the hall."

"You did?" Peter felt his scalp stiffen.

"Emily says it was Nora you rescued, and that Sussanah

should leave you be." James's voice had unconsciously risen in volume and the voices behind the door had correspondingly silenced. "Are you fixed on Nora, then?" wondered James, all mischief, but Peter had turned face about and was following Captain Clayden and Parson Leach to the kitchen.

16

*Of the Road to New Milford, and What They
Discovered at Great Meadow Copse*

PETER THOUGHT HIS HEART COULD FALL NO FURTHER, CONCERNING the events of the afternoon, till Parson Leach told Nora that he and Peter would be leaving. Tears coursed down her face and she trembled so that Peter feared she might fall into convulsions again; but Sussanah and Martha gathered round her and let her cling to them while she wept. Emily appeared more puzzled than troubled, and she watched Peter throughout this with an interest he could not interpret. He feared that Parson Leach might ask him to stay, for Nora's sake, and indeed, the man turned to him with question on his face, but said nothing.

"She will be fine," Captain Clayden insisted, several times over. There were tears in the old man's eyes, and he blinked energetically before turning away.

Mrs. Magnamous prepared them a cold supper and after grace, Peter and the parson ate mainly in silence till James sat with them, wishing aloud that he could go as well. He had gleaned enough from the conversation in his grandfather's den—some of which, to be honest, he may have overheard from the hall—that he believed Parson Leach and Peter were standing into adventure, and James very nearly said as much.

"Getting to New Milford tonight by moonlight will prove enterprise enough for me," said the parson.

Emily turned up next in the kitchen and, deflecting Mrs. Magnamous's mandate to "let the poor souls eat in peace," asked the parson and Peter if they would be coming back.

"I can't promise where I'll be led next," said Parson Leach, "but I'll return in season, God willing."

"I must come back to return these clothes," said Peter, still astonished by the fine things he was wearing. When he first arrived, Emily and the other young Clayden women might have imagined that the state of his apparel had been the consequence of his recent encounter with Nathan Barrow and his men, and of the rigors of the road; by now they must realize that they were his only garments. His father's coat, in fact, had been the finest thing he had ever worn till he came here.

"Did you get that scar rescuing Nora?" asked Emily.

"Peter will be back," said the parson, before the young man could respond.

Emily appeared satisfied with this. She sat at the table and watched them eat.

"How *is* Nora?" asked Peter, though he could almost believe the question implicated him somehow.

"She fell asleep," said Emily. "Sussanah says that Mamma used to cry like that when Papa left for sea, but he takes her with him, now he's a captain."

This intelligence did not ease Peter's heart. Rather than separate him from what happened on the river bank, the ensuing hours had obscured his memories of how it came to pass; the gaps in his recollection had filled with self-damning possibilities, and

he began to place an increasing weight of blame for the unpleasantness upon his own shoulders. His self-accusation was not tem-
pered by flashes of other feelings when he recalled Nora's kiss, or
when he experienced a physical memory of her body beneath his.

They avoided the parlor when they were finished with their
meal, but came into the Captain's den another way. The parson
presented Captain Clayden with a bound and beribboned volume
of *Don Quixote,* and refused any recompense for it. The Captain's
eyes lit with pleasure and anticipation, and clearly he would have
liked to sit with the book then and there, and to leaf its pages lov-
ingly. He laid it aside, however, and offered Parson Leach and Peter his hand.

"I've had Ebulon saddle a horse for you, Peter," he said. Peter
had no idea what to say, but stammered his thanks several times
over. "Bring it back in your own time, lad. With a horse under you,
you'll be that much quicker coming to the next person's rescue."
This last was said with humor, though not without a touch of real
regard mixed with it. "I hope you find your uncle," said the elderly
fellow finally. He did not see them beyond his den, and when they
left the room Peter thought that, if he looked back, Captain Clayden would already be ensconced in his chair, perusing his new
and beloved book.

The temperature had dropped considerably since Peter came
in that afternoon. Their breath puffed before them. The sun had
set behind the western ridge some time ago, and the last glow of
it underlit a bank of airy clouds. Stars had already broken through
a blue-black canvas to the east. In the darkening yard, Ebulon
Magnamous waited by Mars and another horse, which was called
Beam for the streak of white across its otherwise brown forehead.

The animal was a good deal smaller than Mars, but Peter felt she had a sturdy carriage and a steady gait as he moved her in a circle through the yard. He was not an experienced horseman, certainly not in a saddle, but he had always liked horses and he found riding natural enough. He begged a length of rope from Ebulon and with this tied his father's hat and coat in a roll at the back of the saddle.

Peter could see the silhouettes of Emily, Sussanah, and Martha at the parlor window as he and Parson Leach bid goodbye to Ebulon. Mrs. Magnamous waved to the departing guests from the door, and they waved, in a general way, to the entire house as they left the yard.

Parson Leach led the way, past the barn and down a sloping pasture, across a gully and up again. They crossed a road and traveled, to the tune of a barking dog or two, by several houses. A steep ridge loomed against the retreating light, till it was like night itself approaching. When they reached a line of hardwood at the foot of the slope, the parson climbed down from Mars, and Peter followed him as they led their mounts among the trees. Half way up the ridge, they came to a brush fence and skirted it to the north till they reached a stile that the horses could clamber over. Then the slope steepened and by the time they achieved the top of it, Peter was all too glad to climb atop Beam again.

From the height of this ridge, the first light of the rising moon was visible over the rim of the east, but they left the pale light behind as they advanced into the shadow of the land. The parson drew Mars up at the next knoll, and Peter reined in beside him. Stretching a mile or so to the west, and a good deal further to the north, was a treeless progression of low hills, where the night wind could fan the grasses unhindered. Peter strained his eyes in the dimness, but understood that the fields were clear of stumps as well as trees; it was by far the largest, most immaculate expanse of pasture he had ever seen.

"It's handsome, isn't it," said the parson. "But it's nothing, I've been told, to the miles of treeless fields, west of the Ohio. They call them prairies."

Peter had known the close attendance of the forests all his life, with only an acre here or there that had been cleared of stumps; he felt a little dizzy looking out over the rolling fields, as if he might topple from that knoll and fall head first into them. He hardly liked to think of the parson's prairies; the very notion of them was overwhelming.

"They call this Great Meadow," said Parson Leach, "and that crease running north to south is Great Meadow Brook. Beyond— though you can't see it from here—is the Dyers River Valley, and the Sheepscott Valley after that."

Peter did his best to discern what the parson was signifying, but it was difficult to tell the further swells of land from the sky. Stars came to life, even as they watched, and several other lights— the lamp in a window, or the flicker of a distant hearth—also prinked the darkness. The wind, moving among the grasses, made a sound unfamiliar to Peter, and it added to the sense of something remote to his previous experience.

"If we head north," said the parson, "we'll strike a track that will take us north and west, then, to a tavern where the New Milford folk will be meeting."

Peter couldn't have guessed that there was something like a single road between the coastal waters and the backcountry.

"This path we're on now," added the parson, "was tromped down by an old reverend in the days a gun was necessary to ward off Indians. He traveled between two parishes in his day, and its been known as Parson's Path ever since."

So, they nudged their mounts north, and in this expanse of field, Parson Leach slowed Mars's natural pace so that Peter could comfortably keep up, astride of Beam. As their horses' hooves realized separate cadences, Peter fell to wondering on the richness of these acres; how difficult it was, in Sheepscott Great Pond and the other backcountry settlements, to scrape enough feed from a few rocky acres to keep a cow or two, and maybe a horse over a winter. But here, he thought, was pasture for an entire village and more.

They came to the track the parson had spoken of and their speed increased. Peter saw a bluish light to his right, but couldn't find it again when he turned his head. He nudged Beam up beside Mars.

"Something happened this afternoon, Parson," he said.

"What did you say, Peter?"

"Something happened," he said again, his own voice unnerving him a little in that open expanse. "This afternoon."

"Did it?"

"Yes." Peter wondered that the parson seemed uninterested.

But the parson was merely thinking, perhaps, for in another moment, he said, "To do with Nora?"

"Yes," said Peter, a little startled, "to do with Nora," and he wondered, Had she spoken to Parson Leach already?

"Did she tell you something, then?" asked the clergyman.

"No." There was a silence that Peter found awkward. The parson moved Mars to more speed, and when Peter spoke again, his voice jounced with the gait of his mount, as if he were out of breath. "We went out of doors to eat—by the river, on a quilt."

"So I was told. You're learning of the prosperous folk."

"We played some games," said Peter, feeling bashful to tell the parson.

"Hide and seek, no wonder," said the parson.

"Yes! That was one of them!"

The parson chuckled softly.

Peter frowned in the dark, and said, "While James was hiding, and the Clayden ladies went looking for him . . ." He hardly looked ahead of him as they rode and he talked. "Nora and I were supposed to be looking for him too."

"Yes," drawled the parson.

"Nora took me down to the river . . . well, I don't want to put it . . ." Peter fell silent.

"You don't want to put it in such a way that it sounds you're accusing Nora of anything."

"Yes," said Peter, amazed how quickly the parson understood the situation. And what *else* did he understand?

"I'm not a priest, Peter," said the parson, "if this is in the way of a confession."

"I thought I might tell you something," said Peter, hardly audible to his companion.

"Between you and God is good enough for me, my friend."

Peter hadn't thought of dealing with his conscience quite that way. There had been a great deal of confession at the few church services he'd attended, when people were encouraged to bare their iniquities before their neighbors, and most seemed ready—before God, the preacher, and the congregation—to shed themselves of the sins they had committed.

"Did she call on your affections, lad?" said the clergyman.

"Well, it might be . . ."

"It's not a circumspect place, the bank of a river."

"There was a hollow beneath an oak tree . . ."

Parson Leach said nothing, and Peter wondered if he had compounded the wrong by speaking of it.

"But she started to shake," said Peter. "I've never seen anyone shake so—like a drunken fit." They rode in silence for a while, then the parson pulled up. Peter drew Beam to a halt beside the clergyman, uneasy and a little frightened. "She kept pulling me toward her," said Peter, "but she kept shaking worse and worse."

"Why do you suppose, Peter, that she took you down to the river bank?"

After a moment, Peter said, "I thought, then, that she fancied me."

"And now?"

"Perhaps she wanted me to stay with her. Perhaps she thought I would stay if . . . She frightened me, she shook so."

"She was frightened herself, I venture. Frightened of Nathan Barrow, I think."

"Of what he'd do, if he caught us?"

"Of what he'd already done, lad."

Peter said nothing; if he had not understood enough to articulate this very thing, he had at least experienced it on some deep level of suspicion.

The parson turned his horse's head west again and moved on.

Peter took a moment to orient Beam and catch up with him. "You never asked what happened."

"Am I right in guessing, Peter, that, had anything . . . happened, as you put it, you wouldn't have left the Claydens this evening."

"No, I don't suppose I would have."

"Between you and God, Peter."

"Yes, Parson."

They had only ridden half a minute more before Peter asked, "Did you truly snatch a pistol from a man's hand?"

"It doesn't sound very likely, does it," came the reply. "Careful, here."

They had come to the bank before Great Meadow Brook, and looking down at the sparkle of water, Peter was conscious of their shadows leading the way. The moon had risen behind them and the track appeared as if lit by daylight in contrast. Looking back, he caught sight of that bluish light again, but this time he was able to locate it in the broad darkness of the Great Meadow.

"It's a foxlight," said the parson, when Peter pointed it out. "I've seen two or three tonight already. Look over there," and he pointed to the southeast.

Peter saw a second blue flicker some yards away, like pale lightning kindling the ground. "Will-o-the-wisp," said Peter.

"The same, if I am not mistaken."

Peter felt an unprocessed sort of fear fill his chest.

"Those will be wet places, I warrant. I've read Count Buffon, who is a French naturalist and who observed foxlight over swamps and marshes, and connects them with unhealthy air." Peter could well imagine them to be unhealthy, and said so, whereupon the parson chuckled. "I've chased them about myself, and never caught up with one, so I understand why people ascribe mystery to them. But *there's* another light altogether," he added, pointing due north.

Peter saw a tiny orange flicker in that direction and eventually decided that it was coming from the midst of trees on a knoll about a quarter of a mile away.

The parson led them down to the brook, which was not rushing this time of year, despite the recent rain, and after Mars and Beam had drunk a bit, they splashed across to the other side and climbed the bank. They continued along the track they had been following, which would eventually lead them past and away from the unexplained light to the north.

A mound of earth and granite, higher than its neighbors, rose up to their left, and the parson turned Mars aside to climb this. When Peter caught up with him, the parson had his spyglass out from beneath his cloak, and was training it on the grove to the north. "I *am* curious about that light," he said. He lowered the telescope and passed it to Peter.

Peter peered at the light, but could tell little, watching it flicker past the trunks of trees. He was curious also, but didn't know if that meant he wanted to inquire into its disposition. There was something peculiar about it, and though a light to wayfarers is generally a welcoming sight, this looked out of place among the lonely grove of trees in the midst of Great Meadow. It was October, after all, and no other season so compelled a person to believe in trolls and goblins.

But the parson had made a decision, and Peter was not ready to part company with him. The clergyman urged Mars back down the slope, and crossed their previous track when he came to it. Great Meadow Brook meandered to their immediate right, and they had to drift west to avoid its banks, further than they would have otherwise on such a line of sight. Once they splashed through some marshy ground and Peter half expected a ball of foxlight to rise up and meet them.

The fire in the trees looked more and more like a campfire as they approached it, though the parson remarked, half to himself, that whoever was camping was not far from habitation in any direction.

They finally came to a fence and searched some time for a stile or a gate. When a stile was found, the next few yards took them to the edge of the copse.

"I can't imagine someone hasn't heard us," said the parson, and Peter agreed. The parson called out from the edge of the grove. Peter looked up, where the moonlight limned the crowns of several noble oaks, as well as the plumes of birch trees waving in the night wind. No answer was returned. The parson pursed his lips in a deliberate frown, and replied to the silence, "That is stranger still."

Peter was making something of the firelight and its surroundings, by now, craning his head from one side to the other, peering through the trees. He thought he saw something move and that rudimentary apprehension fluttered through him again.

Having dismounted to cross the stile, Parson Leach handed his reins to Peter. He paused, for a moment, over his musket, but decided not to take it from its sheath.

Peter said, "I'll go with you," and he returned to the fence and looped Mars's and Beam's reins over the upper rail.

Parson Leach called out again. "Ho, there, by the fire! We're coming up!"

Peter followed the parson to the edge of the trees, and to avoid being swatted by low branches and bushes, he allowed the man to advance a few steps before entering behind. Their progress sounded thunderous to the young man, or rather the parson's progress did, for the clergyman was making no attempt to move quietly. Though it made little sense to creep along after announcing their presence, Peter found himself walking as silently as any woodsman tracking game. The wind came around for a moment and he smelled smoke and the hint of something cooking.

Parson Leach paused beyond the inner circle of trees and a voice came from somewhere inside the copse. "Come ahead, the both of you." It was a cordial enough address—as much as anyone could ask, coming out of the dark—but the absolute confidence in knowing how many they were gave Peter pause.

"Peter," said the parson easily.

Peter followed the clergyman through the last of the trees, past a low line of thickets and into the midst of a rock-rimmed clearing. The fire they had seen had been built against a stray boulder near the center of the open space—a cheery enough blaze, with some long sticks propping a little kettle against the rock and over the flames.

The light from the fire glimmered against the trunks and limbs and clutches of remaining leaf, so that Peter had the impression of having walked into a room with walls and a lofty ceiling. Against the trunk of an oak, where roots had presented a convenient hollow—like that of the tree on the bank of the river that afternoon—there sat an elderly man with a pleasant enough countenance, a long white beard, and wispy white hair. He might have been a woodsman, or an old farmer, or a wanderer. His kit lay beside him—an ancient musket, a sack or two, a blanket, and some rabbit pelts. A short jug stood next to him.

"Are you hungry, then?" said the old man. "Did you smell the old man's stew?"

"We've eaten well tonight already, thank you," said the parson. "It was more curiosity that took us off the track. We saw your fire."

"Yes, I am curious too," said the fellow by the tree. "And old Pownal, here." He nodded to indicate who or what he was naming, and the two men took note of a dog at the other end of the copse; the creature was as white in the chops and as venerable in the eye as the man, but it stood rigidly, with its back up and its head down. Peter heard a low note rumbling from the animal. "He smelt you half an hour ago," added the old man, which Peter thought was an exaggeration.

"I couldn't help wonder," said the parson amiably, "what a person might be doing, camping here with so many houses nearby."

"Are there?" said the fellow. "I don't put much notice to houses. One of them yours?" There was an inflection to the man's speech that Peter had never heard before, and it occasionally made the fellow difficult to understand.

The parson had no problem, however. "No," he said. "My *horse* is my house these days."

The old fellow laughed at this. The humor shook him a bit and Peter saw something move on his lap. The muzzle of a second musket, trained on them both, lay propped on one thigh, and when Peter scanned the ground within reach of the old man, he saw what looked to be the butt of a pistol peeking from one of the bags.

"I am Zachariah Leach," said the parson. "This is Peter Loon."

"Peter," said the old man, as if the name surprised him. "I am Peter Klaggerfell," he informed them, and the difference in his speech was increased when he spoke his own name. "It's not usual to be traveling of a night, is it?" he asked, registering his own curiosity regarding the motives of his new acquaintances.

"We're going to New Milford," said the parson.

"I hear things are happening there," said old Peter Klaggerfell. Without looking up, he added, "There is an owl in one of these trees," which seemed to Peter a mysterious thing to say.

"Did you hear the call to arms, then?" asked Parson Leach.

"I heard there's another war to be had," said the fellow. "I fought for the King against the Indians and the French, and I fought for Washington against the King. Now we'll see how Washington fares against me."

"Washington is dead, Mr. Klaggerfell."

"Is he? More's the pity. Then some other rapscallion, I'll warrant." The old man's eyes glinted happily in the firelight.

Young Peter thought that John Adams was president, but he wasn't sure enough of this to express his opinion.

"Do you *need* another war, sir?" wondered the parson. "I would have ventured that the two you endured had proved enough."

"Do you think? I'm told they've been fighting in France."

"They were, but the fighting there is done with, I believe."

"Well, that surprised me, you see. For we fought the French, and we fought the British; and the French, they fought themselves, so I figure how, when you run out of other folk, you tangle with your own kin. I never suspected how easy it was to contract a good disputation."

The old man might have been having fun with them, but the possibility did not warm Peter to him. Parson Leach stepped over to the fire, picked a stick from the ground and stirred Mr. Klaggerfell's stew. The smoke from the fire roiled against the rock hearth before it was taken over the trees by the wind.

"Thank you," said the old man. They heard another low rumble from the dog, and Mr. Klaggerfell said, in the most conversational of tones, "That's enough, now, Pownal. Pull it up."

The dog's great age was more apparent as it crossed the little clearing to hunker down at Mr. Klaggerfell's side. The animal walked stiffly, and the fur at its hind quarters was as thin and ragged as the old man's hair. Peter had a queasy feeling when the dog passed between him and the parson, but Pownal settled next to the old man peaceably enough.

"Have you been in the backcountry long?" asked Parson Leach.

"I couldn't tell you, really," replied the old fellow. "The word is strange to me. What they call backcountry in *these* parts, I pass through in a day or so. I've been *back* of the backcountry, here to Canada and gone, more times than I can recall, with a good deal of tramping about in between."

Peter would have expected to feel more comfortable with the old man as the parson conversed with him, but the effect of the man's company proved quite opposite; Peter grew more anxious as he listened to them.

"You're welcome to come with us," the parson was saying. "There might be a bed waiting for you."

"Wouldn't know how to cope with it," said the man.

"They will be gathering, I think, where we're going—the men you're looking for."

"I'll find them, no doubt. They had better mean business, though, or Pownal will likely bite someone. He doesn't mind going places, but he craves purpose."

"You're liable to have more visitors, Mr. Klaggerfell. There are houses about and someone will see your fire."

"Could it be there are people as curious as you and I?" said the elderly fellow. Peter realized that, since nodding toward the dog, the man had hardly moved a muscle other than those necessary to speak. There was something uncanny in his stillness, or perhaps all too canny, like a cat ready to strike.

"It wouldn't surprise me," the parson was saying.

"Let them come. Pownal and I travel till we tire, and then we lay down."

"One of those houses you take no note of may contain someone who owns this copse."

"Yes, there's something like that in all this fuss I've heard tell."

"People have owned *these acres*," said the parson, "and labored over them long enough to lay claim by any measure, that much is plain." He stirred Mr. Klaggerfell's stew again, as if he were in the man's kitchen, and they were talking simple pleasantries. Indeed, they might have been, for all Peter could tell from their words; but the tension in their voices put him on his nerves. The parson pulled something out of the stew with the stick and considered it for a moment. "I think this might be ready," he said.

"The hares around here are tough as corncobs," the old man was saying. "I've been boiling that one for half an hour or more, but I'd wager bottom land to boulders I'll lose a tooth on it if I don't boil it the same again."

"Come, Peter," said the parson. He turned his shoulder to the man and Peter was startled for the fraction of an instant by a sudden stiffening in Mr. Klaggerfell's posture. Peter almost cried out, he was so sure the man was raising the muzzle of his gun. An owl—the owl, perhaps, that Mr. Klaggerfell had suspected—called from somewhere above them, and Peter heard the sound of large wings treading the wind. Parson Leach looked up.

After a moment, the old man said, "Thanks for stirring my stew, Parson," though the clergyman had only spoken of himself as Zachariah Leach.

"God speed, Mr. Klaggerfell." Parson Leach led Peter into the trees.

"Mr. Leach. Mr. Loon."

Peter was amazed, how like a wall the night appeared beyond the sphere of Mr. Klaggerfell's fire. He stumbled against a root, then took the switch of a branch across his mouth. Parson Leach was standing behind him, and the man reached around to hold a sapling back. Peter ducked his head, closed his eyes for a moment, then walked in the direction he expected to find their horses with his hands before him, groping for trunks and limbs.

"This way," said the parson, after a moment, and Peter could see the silhouette of the clergyman's arm pointing to the left a few degrees.

All the while Peter felt as if the bore of that musket was staring at the point between his shoulders. He dared a single look back, and could see Mr. Klaggerfell, in vertical portions between the trunks of trees, sitting with his dog in the light of the fire.

Mars gave out a low whinny, as if telling them where he and Beam could be found. "No need to hurry," said Parson Leach softly.

Peter didn't know he'd been hurrying, but he accepted the parson's word and forced his feet to check their pace. The horses were shadows against the moonlit quarter of the sky, and comforting to reach up and touch when the travelers closed with them.

"As long as we've come this far north," said the parson, "we'll head northwest and the road we reach will take us to the ford at Dyers River." So they skirted the southern and western edges of the copse and rode by moonlight through Great Meadow.

"What do you think, Peter?" said Parson Leach, when they had ridden some distance. "We may have tracked down the foxlight after all."

Peter looked back, now and again, to watch the light of Mr. Klaggerfell's fire dwindle. "That man frightened me some," he said.

Then the parson said, "The hair at the back of *my* neck hasn't settled *yet*."

"He *seemed* pleasant enough, somehow."

"He might have shared his hare with us, tough as it was."

"I don't know if I'd have eaten it."

Parson Leach laughed, but it was a rueful sound in the dark.

"Do you suppose he *did* fight the French?" asked Peter.

"The French and the British, and some wars you and I have yet to hear of, would be my guess." The parson himself glanced back, but the copse was only a dark smudge against the rolling fields and Mr. Klaggerfell's fire was invisible to them. "He's from an ancient race that shows little signs of dying. I only saw fighting at Yorktown, myself, but I met some of his family there, and I must say I wasn't sorry for them then. In battle, they take any soldier at their side as their own."

Peter hoped they wouldn't see Mr. Klaggerfell again, but suspicioned that the old man would not be far behind them in reaching the trouble in New Milford.

"How did he know you were a parson?" he asked.

17

Concerning the Encounter at Benjamin Brook

THE SUGGESTION OF DANGER DRIFTED AWAY IN THEIR WAKE AND ALL but disappeared when they came to the road that Parson Leach had described—a convergence of roads, actually—and he hurried them along the track northwest again. Soon they reached the ford at Dyers River. The current there was salty, but the tide was near to ebb and they were able to splash across on the backs of their mounts without getting very wet.

They saw two or three scattered farms on that side of Great Meadow, as they passed over a road that had been built up on marshy ground; at the top of a hill, they sighted lights in the distance, along the Sheepscott River not half a mile away.

"Does the town look very awake?" said Parson Leach.

Peter thought it did. Lights glimmered from almost every house, and there looked to be a fire in one of the streets. They rode down the slope and when they crossed the wooden bridge over Benjamin Brook—their horses' hooves clumping loudly—a light glared in their faces and several figures stepped from the side of the road beyond and barred the way. Two or three of these persons wore something over their heads, and the others had blackened their faces.

"Stand!" came the nasal twang of a voice from one of them,

who stepped ahead of the lantern light. "Who goes there!" and for the second time that night, the travelers found themselves the object of a musket bore's attention.

"Since *you* are pointing the gun," said the parson, almost with a laugh, "Perhaps we deserve to be answered first."

"What?" said the man, and a second said, "Get down, now."

Peter, who was startled almost as profoundly by the parson's reply as from the original sentry-call, was ready to comply, but the parson put a hand out and touched his arm.

"If you're here to rob us," said Parson Leach, "we can hand over our valuables and stay mounted."

"We are Liberty Men!" declared one of the figures.

"We're the White Indians!" said another.

Shielding his eyes from the light of the lantern with one hand, Parson Leach leaned forward and peered past Mars's large head to inspect the foremost of these figures. The man's face was disguised as an animal of some sort, but he drew back, as if the parson could see who he was beneath the mask. When the parson said, "Are you afraid your wife will come out here and recognize you, Martin Church?" the whole group of them expressed astonishment and dismay.

"Who *is* that?" came a third voice, and one of the men stepped up and peered up at the riders. "Is that you, Mr. Leach?"

"Yes, and I've been greeted with less threat and more flattery when I've come to New Milford."

Some wordless sounds of apology were interrupted by the first man, who came to the fore again and declared, almost in a chant, "The powers of oppression are upon us, and we must be watchful!" Then he considered the two horsemen and added, "Not to speak that the two of you are dressed like gentlemen."

"The sheriff's been about," said a fellow further back in the crowd.

"He's jailed ten men and swears to keep them!" said another.

"Do pardon us, Mr. Leach," managed one man, whose face was black with charcoal.

"Do we take his gun?" said someone.

"The parson?" said another.

"He's one of us, isn't he?"

"You are, aren't you, Mr. Leach?"

"A man for Liberty, I might be," said the clergyman lightly, "but I won't join you for the pleasure of accosting simple travelers."

The Liberty Men replied in harmony of meaning, if not voice. "We're only protecting our own, Mr. Leach," said the one, and "Ten men they took," insisted another, "and not all of them part of the *frolic* the other night." Still a third broke in with, "Roused them from their fields and hearths, Mr. Leach. Put them in irons and marched them to Wiscasset."

The man who had first challenged the travelers took another step forward, shook his musket at Parson Leach, and announced with a degree of belligerence not yet heard in that colloquy, "Mister, you are either for us, or against."

Parson Leach swung one foot over the front of his saddle and dropped from his horse in a single motion. The man with the contentious musket was surprised by this movement and didn't step back as much as he simply leaned away. The bore of the musket leaned away as well and Parson Leach snatched the gun from the man's hand in as quick a move as Peter Loon had ever seen.

There was a great deal of discussion about this, but Parson Leach broke through the uproar with the following quiet, if earnestly felt dissertation. "Step ahead, any man who can say he's seen me demonstrate other than sympathy for backcountry folk. If I speak of moderate means, so much more should you listen to me, rather than follow some mad ranter. But as for being for or against, I feel good will, as a general thing, toward any man not pointing a gun at me. Why have I come here, if not to discover circumstance and offer what stands by my command?" The masked men drew back from this even-spoken lecture, and Parson Leach offered the first fellow his musket back, saying, "I seem to remember writing a successful *answer to writ* for you last spring, George Chaff."

The parson did not wait for anyone to grant permission, but mounted Mars, spoke to Peter, and rode past the group of men. Peter did not immediately understand what was happening, but then he urged Beam forward, with his heart charging in his chest. There was no further challenge or outcry from behind, but ahead of them, the voices of men were raised in shouts and raucous song. There was a bonfire in the midst of the village and the masked and costumed figures milling about it were silhouetted into strange shapes against the flames.

18

How Opinion Differed over the Course of a Few Hours and a Few Miles, and What Was Said at the Sign of the Star and Sturgeon

PETER HAD OCCASION TO THINK OF NORA TILLAGE DURING HIS AND Parson Leach's night journey, but never more than now.

Peter had seen wild behavior before. The severe, drudging life of the backcountry would, on occasion, uncinch—often with astounding, even frightening portions of rum and evangelical fire and brimstone (these two passions not always appearing in mutually exclusive seasons). Peter's mother Rosemund Loon had, on the whole, exercised but a single prerogative over her children by keeping them from the sphere of preachers and Liberty Men, but even an outlying farm will know its neighbors. By mere connection with the community of Sheepscott Great Pond, Peter had experienced a little religion *and* a smattering of squatter's politics. Now, however, riding toward the riotous crowd in the midst of New Milford's central hamlet, Peter thought most on the intemperate Nathan Barrow, and so was sharply reminded of Nora Tillage.

So far, Peter had experienced the events of the night as in a reverie, and particularly the confrontation at the bridge over Benjamin Brook in a troubled daze. While listening to the masked and charcoal painted Liberty Men, he was reminded of the angry visitors and the angry words in Captain Clayden's den; then he understood the Captain's apprehension that Parson Leach was putting himself between reckless adversaries.

Adding to Peter's discomfort was the recognition that he was clothed in a manner that separated him from these men of field and hamlet. He was indeed dressed as a gentleman, and if he had felt ill at ease in those clothes among the Claydens, the clothes suddenly felt ill at ease on him among folk of his own sort. Yet, for all his own trepidation, Peter would not have been anywhere else at that moment.

The bonfire in the middle of the village was being fed, even as they approached. A great cry had risen and Peter blinked to see someone's furniture—chairs and a table—added to the flaming heap. Beam tensed beneath him when they drew near the heat and light; Mars snorted indignantly as the prevailing breeze carried a gout of smoke past them.

The hamlet of New Milford was made up of several houses, barns, and a blocky tavern, ranked on either side of the road along the northeastern shore of the Sheepscott River. The tavern was a door or two beyond the bonfire, and it was in the direction of this establishment that Parson Leach led them.

Peter believed, then, that there were a good *many* people in the world. A throng of drunken men, dressed in mock Indian garb with charcoal-darkened faces, or masked as animals, leaped and rioted between the horsemen and their destination. One group, on the other side of the flames, carried on with song—bellowing a tune, more or less, that Peter recognized, but utilizing verses that had been composed to fit their circumstance and disposition.

No, my son! Independence isn't won!
No, my girl! The Revolution isn't done!
For Great Men sure are wanting killing,
    And Liberty Men are very willing,
To wield the Sword and fire the Gun!

Some of their words were couched in symbols that Peter hardly understood, but the tenor was clear, and those voices gave off a heat to rival the flames.

The Bells of Liberty will be pealing!
The Ghost of Freedom soon be stealing!
    The Lord returns one day to lead us,
And he'll see Great Men rob and bleed us,
And send them, writ and summons, reeling!

Dancing before the fire, filled with rum and the madness of crowds, otherwise terse and toughened farmers and tradesmen had cast aside constraint to howl like wolves and cavort like hysterical children. Peter had heard such carrying on from a distance, watching the light of other bonfires from behind his family home in Sheepscott Great Pond, but he could never have guessed at the immediate noise and confusion.

The parson did not appear to be shocked by what he saw, nor did he seem very amused. Peter had never seen such a lack of expression on Parson Leach, and it made him wary of what this man, who could snatch a gun from another's hand as quickly as the hawk grabs the sparrow, might plan and what he might do. More than one reveler approached them, jug raised or musket lifted to the sky, but they were inevitably brushed back by the peculiar force of the parson's expressionless eye.

Peter kept Beam's neck by Mars's flank as they skirted the bonfire. It was natural to turn his head away from the heat, and doing so, Peter caught sight of several men coming out of the house opposite. One had a jug, and another carried a piece of furniture which he hoisted into the air; the third Peter recognized as one of the men who had been riding with Nathan Barrow.

Peter's first thought was to wonder where Barrow himself might be. He and the parson, meanwhile, did not pass unnoticed, and though Peter averted his own gaze, he could be sure that his own back, and that of the parson's, were drilled by this fellow's scrutiny.

They came to a clapboarded two-story building where a sign hung that bore the likeness of a strange, snout-nosed fish, and a single star. Peter knew the creature was a sturgeon, though he had never seen one before. Tales of sturgeon abounded in the backcountry, fabulous stories of monstrous fish that were first learned at the campfires of Indians. Peter read the sign as meaning "The Star and the Sturgeon."

Some men stood in the doorway to the tavern and one of them shouted something that was answered by the appearance of a boy on the stoop. This small person pressed his way through the crowd and scurried to meet the horsemen. Parson Leach and Peter dismounted and Peter followed the clergyman's lead by handing his reins over to the boy.

"I heard it said you were coming, Mr. Leach," said the boy, who gave Peter—or Peter's clothes, perhaps—a close inspection. "Not an hour ago."

"How are you, Robert?" said the parson. "And who's house is suffering over there?"

"Charles Trall led the sheriff and his men over to Donnell's farm," was the boy's reply, "and they arrested Mr. Donnell and his brother there. Then he led them up to Gray farm so they could take Sam, and Sam hadn't so much as spoken stern to John Trueman, so they say."

Parson Leach stood by Mars and considered the commotion before Charles Trall's house. "He should have foreseen *that* result," he muttered with a shake of his head. There was a renewed howl from the crowd as another bit of the Tralls' furnishings was added to the fire. The men in the tavern doorway made room for the travelers.

The scene inside was several degrees less wild than without; the main room of the tavern was crowded, but many of those making up the crowd were in the latter stages of intoxication, while some talked quietly if earnestly with one another over the dark tables and pints of rum or ale or cider. A fire burned cheerily enough in the great hearth at the midst of the room, but the air was dimmed by the smoke from a score of pipes. Some fellows in less cognizant states still wore their animal masks, and their furred heads, snouts, and long ears seen through the thick atmosphere added to the scene's already dream-like quality.

The identity of the newcomers had run ahead of them, it seemed, for there was little surprise on conscious men's faces when Parson Leach and Peter entered, though there were guarded expressions from those who had been with Nathan Barrow at the lake shore.

One of these stood at the door to the kitchen, and when Parson Leach led Peter to the back of the tavern, this man straightened his bearing and effectively indicated that he intended to bar the way. He looked less certain of his office, as the parson approached, however, and when the welcome (to Peter's eyes) figure of Crispin Moss separated itself from a darkened corner and met them at the door, the watchman left his post with the look of a man who suddenly remembers more important duties.

"Mr. Moss," said Parson Leach, both in greeting and appreciation.

"Mr. Leach, Mr. Loon," said the big man. He had obviously indulged his thirst, as evidenced by the tankard he gripped, but perhaps had done so with less zeal than had some of his fellows. He could, in fact, stand pretty steadily, and his words were clear upon his tongue. "Mr. Cutts and I were in hopes of seeing you before cockcrow. Some pretty wild notions have been thrown about, and the supply of clear heads is lacking." This was said with great indulgence displayed in his expression toward those who proved less temperate than himself.

"I wonder if Mr. Cutts isn't in the kitchen," said the parson.

"Indeed, he is."

"We shall be glad of one moderate soul, at least," said Parson Leach. "Come ahead," he said to Peter, and he brooked no discussion on the subject, but opened the door and stood aside for the younger man.

The revel in the road continued to supply a steady roar behind the quieter environs of the tavern. To Peter, he and the parson were entering decreasing stages of noise and confusion as they progressed, and the room beyond was poised, to a man, in that attitude of interrupted dialogue that is part curiosity and part irritation. Almost a score of sober-faced individuals stood or sat in the kitchen of the Star and Sturgeon, gathered about a long board where many a meal had been prepared, and crock and tankard had been filled. Some gripped crocks and tankards now, but they all seemed respectable enough, at first look, and sober, though in some cases this was a relative business to what carried on outside. Peter thought several of them would have looked the proper guests in Captain Clayden's den.

His attention was quickly drawn to one man, who sat at the further end of the table; Nathan Barrow's hands were on the board, as if he waited for his plate and bowl; his face was dark with barely suppressed animosity. There were those in the room who cast quick glances in the direction of the lay preacher, wanting to be prepared, should there be some sort of explosion. Manasseh Cutts stood leaning against a cupboard and appeared unconcerned; he nodded to Peter and allowed quietly how he admired the young man's boots.

Barrow's head was down slightly, but his eyes were peering up past his brows to glare at Parson Leach and Peter Loon. "I see we have more proprietary agents among us by the minute."

"Those are hard charges, Mr. Barrow," said someone.

"This *Leach*," said Barrow with special emphasis, "has recently absconded with a daughter of the cause, and has been reported to have left her in the care of Captain Clayden himself, who must be as congenial an ally as the enemy can boast of." Barrow hardly stirred, and Peter was struck—and rather unpleasantly—that the man possessed a latent energy, and perhaps a hidden swiftness, akin to that of Parson Leach.

Several men in the room turned to Parson Leach for a defense against these charges, but among the majority of them, Zachariah Leach was not unknown, or disrespected. "I am sure this was a simple misunderstanding," said an elder among these.

"*I* understood that the young woman fled of her own accord, and separate from Mr. Leach's knowledge," said another.

"Nonetheless," said a third, indeed the man who had ridden beside Nathan Barrow at the lake shore, "the girl fled her father's charge, and if Mr. Tillage gave his daughter over to Mr. Barrow's protection, then Mr. Leach must keep her away at her father's displeasure."

Another man, standing in the corner spoke up. "There's little point arguing who owns the land, if a man hasn't possession of even his children."

Peter wondered why the parson did not answer these charges himself, and only realized later that he was taking the tenor of the room by letting the men about the table first speak for themselves. By such means the discussion was somewhat exhausted of its fire, and Parson Leach would have some inkling how camps were divided.

"You wouldn't consent for a man to have such possession of a child that you'd watch him murder her," Manasseh Cutts was saying in a low tone.

"There was no question, I think," said one of the grayer eminences at the table, "of violence against the girl."

"Nor serve her out for a whore," recommenced Manasseh.

"I would tread cautiously, sir," said one of the other older men. "Mr. Tillage could realize a legal suit for speaking of his daughter in that fashion."

"I say nothing against the girl, if you listen," said Manasseh, "but if Tillage cares to answer for what I'd say about him, I won't be hard to find." The woodsman leveled such a direct stare at Nathan Barrow when he said this that there was no mistaking that the condemnation was meant to cover more than the father in question.

"She is a good girl, is Nora Tillage," said Parson Leach, and Peter would remark to himself later that the first words from the preacher's lips were in defense of another. "If she fled her father's wishes out of misunderstanding, then it is easily mended. This gentleman says that a man must have possession of his children, but no one here imagines this to be to all purposes, and even a child has recourse to the safety of the law. Perhaps in my place, Mr. Barrow would not have offered his protection. This young man, here," added Parson Leach with a nod toward Peter, "raced forward himself to rescue her, and Mr. Cutts stood by us as well as Mr. Moss. Perhaps it is more than some think necessary, to harbor a frightened child."

Without warning, Nathan Barrow leaped to his feet, shouting *"Let no man deceive you with vain words: for because of these things cometh the wrath of God upon the children of disobedience!"*

"Ephesians, five, six," said Manasseh Cutts before Parson Leach could respond, and this caused someone in the room to laugh.

"'Who can find a virtuous woman?'" countered Parson Leach, *"'for her price* is *far above rubies.'* How much greater is Miss Tillage's virtue if she must steal it against her father's command? And such goodness in hand we must treat with utmost caution."

Since Mr. Tillage had given his daughter over to Nathan Barrow, the point of this statement—or rather the person who was the point of this statement—was fairly transparent.

"This is libel!" shouted Barrow, and the men nearest him steeled themselves for the task of holding him back.

It did not come to that, however; one of the other men stood and put his hands up till the commotion had died somewhat. He was the elderly fellow—Mr. Pelligue—who had suggested that Nora Tillage fled of her own accord. He wore a long gray beard, and his clothes were clean, if well-worn. "We are not here to discuss this particular case, but to decide our response to the arrest of our neighbors, and it seems to me that the power of our reply will be greatly enhanced if we put other differences aside. Mr. Leach, we would be gratified to hear *your* thoughts on this matter, which I guess must have brought you among us."

Mr. Pelligue then leveled an eye at Barrow, who did not sit down but let out a sound like a piece of wet wood in the fire.

One of Barrow's allies stood and said, "It is Mr. Leach himself, perhaps, who first bred difference by his actions, and feeds it by his argument. There is no more subtle way for Great Men to break our cause then by sending a *whisperer* among us."

"It matters not!" declared Barrow, having regained his voice. He thumped the table with a fist and said, "What cannot be done by many who are timid, will be done by the few who are resolute. The millennium of the Lord's resurrection will soon be upon us, and those who face the enemy in a manner lukewarm will be so greeted by Him when He returns. Our rooms in Heaven will be prepared by the numbers of our oppressors we crush."

Some there were enthusiastic for this vision, and Peter was impressed by their faces as they listened.

Barrow himself looked triumphant. "You may sit here and worry this bone," he pronounced. "I will gather who will follow me and march upon Wiscasset, and watch it burn if so much as a man stands in my way!" Then he strode about the table, past Parson Leach and Peter, and left the room. Two men, including his lieutenant from the earlier encounter, rose and followed him; others who had been enamored of his vision were yet a little less sure of his plan and elected to stay.

"If this is the right thing," said one man, a Mr. Kendall, who stood beside Manasseh Cutts, "we should go with him to be sure of its success."

"If it is the *wrong* thing, we should quickly stop him," said Mr. Briner, who sat near Barrow's vacant chair.

"Men will hie in all directions," said Mr. Pelligue, "and we can surely divide ourselves, following about to help or hinder, but we Liberty Men have known success by careful planning. Mr. Barrow will not march tonight, and we will *never* march, if we distract ourselves at every argument. Perhaps we should find Mr. Leach's opinion by asking what he understands of the matter. Zachariah," said the elderly fellow, indicating the recently emptied chair, "please, join us. Sir," he added to Peter Loon, though with a little more humor, "since you are proved a man of action, attend and advise."

Peter felt deceitful, conceding to such approval and dressed in a wealthy man's clothes, but the old fellow's invitation was enough to cause a chuckle or two, and the room appeared to relax.

"Friends," began the parson as he took the offered seat amid a chorus of agreement. "Word of the arrest you speak of was news to me when I was greeted with it at the bridge yonder, but I *had* heard how John Trueman was driven back to Wiscasset, stripped and beaten, and guessed that something would result. I only know that someone was arrested, but aside from the names of Donnell and Gray, I know neither who nor how."

"Yes, Donnell and Gray," said Mr. Kendall.

"Elbridge Shay," Mr. Briner began, "Henry Bender, Ezekiel Brackett—"

"There were ten of them," said Mr. Pelligue, indicating with a wave that a complete list, at this moment, was not to the point. "The sheriff came with twenty men or so and with Charles Trall as his guide, caught them in their fields or snatched them out of their beds. John Trueman, it seems, recognized certain voices when he was set upon the other night, though they all wore masks, as I understand."

"He didn't recognize every voice!" declared a man opposite Mr. Pelligue, "for they arrested three men who had no hand in it."

"He arrested men whose land he'd like to have for his own," said a Mr. Dodge.

"And you know these men were innocent, Mr. Hook?" said the parson.

"They were *all* innocent," said Mr. Dodge.

"I was there," said Mr. Hook proudly.

"As you have heard, Mr. Leach," said Mr. Pelligue, "there are those who propose a fierce reply."

"There isn't a court in the district that won't show favor against a settler," said Mr. Hook.

"What *is* this fierce reply?" asked the parson. "Does Mr. Barrow expect that it isn't enough to storm Wiscasset and break open the jail? Must he burn the town and kill the people in their beds while he's at it? Better he should be thinking what to do with the prisoners, once they're freed. They'll be charged with escape and hunted down at the very least."

"Some, we believe, will be able to hide themselves, for a time, in the backcountry," said Mr. Pelligue. "The charges against the three are trumpery, and we can't believe they'll be pursued for long. As for the remainder, we have arrangements. Mr. Briner, through his brother, has shipboard berths for seven men on the *Helene,* which is being outfitted at Bath and is bound for the South Seas within a week."

"Then we have only to get them from the jail," considered Parson Leach, "and Mr. Barrow's vision of burning Wiscasset to the ground would prove excessive. A simple foray down river in the night should accomplish your design, and the loosed fellows can be taken to Back River and up the Sasanoa to Bath. Now, *there* you have the beginnings of a scheme, which will fulfill your purpose and lay nothing like arson or bloodshed on your own heads."

A blocky fellow, who had hitherto remained silent, rose from his chair beside the door and, leaning upon the table, cast a bland expression at the parson. "I have no love for Nathan Barrow," he said, "but it is my intent, sir, as it is his, that we inflict more harm than that."

"Is it, sir? I don't know your name."

"Joshua Cargin," said the man. "The fellows who were arrested have been taken to Wiscasset, and it is Wiscasset supports land agents and surveyors and Great Men as much as any town. So we will have our men returned, but burn a house or two as we go *and* rid ourselves of any man who stands in our way!"

"Are you a New Milford man, Mr. Cargin?" asked the parson.

"I am not, though our enemies are the same."

"And you would find it simple enough to melt into the forest, I'm guessing, when Boston sends militia here to quell an armed rebellion."

"What?"

"It's no danger to you to draw fire against another man's town."

" *There* is the voice of the land agent!" declared Mr. Kendall.

"I think not, Mr. Kendall," said Mr. Pelligue. "Mr. Leach has a very good question at issue."

"Are you impugning my nerve?" growled Joshua Cargin. He leaned his large frame a little further over the table, as if considering the possibility of snatching Parson Leach from his chair.

"I am guessing, Mr. Cargin," said Parson Leach, and he never showed a hint of fear or antagonism, "that you might *like* to stir a nest of bees, if you could do it from a distance."

"Or let someone else do it for him," said Manasseh Cutts.

"I'll stir a face or two with *this!*" declared Cargin, and he raised a fist in the air.

Again consternation ruled discourse and voices were raised in argument and anger; but a similar sounding commotion from the tavern room was heard above this—a single outraged voice came through the door and then the door was thrown open. A young woman strode into the room, as might an angry matron who fixes herself to chastise obstinate children. Peter stepped back to avoid her. Joshua Cargin stood his ground however, and she came up short, just shy of colliding with him, took one step aside and cast her indignant glance about the room.

"Here you are *still*, then!" she pronounced. "I see you're good for talk! Such a pack of fools and crows I never believed could account for an entire town! Old women would have done more in a day than you'll accomplish between now and next year!" She was ordinary enough to look at, though her eyes were fine and expressive—a black-haired young woman, perhaps a little older than Peter, her cheek bearing the former touch of the measles or pox— but the anger that enlivened her eyes and tilted her dark brows raised her otherwise plain features to the striking. She did in fact carry inside of her a fire, that was the more attractive for being employed. She gripped a shawl about her, as if fearing one of the men there would touch her and pollute her with their indecision.

"Elspeth!" said Mr. Pelligue. "This is no place for you, nor your place to criticize men who have come of their own to help us!"

"Help you to the bottom of a crock, more like!" she insisted. One or two of the men looked ready to lay hold of her, and she raised a hand, saying, "See if you're brave enough to take a swat or two, since you haven't the pluck to get an innocent man from jail or stand for what's your own! Why, I'd *laugh* if the sheriff came back and took every one of you!"

Mr. Briner sat back in his chair and said, almost with a smile, "Perhaps you'd care to have us go down to Wiscasset without thought or plan and deliver us up so the sheriff won't need to trouble himself."

Parson Leach said, "Well, Miss Gray, Mr. Cargin here suggests we march on Wiscasset, burn a portion of the town, and fire on anyone in our way."

"And what do *you* suggest, Mr. Leach?" she asked, levelling that lofty gaze upon the clergyman.

"Outside, a little while ago," said Parson Leach evenly, "they were singing that the revolution is unfinished, and there are those all through the nation who lend credence to the thought. Daniel Shay rose up with his New England Regulation and escaped hanging, but narrowly. There were Ely's Rebels in Massachusetts and the Whiskey Rebels in Pennsylvania, but no revolt has lasted so long, nor drawn so little governmental attention as ours."

"The reason is clear enough," said Mr. Kendall. "We're a long way from Boston."

The parson answered, "The miles from here to Boston *are* in our favor, but our greatest power has been to avoid organizing an army, or justifying retribution by acts of willful murder and destruction. The courts and the sheriffs and the government know we are here, *and* they know—by our acts against the French and the British—how capable we are. The fear of our capacity keeps them at arm's length, experience of it will bring them down upon us. A fox in the neighbor's yard might seem too distant to trouble with, but not a wolf."

"And with that," said Elspeth Gray, "you suggest we do nothing."

"Your father was arrested," said the parson.

"Yes, he was! And he never was with those who drove out John Trueman, though there's a man or two in *this* room who knows more than I do! It wasn't difficult raising a troop to set upon a lone man, but they're thinking twice about coming out of the woods to save one of their own!"

These words occasioned some general discomfort in the

room, and more than one man began to agree with Mr. Pelligue that this was not a proper place for a young woman—or, at least, *this* young woman.

Joshua Cargin was not one of them, however, and he made so bold as to promise Elspeth Gray her father's rescue. Miss Gray, strangely enough, was not impressed by this assurance, and she looked the big fellow up and down as if she wondered there was enough of him to answer the task.

Parson Leach had seen, on the table before Mr. Pelligue, a wide strip of birch bark marked with lines and figures; he turned this slightly to understand what this chart represented. "How many men are here?" he wondered. "All told, the Indians in the yard as well. A hundred? A hundred and fifty?"

"I counted ninety-three men this afternoon," said Mr. Kendall. "But more have arrived since, including yourselves."

"Do you think a hundred men are enough to quell an entire town?"

"The word is abroad," said Mr. Pelligue, almost regretfully. "More will come."

"I think we should wait to know how many more they'll be," said the parson. "Then, perhaps we can decide whether we have enough for a show of force, or no more than would warrant stealth instead of riot. You wouldn't object to waiting for more fellows, would you, Miss Gray? Perhaps in numbers we'll find the courage you suspect we lack."

"Time is a difficult coin to come by in the backcountry, Mr. Leach," said the young woman, "and a day's labor lost might decide who won't last the winter. My brothers are young and my sister is ailing, and what my mother and I accomplish may not answer for the entire house. But I suppose there is nothing for women to do but wait when the men find there's rum and ale still to be had."

"We thank you for your forbearance," said the parson. "I will be satisfied to wait as well, then, and suggest no great plans be made till we know we have the men to perform it. I, in the meantime, must find a place to put my head."

"Grandmother will ask after you," said Elspeth Gray, "and you can't be staying in this mess. Come back with me and we'll feed you, unless you want to dance around the fire. The bed will be a rick of hay, but it will be peaceful."

"Peter, here, is with me."

The young woman inspected the well-dressed young man, and said, "He is welcome, too."

Peter was amazed by the invitation, coming as it did on the tail end of a harangue, but the parson took it in stride. "I will come, then," said the clergyman, "and take some abuse from your grandmother." He rose from the table and Mr. Pelligue thanked him for his sentiments. Parson Leach tapped at the map on the piece of birch bark, and said, "There is no door at this end of the jail, by the way."

19

Concerning Matters with Elspeth Gray and Gray Farm

PETER LOON HAD LISTENED ATTENTIVELY TO THE TALK AND ARGU-
ment in the kitchen of the Star and Sturgeon, but he hadn't had
time to consider what it all meant. Manasseh Cutts followed Parson Leach, Elspeth Gray, and Peter into the tavern room where
several heads came up and Crispin Moss greeted them cheerily
from a nearby table. More than the gentlemanly appearance of the
parson and Peter, the presence of a young woman drew its own
particular attention from some, but Elspeth kept herself wrapped
in her shawl, as in armor, and her head up in that same commanding posture. Peter noticed that she was considering him with
particular interest, and without thinking he lifted his hand to the
scar on his forehead.

"Did Mr. Barrow ride off to Wiscasset, then?" asked Parson
Leach of Mr. Moss, with more irony perhaps than was evident to
the big woodsman.

"He couldn't find any men, but one, who was sober enough to
sit a horse," said Crispin Moss.

"A shame," said the parson, and Peter thought he might be half
in earnest. "He might have saved us a deal of trouble."

"Barrow?" said Miss Gray. "You wouldn't send *that* man after
my father, would you?"

"No, I don't suppose I would."

Peter considered the opinions advanced in the kitchen and the men (and woman) who had offered them. Mr. Pelligue seemed a steady fellow in search of a commander, while Mr. Kendall and Mr. Brine seemed contrary sides of a coin—of the same weight, but opposing views. Joshua Cargin was a gun waiting to go off, but Miss Gray, who seemed to be looking for just such a man, had been unimpressed by him. Nathan Barrow was himself off somewhere, having his visions or exhorting men to wild behavior. Mr. Cutts and Mr. Moss were of less opinion, it seemed, though more ready than some to act, Peter thought, if called upon.

"We're going to the Gray farm, north of town," said Parson Leach to the woodsmen. "Perhaps I can cull some sense from all the *non*sense. The ladies Gray may have more intuition than these gentlemen possess in their present state." He indicated those who were flopped about the perimeters of the tavern room; their numbers had grown in the short while that Peter and the parson had been in the kitchen. Noise continued to jar the night, however, and through the tiny-paned windows at the front of the tavern, the light of the bonfire wavered. "Anyone can tell you where the Grays live, if something happens that I should know about."

Manasseh Cutts and Crispin Moss accepted these subtle orders placidly. "We're glad you've come," said the older woodsman.

Parson Leach did not look so sure himself. He followed Elspeth Gray into the tavern yard and he and Peter went to the stable to retrieve Mars and Beam. "Did you walk in?" asked the parson of the young woman.

"Yes, I did," she answered, "and it is a good thing, as my temper had time to cool."

"Very right, of course," said Parson Leach, and he gave Peter an odd expression when Elspeth turned away.

"You may take my horse, if you like," Peter said quietly to the young woman.

"I will ride with you," she said, and she indicated with a wave of the hand that he should mount before her; then she reached up and let him pull her behind him. Beam fidgeted for a moment, then relaxed beneath the extra weight. Peter did not relax very much himself, particularly when Miss Gray locked her arms about his middle and for the sake of a secure seat pressed herself against him. He thought that for a plain farm girl she smelled very interesting—that is of more than cows and dust—and whenever she spoke on the ride to her family's farm he could feel her voice resonate against his shoulder.

It occurred to Peter after they had ridden a mile or so that she reminded him of Emily Clayden, if Emily Clayden had been older and made a little bitter with life. It was Miss Gray's directness that both daunted and intrigued him, and if she did not otherwise look like Emily, her eyes were similar to those of the young Newcastle girl—pale blue, direct, and comely.

They rode two or three miles along a path that was marked only by the passage of other horses and rows of stumps. The moon was riding high by now, and Peter fell to wondering about Peter Klaggerfell and his dog Pownal, and had they finished their meal and pressed on toward New Milford beneath this very moon? The trail rose and fell among alternate acres of forest, cleared land, and fallen trees. Quartz veins in granite hillsides glowed, and somewhere in the blue shadows of a pine wood a wild creature coughed. The Gray farm was first sighted from one of these rocky knolls, and it was a pretty enough situation as seen in the half-light, tucked against the opposing hill by the narrow reaches of the Sheepscott River.

Miss Gray dropped down from Beam's back without warning and strode the rest of the way, keeping a brisk pace down the slope. She led them through a gate, then showed them the easiest place to ford the stream. Lantern light fell across the yard when the door to the cabin opened. A woman's silhouette appeared there.

"El?" came a voice akin to, but older than Miss Gray's. "That you? You didn't bring your father, did you." This last was couched in assertion rather than query. "Who is that, then?" she asked, hearing, perhaps, rather than seeing the horses and the extra bodies.

"It's Mr. Leach, Ma, and a friend."

"Mother Gray," called Elspeth's mother into the cabin. "Zachariah is here to argue with you."

"God bless the sinner!" Peter heard coming from within.

Two or three other, smaller forms filled the doorway behind the mother, and Mrs. Gray—that is Mrs. Gray the younger—shooed her children aside so that, once Mars and Beam were tethered, the parson and Peter could follow Elspeth in.

"We killed a pig about a week ago, so there's something on the table," promised the mother. She turned her back on the guests as she went to the hearth, barely showing interest in who the parson's friend might be.

The cabin was not as old, nor as large, as the one Peter had been raised in. The barn behind the cabin *was* large, however, and evidenced the labor of the surrounding community. It hovered darkly over the cabin as Peter stepped inside the Gray home. An ancient woman sat by the hearth, toothless and sightless, by Peter's guess, but indicating great curiosity by the posture of her head, which was craned up, as if she were considering the weather.

"Go out and take those horses to the barn," said the mother to a small boy, who immediately jumped to the task. "And give them hay and water!" she shouted after him. She looked at Peter, glancing from his clothes to the scar on his head, before turning back inside.

"Zachariah, you awful heathen!" declared the elderly woman when they entered the cabin. "Have you come finally to confess all your devil-notions?"

"I come to offer you truth and beauty, Mrs. Gray," said the parson happily. "I've come to court you, as always."

The woman made a noise to indicate her disgust. "You think just because these eyes can't read, you'll overwhelm me with your high talk. But Elspeth here can read, and she tends me my Bible every day. Elspeth? You're there, aren't you?"

"Yes, Gran."

"Tell him you can read as ever as your old Gran could."

"He knows that Gran."

"He might forget. Don't let him get ahead of you, that's all. He talks high, but *'devil, get thee behind!'*"

Peter was sure that he had entered a perpetual state of astonishment, and that this treatment of Parson Leach was just one in a series of ongoing surprises. The parson however seemed unaffected, and spent this harangue in inspecting the pot that steamed by the hearth.

"What have you done for my son, Zachariah?" asked the old

woman, and the use of the parson's christian name seemed at odds with her previous abuse.

Parson Leach answered her with all the ease in the world. "I may have dissuaded some gentlemen from getting him killed in an attempt to break the jail."

"Gentlemen, I'm sure!" she said. "That's something, anyway. And who is *this* high-handed fellow?" she asked, considering Peter sightlessly.

"This is my friend, Peter Loon," said the parson, "and you're not to convert him."

"So the devil says!"

The younger Mrs. Gray turned from the plank table where she had been laying out bowls and said crossly, "What is it to be, then?"

"Perhaps you should tell me," said the parson. "I only know that he was taken to Wiscasset, but neither how or why. Where *we've* been, discussion has shed more heat than light."

Peter was standing by the door, feeling as out of place as he had in the Clayden's kitchen; he did, in fact, feel so very out of place, partly because of having *been* in the Clayden's kitchen. He looked down at his clothes then—the fine attire of the younger Captain Clayden—and met the curious stares of two small children, a boy and a girl, who stood on either side of him. Their faces were glum and dirty. The little boy showed the same marks of disease that speckled Elspeth's cheek. Peter was reminded of his little brother Amos and he smiled at the boy.

"I told Sam to go with them, when they drove John Trueman out," the mother was saying bitterly, "and maybe he'll wish he had, when all is said and done, as he'd have reason to be where he is now. I told him to garb up and take his gun, if he had to, but he'd have none of it."

"Been talking to you!" said the ancient Mrs. Gray to the parson. "I told him he lacked sand and he preached moderation to his own mother!"

The parson seemed unaware of, or at least unconcerned with, the triangle he occupied—the grandmother at the hearth, the mother at the table, and the daughter—her arms crossed and her face grim—by the curtain that hid the single bedroom. A voice came from behind the curtain, and Peter remembered that Elspeth had spoken of a sister who was ill.

"He is a temperate fellow, is Sam Gray," said Parson Leach, as if he were praising a congregant after church.

"Moderate never does, I say," pronounced the elderly woman.

"Perhaps one of you good women should have taken up a gun and gone yourselves."

"Don't think I wouldn't have," said Elspeth's mother, and her manner left no room for wry response. "The men assemble for their drunken meetings, and ramble off on their hunts when things are hard, and when things are harder still, they get it into their heads there's treasure in the woods and half lose a harvest digging up rocks and bones."

"There *is* treasure in the woods," said the older Mrs. Gray, almost to herself, as she rocked by the fire.

"I have no more than the house to talk with," continued her daughter-in-law, "and rarely see another like myself from month to month. And when there's sickness or we come up half starved to the end of winter, it's me that bears the hardness of it. It's woman knows the first injustice."

"Yes," said Parson Leach. "I know it's true. Adam took the rule and Eve took the curse for breaking it. Woman knows the first injustice, but it's the children know the worst."

"That's blasphemous talk!" said the elderly woman, delighted. "There *is* treasure in the woods," she repeated. "Edward Bailey saw it in the pit he dug, but his son sneezed and it whisked away. That was fifteen years agone."

"You speak of drunkenness," said the parson to the younger Mrs. Gray, "but I was always of the opinion that Sam was as temperate toward drink as he was toward the use of violence."

Mrs. Gray recommenced her business at the table.

"And I remember—three years ago, wasn't it?—" he continued, "when half the settlement was up on the Dresden line, digging for treasure, and Sam was clearing the acres across the river."

There was nothing replied to this.

"I expect," he added, as if only by the way, "that Sam was sharpening an axe or getting some sleep while the White Indians were out putting sticks to John Trueman."

"Perhaps he should have been gone with them, instead of hovering about here!" said the wife with audible vehemence. She was weeping suddenly and she went to the pot over the fire and stirred it as if *it* had made her angry. The entire business seemed contradictory to Peter.

"Ah, well," said the grandmother, softly now. "He's never raised a hand to any of us, has he? We must take the good with the bad, you know."

Peter wondered if his father and Samuel Gray were a bit alike.

"You still haven't told me why he was arrested," said the parson.

"Charles Trall," said Elspeth, her arms still crossed before her. "He has his eye on this bottom land, now it's cleared and plowed, and a cabin and barn are raised."

"Surrounded him and the little boy and girl, up in the high field," said the elderly woman, nodding in her chair by the fire. "Set upon them, and put him in chains, so the children said."

"Charles Trall? The man who led the sheriff up here?" said the parson.

"Yes," said Elspeth, "*and* John Trueman, his cousin."

"The sheriff might have suspected . . ." began the clergyman, but the very silence that greeted this thought cut it short as well.

Supper began as a fairly silent affair. It was a late hour for farm life, and though the children had eaten, they sat down as well and watched the guests avidly, and listened to the parson's talk, which was pointedly meant to entertain. The elderly Mrs. Gray stayed by the fire and fell asleep.

The fare was plain pork and potatoes and beans, and Peter felt he was back home again. He tucked in with some appetite, despite the discomfort that he sensed hovering over the table. Twice he found Elspeth watching him, and after the parson regaled them with the tale of Nora Tillage's rescue—told in such a way that Peter seemed to have accomplished the business entirely on his own—Elspeth's stare came more often and became more insistent. Peter tried his best to deflect the parson's hero-making, but managed only to sound modest.

There were five living children to the Gray family, besides Elspeth, and besides the sister in the room behind the curtain, they were much younger than she; an influenza had raged through New Milford some years ago and taken several other brothers and a sister between. After supper, when Elspeth led the guests out to the barn, Peter saw the shadows of wooden crosses in the little yard on the slope above and behind the house.

The barn was dark and close with stacks of hay on two floors and the remnant heat of the day. There were two cows and a goat that stirred when the parson and Peter followed Elspeth inside. Peter found Beam's saddle and untied his father's hat and coat.

"I want you to stay with the Grays tomorrow, Peter," said Parson Leach. He glanced from the young man to Elspeth Gray when he said this. Something flashed in Elspeth's eyes, and Peter looked ready to speak, but the clergyman added, "They could, perhaps, use an extra hand while Mr. Gray is gone," which seemed to arrest any discussion on the matter. "I'll be back, the day after, or the day after that, perhaps, and we will go looking for your uncle."

Peter had expected to go with the parson on the morrow, not because he thought of himself as part of the discord in New Milford, but because he felt far from home and separate from his entire life and Parson Leach was his only landmark—steady, if yet unfamiliar. Peter thought he *might* say something, but a yawn overtook him.

"There's a place in the corner over there," said Elspeth, holding her lantern up and pointing. "And there's the loft, where you've slept before, I think, Mr. Leach."

The parson was already crossing to the rude ladder pegged to the end of the loft. Peter heard him yawn, as well, then the man muttered a good night blessing and climbed into the shadows.

Elspeth stood and watched Peter, as if she required something from him. He thanked her, for perhaps the fifth time, for supper and the place to sleep, but this did not appear to satisfy her expectations. She looked away from him, after a moment. Peter thought he could hear the parson's breath, rumbling in sleep above them. "Will you go with Mr. Leach to Wiscasset?" she asked.

Peter was startled. "He's told me not to," he said, and looked as if he might have heard wrong—either the parson's directive or her question. He hadn't thought of going to Wiscasset, really, where Elspeth's father was in jail; his imagination had taken him no further than New Milford. "I don't know that he's *going* to Wiscasset," he said, hardly moving his lips.

She looked at him some more, and particularly at the scar on his head, as if it indicated more than his words. She said "Good night," and Peter scrambled into the corner before the only light was gone with her.

In the complete darkness of the barn he was conscious of the heat rising from the hay, the sound of the parson's soft snore above him, and the movement of the animals in the stables close by. A bird of some sort called mournfully. A fly was buzzing. Peter patted down a mound of straw, sneezed at the dust he raised, and made himself as comfortable as possible—more so than at home, actually, where he shared a short trundle bed with his brother, though less so than his single night at the Clayden's. He used his father's coat and hat for a pillow.

He woke and was conscious of a soft light in the barn. He barely opened his eyes, watching from beneath his lashes as El-speth Gray stood over him with the lantern. She was dressed in her nightclothes; her bonnet was off and her hair spilled over her shoulders. Peter did his best to feign sleep. He watched her till he feared the lamplight would catch a telltale reflection in his slitted eyes. The blemish on her cheek was invisible in the lantern-glow, and if her form was hidden behind the loose gown she wore, the cut of her shoulders and the length of her neck were all that were needed to mark her as a woman.

Peter imagined that if he opened his eyes and stood up, she might kiss him, or that if he simply put his arms out, she would lay down beside him. He was a farm boy and had some notion about the merging of male and female. The thought was pleasing and frightening at once; then the recollection of Nora Tillage, trembling beneath him, shaking into a helpless fit, gripped his heart, and he closed his eyes and wished Elspeth Gray away from him.

Later, perhaps after he had slept again, he opened his eyes in the dark, wondering if he had dreamed her.

20

How the Parson Was Accused by
—and Peter Attached to—
Nathan Barrow

ELSPETH GRAY WAS WALKING FROM THE HOUSE WHEN PETER CAME out of the barn. "You're not going with him to Wiscasset, if you don't catch him up," she said, contrary to everything discussed the night before. It was barely light out, and an ash colored mist rose off the river in the pre-dawn; nothing else moved besides them—not a crow called or a twig of brush shifted. Peter had known mornings like this, when a conscious body might seem to be stirring separately from the air and life around it.

The intuition he had known regarding her willingness toward him returned, and it was like being struck in the face, so that he wondered she hadn't heard the thought hit him.

She was dressed in men's clothes, and her hair was tied back in a kerchief. She had a hat in hand that a young man might have worn at work. "They're my brother Samuel's," she said, mistaking his expression. "He would have gone with Mr. Leach, if he were alive." Peter heard a clattering and one of Elspeth's younger brothers came around the corner of the cabin with a milk pail.

Elspeth turned away from the barn and walked toward the river. "Mother has biscuits and bacon," she said to Peter. "Eat and get your horse. I'll be along." She had a length of rope and a blanket in her hands.

Peter wondered what to say when he went into the cabin. The ancient Mrs. Gray sat by the fire, as if she had never moved all night. Her daughter-in-law appeared from behind the curtain to the back room. A face peered down at Peter from the loft.

"Mr. Leach said you were to stay," said Elspeth's mother, though the ratio between information and accusation that was intended in the statement was difficult for Peter to judge. "He left two hours ago. There's a fork on the table," she said. "You can hang the bacon over the fire if you want it hot."

"It's fine," he said, but his voice hardly worked. It was the first time he had used it since rising. He coughed as he crossed the room, and resolved to eat Mrs. Gray's biscuits and bacon without compunction. His boots sounded loudly on the plank floor.

"Are you one of Mr. Leach's sinners?" asked the elderly woman while Peter ate. She peered at him with sightless eyes.

"No," he said, which sounded lame as the ensuing silence seemed to echo with the word. "But I don't find any fault in him," he added, finally.

"Don't you?" said the old woman with a laugh. "He has a simple way of seeing things that would appeal to most folk, I suppose. The world would be a pleasant place, if it worked the way he saw fit."

"I don't find fault in that, either," said Peter, wondering how she could.

"It doesn't work that way, lad," she said, almost affectionately, "that's all. It isn't meant to."

It occurred to Peter, then, that Elspeth's mother, and probably Elspeth herself thought the same. He wondered why he didn't. He didn't live so very different from these folk. His parents had known much the same hardship and, if truth be known, they didn't look out upon so pleasant a scene when they got up in the morning.

Peter was hungry, and his hand hovered over another biscuit. He was thinking of his mother, his dead father, and his brothers and sisters. He tried to count the days he had been gone, and wondered how they fared, without his father and without the oldest son. People thought his mother mad, he knew, but she often said something, now and again, around this time of year.

"The leaves fall," he said, directing his mother's words to the elderly woman, and to Elspeth's mother who had disappeared into the back room, and to Elspeth who was outside and long out of earshot. "The leaves fall, and winter's cruel. But nothing says the leaves have to be so pretty before they come down." He rose from the table and snatched up his father's hat. "Thank you, Mrs. Gray," and he nodded to the back room, then to the elderly woman by the fire. "Mrs. Gray." He left the cabin without first seeing the mother, but the door opened behind him and she called to him.

"You watch out for my Elspeth, Mr. Loon." She stood, just as her daughter had the night before, her arms folded, but she was without expression.

Peter simply wanted to catch up with Parson Leach, despite what the man had told him.

When he came out of the barn with Beam, Elspeth rode up on

a brown horse. "He's meant for plowing, mostly," she said about the animal. "He's usually frisky, but I guess he knew better than to cross me this morning." She had no saddle but the blanket, and she rode like a boy. She wore her brother's hat and in his clothes she might have fooled someone who didn't know her into thinking she was a young man. The roughness of her cheek, however, gave her away to anyone who had seen her before. She needed to pull her collar up around her slender neck.

"You look too much like a woman," Peter said, as he fixed his father's clothes, as before, to the back of Beam's saddle.

"Don't talk to me like that," Elspeth said grimly. "There's a man on the farm north of here who's asked me to marry him twice already, and if he asks me a third time, I might say yes."

"Pull your collar up," he said.

She reached up to her neck, as if she had revealed something vulnerable to him. "We'll see if there are any other women with us," she said.

Peter couldn't guess her meaning, but she nudged her horse forward and he swung onto Beam and hurried after.

The landscape that had been hemmed in by night on their journey to Gray farm was now closed to the far-reaching eye by fog that lifted out of the valleys and bottomland. A diffused light radiated from above where higher vapors caught the first beams of the sun. Peter trusted to Elspeth's knowledge of the way and stayed a length or two behind her. When they came out of the mists briefly, ascending a steep slope, a voice called out and along the next ridge to their right they saw a backcountry fellow on foot and hailing to them.

Elspeth pulled her horse up for a moment, then let out an unhappy sound and kicked the animal into some speed. With a wave
to the man, who was staring intently after them, Peter righted
Beam's head and followed. They hurried down the far slope and
into the fog, with another cry at their back. She trotted ahead
some yards before she pulled up again and veered away from a
granite escarpment that loomed out of the cloud. Peter came up
beside her, but she would not explain herself, or even look at him,
though they proceeded with less haste. Peter wondered if the man
had been Elspeth's suitor, and was it her brother's clothes or Peter's company that caused her to hurry off?

For a while, the fog blew in thick patches, like tattered clothes
in the wind, though it exhibited new resolve as they neared the
trough of the river valley. Elspeth dismounted at one point so as
not to lose sight of the trail. Her horse balked as she tried to lead
it, and Peter got down himself and took both animals, but soon
she snatched the reins from him, and before *he* would have cho-
sen to mount again, she rode into the deepening fog.

Only once after that did she slow her pace, and that was when
some large creature passed before them. Her horse shied to one
side and Peter had only the glimpse of a dark form moving from
fog to fog—a deer perhaps, as uncertain as they in the white murk.
Almost immediately, a building shouldered itself from the fog and
watched them from two pale reflecting windows as they passed.

They came into the settlement of New Milford on the gathering presence of smoke and the note of a single voice that rang like
metal from a distance. Peter did not consciously recognize the
voice, sound was so altered in the fog, but it made his hackles rise,

so that he guessed that he was hearing the declamations of Nathan Barrow.

Elspeth took them past the expired bonfire, now roiling smoke and steam into the mist, but barely glowing beneath the ash and char. Rather unwillingly Peter followed her as she followed the sound of the voice in the direction of the river. A disembodied head was the first to startle him; it turned toward Peter and Elspeth, even as its associate form materialized beneath it and still other shadowy men rose out of the fog.

The voice, which Peter definitely knew to be Barrow's now, rose up in a declaration about the devil and the designs of Hell. There was a small grove of birch and scores of men, some still in their White Indian garb, or with their hideous masks in hand, standing in the fog where the sound of moving water was near. They were a daunting sight to Peter, and he had the inkling that he had veered too close to a nest of barely dormant hornets. The sun had gained prominence just over the eastern ridge, and its reflective strength was enough to make further shadows of more men standing in the shoals of the upper Sheepscott.

"And seeing Heaven, I returned," came the voice in a loud cry, "to lead you against oppressive men and to complete the revolution started twenty-five years past!" Peter could see Barrow standing knee deep in the current, his bearded face lifted, his arms raised.

Murmurs ran through the crowd of men on shore, and every extreme and mixture of opinion was to be heard therein. Some watched with awe, and some with something like disapproval; some expressed amusement or simple patience.

"Do you accept this vision of Christ?" called Barrow, as if to the entire congregation, though he was speaking to the first man before him.

"Yes," wavered the fellow, who may have been daunted by Barrow's fierce revelations, or simply unsure of being dunked in the cold water in a state of partial drunkenness.

"In the name of Christ, then!" shouted Barrow, and he took hold of the man's collar and proceeded to half-drown him. Barrow's shaggy countenance was already glaring at the next man to be baptized as he jerked the first man's head from the water and set him on a course to the shore.

"Yes, yes!" shouted the second man, even before Barrow could question him.

"Death to Great Men!" shouted the third and Barrow never leveled his query but plunged him into the river like a piece of laundry.

Some of the men on the bank seemed to think this was poor entertainment after all, and while the first of the wet men clambered onto the bank and hurried for cover or another pot of rum, these less convinced fellows broke away as with a single thought. "This is Mr. Leach's friend," said one man and several of them gathered round Peter and Beam. Elspeth let herself be brushed aside and in the lifting fog and the distraction of Barrow's baptizing, there were none who looked close enough to tell her apart from a boy.

"So, you sprung from a dead buck, did you, lad?" said another man.

Peter couldn't guess where they had gotten that tale if not from Manasseh Cutts or Crispin Moss, but he was disconcerted by the attention that this report lent him. Nathan Barrow continued to baptize as the line of men advanced, and while Peter talked with those disinterested in the ceremony, dripping men continued to race past.

"How from a dead buck?" wondered someone and the fellow told a barely recognizable variant of the tale, that went a long way toward suggesting that Peter was something other than he seemed.

"That was a trick," said the first fellow.

"I was asleep behind the deer when it was shot," said Peter, though he shifted on Beam and his eye did not light on anyone; he had a culpable look about him, and there were those watching him who might have believed the wilder tale, though they hadn't till now.

"That's a fine horse," said someone.

"I was given the use of it," said Peter.

Barrow had paused now in his labor to venture more thoughts on the nature of paradise and the evil of men who claimed land without settling it. The fog was rising.

"Were you and Mr. Leach down in Newcastle, then, at Captain Clayden's?" asked the first man.

Peter was concerned to answer this, but did so with a simple "Yes."

"Where *is* the parson?" wondered his questioner.

"I came to catch him up," said Peter. He sensed that Elspeth had nudged her horse further away from him, and soon she was on the other side of the small crowd. Again Peter realized how the horse, its handsome harness and gear, and *his* handsome borrowed clothes set him apart from those before him. The ache in his scalp seemed to reawaken.

"What did the Captain have to say?" came the next query.

Peter did his best to answer as he imagined the parson would. "He was unhappy about what was done to John Trueman, but he had little against us otherwise."

"Us?" said one of the older men. He pushed his way through the gathering crowd, and fixed on Peter's face with a belligerent eye. It was one of Barrow's fellows, and Peter was beginning to wish he had listened to Parson Leach and not Elspeth Gray. He was wondering whether sudden retreat was in order, when the first man gently took hold of Beam's halter. "Us?" Barrow's man was saying. "What do you mean by *us?* Do you mean Leach and yourself, or do you mean those of us in New Milford, for the word won't cover all."

"I *do* mean all of us," said Peter, "the parson and I included. I'm from Sheepscott Great Pond."

"You don't look it," said the man.

"Have they dug up treasure, then, in Sheepscott Great Pond," said the man at Beam's halter.

"These are borrowed clothes," said Peter.

"Borrowed from Captain Clayden, I warrant," said Barrow's man.

Everything was laid like an accusation toward Peter and he found it increasingly difficult to answer, except in a faltering series of mumbles.

A man appeared from the direction of the road, and when he saw the first of them, he broke into a half-hearted run, as if he wanted to be seen hurrying. "Where is Mr. Pelligue?" he demanded, as if his mission made him important.

"Mr. Pelligue is not here," said the man who first spoke to Peter. "He went home last night."

"Well," said the newcomer, "he should know that Zachariah Leach is heading east this morning."

"East from where?" came the question.

"East from the bridge over Benjamin Brook."

"He's heading back to Newcastle," said someone.

Faces turned back to Peter, and the man with Beam's halter in hand asked, "Where is he going?"

"I don't know," said Peter honestly.

"You said you were to catch him up."

"I thought to find him here."

"*Did* you?"

Peter looked around to seek Elspeth's support, but she had ridden off. The questions grew more suspicious and even angry, when Beam shied and pulled at the man holding her, which gave the look of Peter trying to back away. Two other men took hold of the animal, one at the reins, the other at the bridle on the other side of her head.

"You had better get down," said the first man, and Peter unhappily obeyed. He eased off the horse, as if any sudden move might be mistaken. He remembered how deftly Parson Leach had dismounted at the bridge last night and disarmed the man who had challenged him.

There was something of a hubbub about Peter and Beam, and the horse shied again and was taken from him to the periphery of the crowd. Everyone wondered aloud what the parson was up to, and a second fellow arrived to say that he had followed Mr. Leach in the fog and the man had indeed crossed Great Meadow in the direction of Newcastle. Interest was so great among the crowd that several shivering wet men stopped in its midst to discover what was about, and finally Nathan Barrow himself came dripping up the bank and pawed his way through the ranks of men.

It was about this time to Peter's great relief that Mr. Pelligue and Manasseh Cutts rode across the road, and Crispin Moss came walking not too distant behind them. The fog had mostly burned away.

"It is not too much to ask," said Mr. Pelligue, when he heard the controversy, "where Mr. Leach has gone."

"He left the Gray's farm, before I woke," said Peter. "I only thought to find him here."

"He's gone back to his friends in Newcastle to raise the alarm," declared Nathan Barrow, who had pushed himself to the fore.

Mr. Pelligue raised a hand to stifle the commotion that this statement provoked. From the back of his horse, he was an impressive old fellow. "We know nothing of the sort," he said. "But Mr. Leach has not considered the appearance of things, by leaving as he did."

"He would just as soon our fellows rot in jail," said someone.

"He never said anything like," countered another. "He only counseled moderate behavior, is what he did."

Other voices were raised, scoffing at the thought of Parson Leach turning coat, while others declaimed the punishment for betraying Liberty Men; Peter recognized some in both camps from the debate in the tavern the night before.

"He didn't appear to me to have the cause at heart," said Mr. Briner.

"It's no sin for a man of God to point toward peaceable means," said Mr. Kendall.

Peter said, "He wouldn't have come past the tavern and over the bridge if he'd had reason to be sneaking away," and Manasseh Cutts, and one or two others made sounds of agreement.

"Here is one that knows what it takes to sneak," said Barrow.

"I can only guess," returned Peter, "that a turncoat would hesitate to let men know what direction he was taking their secrets." He had surprised himself more than anyone by his quick reply, and he gaped to find himself standing there, as in court, before these men.

"He said it himself!" shouted Barrow. "He's admitted Leach was raising the alarm against us!"

Peter was astounded, for others in the crowd joined the lay preacher in this absurdity.

"Come now!" said Mr. Pelligue. "Nothing of the sort has been said, and if you insist on willfully misinterpreting any man's words, Mr. Barrow, I will do my utmost to have you thrown from this assembly." This promise was greeted by some low exclamations; the elderly fellow may have been pressing the limits of his jurisdiction, but he offered no one the time to debate the point, returning immediately to Peter, saying, "Did Zachariah say anything to you, Mr. Loon, that might indicate his destination this morning."

Peter was momentarily speechless, his blood running cold with the knowledge that there were men ready to surrender their understanding to someone like Nathan Barrow—that some could

hear what he had said and yet accept Barrow's complete and pur-
poseful corruption of it.

"Mr. Leach is of his own mind, Mr. Pelligue," said Peter finally.
"I have only known him for three days, myself, but I consider him
a man of great fairness and honesty. If he weren't honest, then he
certainly wouldn't have disagreed so openly with Mr. Barrow yesterday."

"The pup has all but accused me of dishonesty!" shouted Barrow again, which is how Peter's statement might have been con-
strued.

Peter realized that he had misspoken. "I only mean that, if he
had intended to make you confide in him with your plans so that
he *could* raise the alarm, he would have done his best to agree
with them. He would not have argued, and left himself exposed to
such an accusation as this."

"The lad has sense," said Mr. Kendall.

"It's what he wants us to think," said one of Barrow's allies,
though Peter couldn't say if the statement was referring to the parson or himself. There was such dissension between men throughout the crowd on this point that Peter wondered they didn't fight
among themselves and leave the sheriff and the town of Wiscasset
in peace.

Mr. Pelligue, however, made himself heard among the angry
talk. "A man's deeds must be understood by what is known of
him," he pronounced, "and I know nothing untoward about Mr.
Leach, nor do I believe any of us have ever heard anything to suggest that he is other than direct in his opinion."

"Will you be accompanying us to Wiscasset, Mr. Loon?" asked
Nathan Barrow, with an ugly sort of smile on his face.

Manasseh Cutts then broke in before Peter could reply. "Mr. Leach has told me to keep the lad from harm's way. I'll be going myself, but he wished Peter to stay behind."

Another commotion greeted this intelligence, but Peter shouted above the hubbub, "I'm going," and when they quieted for a moment, just to understand what he meant exactly, he said, "I'll go with you."

"What do you intend?" wondered Barrow. "To follow us south till you can steal away in the night and assist Leach in raising the country?"

Peter did not respond, except with a meaningful look.

"Perhaps you would like to accompany those of us who are going straight to the jail," continued Barrow.

"He isn't to do any such thing," said Manasseh.

But Peter took a deep breath and said, "I will be the first through the door."

"It isn't necessary, lad," said the woodsman.

"We'll not have this boy's blood on the head of the assembly, Mr. Barrow," said Mr. Briner.

"I will be the first through the door," said Peter again. "And *there* to your saying Mr. Leach is turncoat!"

"Bah!" said someone. "It means nothing!"

"It's no place for you, lad," said Mr. Pelligue.

"You mustn't concern yourself, Mr. Pelligue," said Nathan Barrow. He gazed about himself with a smile. The fog was gone, the day was upon them; the sun had spotted its first rays upon the tops of trees across the river. "I will be right behind the boy," said Barrow.

"Very good," said Manasseh Cutts, "and I will be right behind *you*, Mr. Barrow."

"I am anxious, myself, to be there," said Crispin Moss (whether this meant at the jail or behind Nathan Barrow) and no one could say that his smile was not good natured.

21

Concerning the Disposition of Two Hundred

THERE WERE THOSE WHO THOUGHT PETER SHOULD BE DENIED HIS horse, for fear he would make good an escape and help Parson Leach warn the people in Wiscasset, but Manasseh did not let the young man linger to answer this.

"I can't take her with me," Peter said as he was led away from the shore and Nathan Barrow. "Captain Clayden gave her to my safe-keeping."

"We'll put her above the tavern," said Manasseh. "The landlord has a pasture fenced off." As they walked, they met with the stares and greetings of men recently arrived, and the woodsmen recognized two or three. "That was a hasty business back there, lad," the older woodsman said to Peter. "The parson will not be pleased I didn't keep you safe."

Peter thought he hadn't had much choice in his decision, but felt it an act of faith against the parson's accusers, and refused to regret his promise, though he was a little fearful.

Elspeth had already driven her horse into the pasture and she watched beneath the nearly barren branches of an old apple tree as Peter and the woodsmen approached. Peter realized she had not wanted to be discovered for a woman by speaking out, though he still felt she had abandoned him. He said nothing to her, and left her, when they went off, to her own solitary devices. She stayed by the fence or at the margin of the crowd the most of the day.

When they returned to the common, Peter was amazed that more drink had been found—he would have believed the entire settlement had been dried up by the previous night's revels—but tankards and bowls were out and barrels were being dipped. More men arrived as the morning wore on and Mr. Pelligue led a meeting before the Star and Sturgeon, where they planned a raid upon Wiscasset, and more specifically upon the county jail, to be conducted that very night.

A good deal of martial speech was heard, and White Indian garb and paint was employed again and those with bestial masks raised them in place of human faces; but as the plan was hammered out, the men in charge, and those who would put themselves the closest to harm's way seemed of moderate inclinations.

"We go together as an indication of our strength," Mr. Pelligue avouched when the plan had been expounded. "We go to protect one another, and in numbers to prevent the loss of life and property rather than to prompt it. We will cordon off the roads to the town and release our fellows, and leave with no more than we came with." Even Joshua Cargin, who had spoken of "inflicting more harm" upon the denizens of Wiscasset, seemed less warlike as the consequences of their intentions drew near.

The sun was brilliant on the common and the surface of the water beyond, but the wind was out of the northwest and the day had come off cold, so that the shadows of trees and houses felt like the breath of winter rising out of the ground.

Manasseh, by dint of having said little (and that with quiet conviction) had been given the leadership of some thirty or forty men. Barrow had not waited to be allotted a command, but gathered his own men about him; they numbered sixty or more. Before the afternoon was done more than two hundred men had gathered in New Milford, and they had come from every back-country settlement within a three day tramp.

"How far is Wiscasset?" asked Peter, who had not thought about this till they were being fed by the remainder of their kits on the common.

"It'll be four or five miles down river," said Manasseh.

"Where do you think Parson Leach has gone?" asked Peter. He had had little else on his mind since the morning, unless it were Nora Tillage, or Emily Clayden, or Elspeth Gray.

"He had reason to leave without us," said Manasseh. "*And* reason to say nothing, I warrant."

Crispin Moss lent his good-natured concentration to this thought, but could not imagine the parson's motives and looked it.

"I wish he were here," said Peter without shame, though he thought he might cry when he said it.

"If I know the man," said Manasseh, "and I guess I know him right well for having met him just the other day . . . but if I know him, he's put himself between more danger than you or I will know tonight."

Peter himself tried to imagine why Parson Leach had ridden off in the direction of Newcastle, where lived Captain Clayden and (more importantly) Captain McQuigg and his horsed militia.

22

Concerning the March to Wiscasset

THERE WAS AN OLD PLANK BRIDGE OVER THE DAM AT THE HEAD OF the tide above the New Milford settlement, and Peter thought it would be worn out before half the rabble of Liberty Men were across it. They were a strange company, like celebrants on Mummer's Day, which Peter had heard tell of from long-memoried folk at Sheepscott Great Pond. Their costumes were preposterous and bizarre; there were men whose masks bristled with bear-claws for teeth, or who wore wolf heads with antlers. The *Indians* looked like no Indian Peter had ever seen, but were cut out in outlandish headdresses and daubed with charcoal and ocher. Most of the men were armed with muskets and squirrel guns. They had lost their identities as well as their faces, and Peter understood on some unspoken level that any outrage they committed would be recalled by them as belonging only to the masks they hid beneath.

Disguise might hide a man from himself as well as the world, and Peter carried his own mask perhaps in the form of Captain Clayden's clothes. His father's hat and coat he had turned into a thin roll and looped with the length of borrowed rope over one shoulder.

Nathan Barrow had endeavored to attach Peter to his own group of men, but Manasseh Cutts drove off such proposals with something less than diplomacy, and the threat of something more than the toe of his boot. They were benefited by several imprecations from the lay preacher, till Barrow was encouraged to retreat to his own company by several who were less moderate than old Manasseh.

The journey to Wiscasset commenced in the forest's shadow, west of the Sheepscott, and soon they entered the woods where the trails were narrow and less traveled than those along the river. The company was mostly afoot and even Manasseh's men were largely in disguise so that Peter felt strange to look so much like himself. The aspect of those about him grew more unearthly with evening's approach. Torches lit the paths. The men sang at intervals, their rough-made songs brewed from ancient melodies and bittered with discontent; but then they would fall silent and the forest would be filled with the tramp of their feet—a disorganized sound—and the snap-and-stumble presence of humans among the trees. Peter was ever conscious of the ranks of men ahead and behind him, and found himself falling under the warlike spell of their numbers and purpose.

Rum and ale had been brought with them—some carried their own libations, while one group of men had forded horses across the upper river to pull a cart and barrels with them.

Night came on suddenly among the pine and fir. The moon had yet to rise; the torchlight rose almost to the tops of trees. The company had been moving two hours or more through the woods—Manasseh's men, along with Peter, being in the middle of the line—when Peter caught sight of a rider who was knocked from his horse in the dark by a low lying branch.

The horseman managed to clutch on to his reins, and he scrambled for his hat and to his feet as someone with a torch halted to lend a hand. The rider cast a glance in Peter's direction once the hat had been replaced, and Peter recognized Elspeth Gray. From there, she walked her horse, till some jolly fellow offered to ride it for her. The young woman gave out a low grunt, tugged the horse away from the man and swung onto its back, which caused some laughter.

Elspeth may have thought she had come dangerously close to discovery, for she eased her horse to the other side of the path where Peter walked. He did not give her much regard, and was in fact doing his best to ignore his concern for her. Spitefully, it seemed, visions of the young woman in her nightclothes with the lantern light shining in her hair crowded other thoughts from his mind.

There was little chance of the company meeting anyone on this trail, but they did pass some farms along the way and it was clear from the dying lights in the tiny windows of the houses that they had been heard. On one hillside they caught a glimpse of lights beside the river and realized they were passing Sheepscott Village.

The main road wandered some, avoiding difficult climbs or steep descents when it could. It circled a tall hill, which maneuver Peter was only conscious of because of the eminence to their right and the stars wheeling above them. Word came back through the line that Nathan Barrow had taken his men off the main trail and struck westward, where they would cordon off the landward approaches to Wiscasset. Peter was glad to have them go, but Manasseh seemed to think that Barrow was capable of mischief once he separated himself from the main body of men and Mr. Pel-ligue's command.

Almost a mile above Wiscasset the woods began to thin away, till the head of the company halted and they gathered atop a low ridge to consider the open fields and the port town lying in neat rows along the shore. The moon had risen over the opposite hill, its reflection fractured in the river currents. This was a landing of some significance and several vessels of various sizes and descriptions shadowed the water with their hulls.

Peter was not alone in his curiosity and wonder; there were others in the company who had never seen the town, or anything like it—younger men, who had been born and raised in the back-country. Most had not seen anything like it for a long while. The surrounding fields were clear of stumps; the center of the settlement was populated with fine houses and one or two official buildings, and in the moonlight, even the ruder constructions along the outskirts looked neat and orderly. The wind was in the northwest, but a salt tang permeated the air even so far from the water; it left Peter with an odd melancholy, which emotion brought his mind to Nora Tillage and he wondered how she fared since the parson and he had left Clayden Farm. He looked over his shoulder for Elspeth, and thought he could pick her out, astride her horse, some distance behind the crowd.

"It looks quiet enough," said Crispin Moss. Few in the troop, including those disposed to trust Zachariah Leach, had entirely left off the idea that the saddle-parson had raised an alarm against them.

"Is that a tavern down there?" asked Manasseh. From his crouch he pointed toward an imposing building near the northern margin of town. Smoke roiled from the chimneys atop the house, and lights burned in its windows, but Peter knew that the horses tethered outside the building were the source of the woodsman's concern.

"There's your alarm raised," said someone, and the effect of this thought ran through the company like the rumble of a dull and distant storm.

"What do you think, lad?" asked Manasseh. "There must be twenty or thirty horse down there."

"It's Captain McQuigg and his militia," said Peter, even as the thought came to him. "They were leaving for Wiscasset two days ago, before the parson and I ever came to New Milford." They were a hundred yards from the horses, with only moonlight to illuminate the scene before them, but Peter could almost place the broad-shouldered mount of Martha Clayden's admirer Edward Kavanagh.

The company retreated into the forest behind, and as Manasseh mustered his men together, Mr. Pelligue rode up among them—a gray old man, hardened by his years in the wilderness—and he dismounted and threw his reins to someone. He hunkered down beside his chief men, including Manasseh Cutts, and considered the horses below.

"Peter says that Captain McQuigg gathered a troop together days ago," said Manasseh, before the question could be asked.

"I know the man," said Mr. Pelligue.

"What will they do?" wondered another fellow. "Will they come out and shoot at us?"

"I would lay wager they're not carrying hoes and shovels," said Mr. Pelligue.

"Well," said the man, "I don't want to be shot, and I'm not *very* anxious to shoot at *them*."

Mr. Pelligue looked over his shoulder at the company behind him. "We won't, if we can help it," he whispered, and Peter wished the whole body of men could hear this, though more as directive than comfort.

"What house is that?" asked someone.

"It's the Whittier," said the old man, and when the fellow frowned, Mr. Pelligue added, "Some know it as the Three Sisters, after the elms out front of it." Mr. Pelligue turned to Peter and said, "You saw McQuigg at Captain Clayden's?"

"I met him there," said Peter.

"You're dressed for it," said Manasseh, which was not meant unkindly. An odd expression crossed his face when he said it, though. "There were others there, you said."

"There was an Edward Kavanagh, a Mr. Flye and a Mr. Short-well . . ."

"Kavanagh," said Mr. Pelligue. "He's a big man—knocked down the two Mulligan brothers last harvest fair at Newcastle."

"They'll be down there as well," said Manasseh.

Peter considered the horses outside the Whittier Tavern.

"Did you make a good impression, lad?" asked Mr. Pelligue.

"I don't think I made any impression at all."

"That will do, as long as they remember where they met you."

"Mr. Kavanagh, perhaps . . ."

"Will you do it, then?"

"Go down there?"

"Set them off course," said Mr. Pelligue. "Up the river road to New Milford, if you must."

"What if he raises the alarm?" asked someone, meaning Peter, but Mr. Pelligue paid the man no heed.

Peter set his jaw and gave the fellow a hard stare. "What will I tell them?" he asked.

"What you will. But you must have a horse. No, not that beast of mine. There must be a creature that better suits your clothes."

"The fellow who was knocked from his horse," said Manasseh, almost as to himself. "I see him over there." Before Peter could say nay to any of it, Crispin Moss had gone off to collar the *man* and take his mount.

"What will I tell them?" asked Peter again.

"You're only there to warn them," said Mr. Pelligue. "Tell them a troop is coming, but don't make it so big as it will frighten any of them away or encourage them to raise the town."

"We just want them to head north and out of sight," said Manasseh.

Peter was thinking that after this adventure he would never be able to set foot in Captain Clayden's home again; and he had hoped to remain unseen and unchallenged. The uncertainty might have showed upon his face, for Mr. Pelligue said to Manasseh Cutts, "Do you trust the lad?"

"As I trust Parson Leach, and as I *don't* trust Barrow."

This seemed enough for Mr. Pelligue and he did not pursue the subject. Peter was unoffended by the question, coming from the old man, and thought it only sensible, couched in such simple terms.

"I might have mistaken that fellow for a woman," said Crispin Moss, when Peter and Manasseh met him below the woods. "If I didn't know better," he added. Manasseh had given him an odd look, and out of shock Peter had himself looked astonished by the idea. Crispin glanced back at Elspeth, who managed to look angry though she was some distance away and her face was in shadow; Crispin was uncertain *yet* what to think of the small figure at the edge of the company. "He didn't want to give up his horse, but he didn't hit me very hard." He passed the makeshift bridle to Peter.

"Who told folks about my climbing out from under that buck you shot?" wondered Peter suddenly.

"That was me," said Crispin, a little abashedly. "Did it cause you any difficulty?"

"Well the story hasn't gotten any less strange, and the buck hasn't gotten any smaller in the telling."

"It's too good a story to let go, lad," said Manasseh, then falling to more immediate concerns he said, "Just send them north. But don't, for Heaven's sake, get dragged along with them."

That was an awful thought, and Peter did not linger over it as he led the horse along the wooded ridge above the road. At one point he hurried down the slope opposite the river and traveled a creek for some yards before cutting right again and making for the trail.

He followed moonlight through the skeletal branches and the underbrush, leading the horse till they broke onto the hall-like aspect of the road, north of town.

He stood for some time, gazing up the dim path in the direction from which they had come. He could quite easily take Elspeth's horse back to New Milford, gain Beam at the pasture above the Star and Sturgeon and never be seen again outside Sheepscott Great Pond. He considered the other direction and Wiscasset and the conflict he would enter therein. It was not at all what his mother had sent him for. *If there were this many people between here and home, how many were there on the way to Boston, or on the way to the prairies of which Parson Leach had spoken?* He was both daunted and compelled to consider it.

23

How Peter Came to His Third Tavern, and How He Put the Night's Adventures into Motion

THE WIND MET PETER FROM THE NORTHWEST—AT HIS BACK, AS IF hurrying him along. He *did* hurry Elspeth's horse, hoping to give the animal some appearance of having labored to get him there. He rode down through the fields, into the air of the port town, which was heady with the scent of salt and water and mudflats; except for the smell of burning wood, the air itself was alien to him who had only known the inland forests.

The town of Wiscasset seemed immense as he neared the outlying houses and barns. Prosperity was evident—there were regular wooden fences before some of the homes, and the streets were straight and barely muddy. The horses outside the tavern stirred as he rode among them. He took a moment to count twenty-eight before tying Elspeth's horse to a lilac bush at the corner of the building. He crossed the pools of light cast upon the ground by the brightened windows, patted a horse's nose along the way, and though he could hear voices and laughter within, he approached the front door of the Whittier Tavern as he might a sleeping giant.

The board by the door said: DRINK FOR THE THIRSTY, FOOD FOR THE HUNGRY, LODGING FOR THE WEARY, AND GOOD KEEPING FOR HORSES. Obviously there was not *enough* keeping for all the horses tonight, though Peter imagined that the men inside wanted their mounts saddled and close to hand in case of alarm.

Well, he thought, *I shall give them one.*

Like a small breeze, knowledge of the front door opening and of Peter's consequent presence touched the men in the common room one at a time; the nearest of these ceased to talk as they turned their attention to him. Islands of conversation persisted, however, in the further corners of the tavern, though all eyes considered the well-dressed young man with the roll slung over his shoulder.

"Mr. Loon," came a voice by the fire and Peter recognized Edward Kavanagh, lit like Vulcan by the nearer hearth. The brawny fellow's shadow seemed to cover half the ceiling, but he himself called out to Peter with that same wry smile he had used to such advantage with the Clayden's women.

"Mr. Kavanagh," said Peter.

"Loon?" came another voice. "Loon? Who is Loon?" And at the other end of the room, Captain McQuigg half rose out of his chair to look at the new arrival.

The tavern was of finer workmanship and filled with finer things than either the Ale Wife or the Star and Sturgeon. The hand-hewn beams had been smoothed with care and the wainscot along the lower half of the tavern common room walls was paneled and stained. Bright brass fixtures caught the fire light and fine tankards of more precious metals than pewter hung behind the counter.

The men themselves seemed of finer stuff, dressed as well or better than Peter, and he recognized several from their visit at Captain Clayden's house. It was a moment before he could speak beyond greeting Edward Kavanagh. "The backcountry is risen," he said, in a low choked voice, at first, then more loudly he repeated himself. "The backcountry is risen."

Anything else he might have said was drowned in the sudden chaos of exclamations and questions, and Mr. Kavanagh proved a surprisingly calming presence when he shouldered his way through the sudden press and made a way clear before the young man. "Get the lad something to drink!" shouted Kavanagh, and he almost pushed Peter to the back of the room.

"Loon?" Captain McQuigg was saying still. "Loon? Who is he?"

The tavern keeper put a tall, highly wrought tankard on the counter, where the head of froth splashed. Peter *was* thirsty as it happened, and he used the excuse to drink deeply as an opportunity to arrange his thoughts.

"Where have you been, Peter?" asked Kavanagh.

"I've been to New Milford, looking for my uncle," said Peter, and thinking this was a good start, he took another draft. The ale was sharp and vigorous; it stung the nostrils, and it roused his mind as well as his tongue. He couldn't say anything about the parson, whose position in this struggle might be questioned among these men as it was among the company Peter had recently quitted.

"His uncle?" some were saying, but Captain Clayden had unknowingly laid the foundation of Peter's next fabrication two days before.

"He's been sent to find an uncle," said Mr. Shortwell. "That much Captain Clayden did explain."

Peter nodded to the man.

"You stepped right into the hornet's nest, if you went to New Milford," said Mr. Flye.

"Winslow was the man's name, wasn't it?" asked Mr. Shortwell.

"There are Winslows in Bath," said someone.

"But the backcountry is raised," said one of the younger fellows, who looked as pale and frightened as Peter felt. "He said the backcountry is raised."

"What of it, Peter?" said Kavanagh.

"I was in New Milford and there was a mob gathered at the tavern."

"The Star and Sturgeon."

"That was it."

"How many, do you reckon?"

"Oh . . ." Peter cast his mind, not to the actual scene before the tavern but to Mr. Pelligue's admonition to raise an alarm without frightening these men into mounting barricades and raising the town. "Fifty or sixty," he calculated aloud.

"Fifty or sixty!" came the general cry, and "That's twice our number!" followed a more specific one.

"Were they mounted, Peter?"

"Only two or three, I think. The leaders had horses, it seemed."

"How did you ever get out, once you discovered their plans?" wanted to know Mr. Flye.

"In the fog, this morning," said Peter, which did not go a long way to explaining why he was only now showing up. "I've never been to Wiscasset," he added hastily, "and got lost on the way."

"You've gotten here on time, it seems, lad," said Mr. Marston, and this was meant as praise.

"Is this the boy at Captain Clayden's the other day?" demanded Captain McQuigg as he pushed his way to the counter. He leveled a hard stare at Peter. "You were with Zachariah Leach, weren't you? Where is he in all this? *He* spoke like an Indian himself."

"Parson Leach is in Newcastle, I think," said Peter, which was close to the truth. He put his tankard down after another draft and met the Captain's eye.

Captain McQuigg was accustomed to being addressed with his rank or sir, and it was a moment before he realized that Peter had finished speaking. "I wouldn't trust that Leach," the old warrior inveighed.

"You could with your life, I am quite sure," said Peter.

Neither was the Captain accustomed to contradiction. "What?" he said, sounding a little like an outraged mallard.

Edward Kavanagh found this exchange amusing; he gripped Peter's shoulder as he might a younger brother's, and chuckled deeply. Peter could not hear the laugh, but he could feel it through the man's ironlike arm.

"But the backcountry!" said someone again. "Tell us what is happening!"

"Fifty or sixty? Are you sure?" asked one of the younger men.

"I couldn't count them exactly, no," said Peter, afraid that he had overtaxed their resolve. "But no more, surely." What would they have said to two hundred?

"It's barely enough, by my reckoning," said Kavanagh.

"Bah!" said Captain McQuigg, as if he disdained the grit of his opponents.

"Barely enough?" cried the young man.

"It'll hardly be worth the effort to go out and meet them," assured the brawny fellow. "There won't be half of them armed with anymore than squirrel guns, nor will they be prepared to take on a force of mounted men. We'll drive them back to New Milford with no more than a good shout." And he laughed and appeared so confident that Peter almost believed him, and almost felt sorry that his lie would deny Mr. Kavanagh an enjoyable quarrel. "I thought better of them," finished the big man. "What road are they traveling, or do you know?" he asked Peter. "By the river or in the woods?"

"By the river," said Peter, and he was immediately sorry for it, for Mr. Kavanagh and Captain McQuigg looked as if they doubted it. Perhaps the question was meant as a trick to find him out.

"They'll raise the alarm themselves," said Mr. Flye.

"Perhaps that is what they meant you to think," said Mr. Whitehouse.

Peter decided to stick with his story, rather than look unsure and cast doubt upon it all. "No, sir, it was all the talk."

"They aren't very careful with their talk, we know that," said another man, who was almost as tall as Mr. Kavanagh.

"Nor very clever, it seems," said a bearded fellow beside him.

"They can move quietly, when they want, I think," said Peter. "It's why they call themselves *Indians*."

"It is the quickest road," admitted Kavanagh.

"Certainly John Trueman didn't know they were coming," said Mr. Flye.

"Let's break this frolic up!" exclaimed Captain McQuigg. He raised a tankard above his head like a weapon.

Most of the men were ready for this order and let out a happy shout. The tavern keeper and several other fellows outside the group cheered them on.

"Come along, Peter," said Edward Kavanagh, amid the noise, and with a companionable hand on the young man's shoulder, he led Peter with the rest of the militia to the door. "You'll have some excitement to tell your lady friends about. They're not bad men really, these Liberty Fellows, but they're a rough lot. They know enough to keep out of trouble, as a general thing, but take cover if you see a musket bared. Have you a gun?"

"I haven't," said Peter. They were squeezing out the door like water through a hole. The horses were nickering and shifting feet with sympathetic excitement; the men noisily harangued one another.

Captain McQuigg laughed humorlessly, baring his teeth like a wolf. "We'll have *this* little riot down and be to bed before cock-crow."

"Here," said Kavanagh to Peter, when he reached his horse. "Take this," and he handed Peter a pistol and priming pouch. "Can you load it?"

"I think so, Mr. Kavanagh, thank you, but—"

"It'll be like firing off guns at Christmas," said the big man with a smile meant to reassure.

Peter found himself mounted and trotting out of town with the militia, like flotsam pulled along by the current. The moon had risen to a position of authority and its crescent lent a silver contour to every object. Breath steamed from the horses. One of the men was knocking the coals from his pipe and shifting it to his coat pocket; the sparks from the bowl flew like cats' eyes in the breeze.

The militia thundered out of town and were half the way to the line of trees, where the forest first asserted itself in small clumps. Beyond and above the silhouette of the woods, the mound of a low hill blocked the stars.

Peter pulled up and called out to Mr. Kavanagh. He had expressly kept himself beside the man, and Kavanagh's head turned first, and then his mount. Peter held out the pistol. "Thank you, Mr. Kavanagh," he began, "but I have to go the other way."

"Do you?" Kavanagh's horse danced impatiently. One or two of the other riders had slowed their mounts a short distance away; the rest rumbled off unheeding. "What is it, Peter?" asked Edward Kavanagh.

"I must warn the others," said Peter lamely.

"There's no need, I promise you," said the man. One of the other riders trotted up to them.

"Well, there's my aunt," said Peter.

"Your uncle's wife?"

"I have to tell her what's happening."

"Do you? Well, she keeps late hours if she's waiting for word now."

"I told my mother I would keep out of trouble," added Peter with an uncomfortable shrug.

Kavanagh nodded with a smile. The other rider, who had caught the end of the conversation, looked askance at Peter. Clearly they thought he was afraid and simply making excuses.

"Well," said Mr. Kavanagh, "it's better, perhaps, that the Liberty Men don't see you, after you'd been among them. No need to let them know who warned us."

Peter only looked more uncertain. Kavanagh let out a short

laugh, said something that was lost in the breeze and spurred his horse after the disappearing troop. The second fellow turned his horse's head without a word and followed.

Peter watched them go, watched the contour of the land and trees and the darkness swallow them. *I must get up to the company,* he thought and with another glance toward the river road, he turned Elspeth's horse up the slope.

But the Liberty Men were already flowing down to him like silent wolves. Peter saw the occasional gleam of a musket bore, or perhaps the flash of a face in the moonlight. He unshouldered the roll at his back and shook out his father's hat and coat. It had grown colder; there was a bite in the air, and he was glad to have his father's things wrapped about him.

Then the men in the van of the company, running softly in their outlandish dress, were almost upon him. He could hear their feet as a low rumble in the ground, though unlike the pounding of horses' hooves. They were already dividing toward their separate objectives, each loose group of men turning aside to block some course or road, or to confront authority at the jail itself.

Manasseh and Crispin reached him first. "Good lad," said the older woodsman, and the big man simply nodded his approval.

Another figure hovered just within the jurisdiction of Peter's moonlit sight. "There's that strange fellow," said Crispin, pointing. "Wants his horse back, I warrant."

24

*How Peter Loon Came to the Jail at Wiscasset
and What Happened There*

LIGHTS ROSE IN SEVERAL HOUSES IN THE NEIGHBORHOOD OF THE Whittier Tavern. The sudden gallop of twenty-nine horses, it appeared, had wakened townspeople to the possibility of danger; Peter wondered how conscious they would be—or how quickly conscious—of the hundred men and more who tromped through their yards.

The company was like an army of ghosts, passing in and out of the moonlight, disappearing among the shadows, with nary a sound but the occasional nicker of a horse and the hush of stealthy movement that gathered in the ear like the wind. Peter felt as if he had become a part of the deer herd he had encountered in the forest, and he was astonished how silent these men were, till someone cut through a fenced yard and stumbled over a sleeping pig. This led to some night-piercing squeals and a shout or two, and every man in the company felt his heart rise to his throat.

Contrarily, once the startled animal had settled itself again, some of the house lights dwindled.

"Step carefully," said Manasseh in a whisper. "There will be muskets at every door, and in nervous hands." And then he led them southwest, catty-cornered among the houses and outbuildings. They ran alongside a brook and below a graveyard, where the slate markers formed regular silhouettes against the western sky. Peter could see dark clusters of men fanning out on either side, drifting toward the wharves or disappearing over the next rise. Through the alleys and over the roofs, he saw glimpses of the shoreline and vessels at anchor in the moonlight.

They left the brook and had crossed a second narrow water when Manasseh stopped them and pointed out a building that stood against the sky about half a mile away. The splash of a horse through the brook, however, merited the old woodsman's attention and he told the rider to stay back.

"My father is up there," said Elspeth Gray, endeavoring to alter her voice by lowering both pitch and volume. The result sounded false and suspicious.

Manasseh Cutts moved closer to the horse and peered up at the rider's face. "Your father?" he said. "You come along, then, but stand down from that animal and stay back when I tell you to."

Elspeth had been discovered, it seemed, but Manasseh was not going to send her back in the night alone. The woodsman cast a glance toward Peter, though Peter couldn't quite see, in the shadows, the old fellow's expression. "Let's have done with it," said the old man.

There were several houses along the well-kept road to the jail, and as they passed these homes, Peter had the uncanny sense that their progress was observed, and not only by human eyes, but by the sights and bores of several firing pieces. They moved through back fields; men dropped off to watch the crossroads and their numbers dwindled till there were only twenty or so that actually came within a few yards of the jail.

It looked an imposing structure, standing on a small eminence above the town. It wore weather-darkened shingles along its forty-foot length, and only the jailer's house had more than slits for windows. Two chimneys smoked above the building. Peter was surprised to see the vicinity dark and apparently unguarded, though he recalled Manasseh Cutts's forecast of muskets and nervous hands in the town below.

The jailhouse itself had a single iron-bound door on its eastern end, which faced their approach. This door may have been a small thing to anyone having entered Newgate or the Bastille, but to the silent company approaching in the moonlight with the barren trees about them and the bushes rushing in the cold breeze, it seemed the very Gate of Perdition.

They were finishing the distance to the jailyard when the glow of a torch, and then the torch itself, and finally the man carrying the torch appeared from over the further slope of the hill. A man on horseback came next, almost leaping to the top of Jail Hill, and he was followed by a small mob of men who carried torches and waved their weapons above their heads.

The vicinity of the jailhouse had transformed from secretive darkness, where only the breeze spoke above a whisper, to fierce torchlight and bounding shadows. The eastern wall of the jail was orange with reflected light and the air was dense with, if not shouts, then barely muffled growls and invective.

Manasseh's company fell into a defensive posture; several veterans of revolution among them found rocks and pockets of ground to either side where they laid down as flanks for the line.

With reins in hand, Elspeth looked uncertain where to go, and Peter was ready to shoo her horse away and force the young woman to take cover when Manasseh said aloud and gruffly, "Barrow! It's Nathan Barrow!" and, indeed, it was; if Peter could not recognize any particular man in that mob, he had understood, even before the old man had spoken, who they were by their collective demeanor. Once his eyes had adjusted to the sudden glare of their torches, he could plainly see the grotesque spectacle of their dress—the animal furs, and the antlers, and the feathers—the whites of their eyes looking feral and mad, peering from their charcoaled faces.

The men atop the hill had not detected the company below and it was easy to see how vulnerable Barrow and his men were, had Manasseh and his fellows been Captain McQuigg's militia instead. Barrow himself was mounted and he stood in his stirrups and roared at the jail an imprecation meant for the devil.

"They'll bring the whole town on us," said Crispin.

"Well," declared Manasseh, "the entire town will have to contend with *me* to be the first to shoot *that* fool off his horse!" and he led his company the final rods to the jailhouse door. "Barrow!" he shouted, now that silence was a useless artifice. "You and your men were to watch the western approaches!"

"And you were to break our fellows from jail," said Nathan Barrow. The torchlight caught a wild and heedless expression in his eyes. Those eyes shifted past Manasseh's company, but settled for a moment on Peter. "*You* were to be the first through the door."

There was a concerted shout from several stragglers among Barrow's men as they dragged a large piece of timber up the opposite slope, and advanced with it toward the jail. Between the great pole and the torchlight, it was a primitive sight that might have been enacted at the gates of a thousand battlements. Peter had never imagined anything like it. Elspeth's horse shied back from a torch that was carried too close to it and Crispin had to take hold of the animal's makeshift bridle to keep it from bolting. Elspeth's hat—or, rather, her brother's hat—was brushed from her head, and in the confusion she stood among them, quite obviously feminine with her dark hair falling out from beneath her kerchief.

The effect of this was to confound everyone but Peter and Manasseh Cutts. The scar of disease had not entirely marred the handsome cut of her features, and the torchlight caught something that was fierce and striking in her eye. "Are you going to break it down, then?" she demanded of Nathan Barrow.

"I will *burn* it down before I'm done," said Barrow.

"You'll break and burn nothing, that can be taken peaceably," said Manasseh, and there was a perceptible wariness between the two bands of men that suddenly focused into something more dangerous as Barrow jerked the head of his horse around and faced the old woodsman.

"When I give the word," said Barrow through his teeth, "you had better stay out from between."

"It's a wonder," maintained one of the veterans in Manasseh's company, "if there aren't guns in those slots, just waiting for the first attempt on that door." He pointed to the window slits in the eastern wall, which did indeed look like the gunslots used in forts and barricades. The notion appeared to dispel somewhat the enthusiasm of Barrow's men, and Barrow himself cast an uncertain look at the jailhouse. There was a moment of near silence. Elspeth's horse shifted its feet. The torches crackled in the breeze.

"It *was* a woman," said Crispin Moss, who was still weighing his earlier impressions of Elspeth Gray.

Most of the men in the yard considered the jail as if its walls were ready to bristle with musket barrels and pistol bores at the slightest threat. The building itself seemed to grow, looming in the night, as it loomed in their thoughts.

"We didn't come here to serenade," said Manasseh Cutts finally, and with Peter and Crispin beside him, he moved up the last of the slope. The two companies tensed like nervous horses as they closed. Peter considered the great timber that lay before the jail, and to the men who had carried it there he said, somewhat amazed, "That's a battering ram!" He almost laughed to recall the image of a large goat he had conjured only a few days ago. He stood before the jail with Manasseh and Crispin, and with a nod the older woodsman gave the young man the opportunity to remain true to his word. Before he properly knew what he was doing, Peter had raised his fist and banged upon the door.

The room beyond the door resounded with three hardy thumps. There was a moment's near silence, and then there came a voice from inside that sounded remarkably cordial. They could not quite hear what was said, and Peter thumped again. "We're here to collect our fellows as peaceably as we can," he shouted.

"Don't make any pledges you can't keep," said Nathan Barrow from his horse.

Then, very distinctly, the voice repeated itself, saying "Come in, come in! The door's unbarred."

Nervously, Peter reached for the latch and Manasseh grabbed his arm. "There might be a trap gun, or *any* sort of trap inside," said the woodsman, who mistrusted something so easy.

"Come in," came the voice again. Peter thought it sounded familiar. Elspeth had wormed her way to the fore and she said something silently to him when he glanced her way. The two companies waited in the light and crackle of the torches.

Barrow, however, leaned over his horse's neck and scoffed at Peter. "You *did* say you'd be the first through the door."

"The door is unbarred," came the voice from within.

"We'd cherish greatly to see it opened from the inside," called Manasseh Cutts and this raised a laugh from the other side of the door.

A long interval followed, then the outside latch jumped and the door swung out. Peter stepped to one side and several men moved back. Like a father gripping the arm of a child who insists on peering over a great height, Manasseh had not let go of Peter; with a tug, he encouraged Peter to step back from the door, which opened to reveal a man standing at the threshold of the jail.

"I'm not sure you didn't come at a bad time," said the fellow pleasantly. "The old knight was about to attack a flock of sheep."

Very little could have disarmed the mob outside the jail as surely as this extraordinary pronouncement, and perhaps it was meant to do just that, for the man smiled at the effect.

"Poppa," said Elspeth, and there was more reprimand than surprise or relief in her voice.

"Elspeth?" said the man, and it was his turn to be surprised. "What are you doing here with these Indians?"

"I've come for you, Poppa. Momma is about fallen out of mind."

Sam Gray appeared touched to hear it, but he said, "Whose clothes are those you're wearing," and to the rest of the company, "What are you fellows about, taking my daughter on such a business?"

"We didn't know it was your daughter," said Manasseh. "She's dressed like a man."

"Did you think a boy was that pretty?"

"Poppa!"

"You come in here, now, girl. This is too rough a venture for any of my children."

"Are the prisoners guarding themselves these days, Mr. Gray?" asked Manasseh Cutts.

"The jailers here have proved a pleasant lot, in the end, sir," said Sam Gray. "But, come in, two or three of you, and we can all go home, it seems, when this is done."

There were uncertain looks cast about the company, and Manasseh was tugging at Peter's arm again—pulling the young man back as he pulled himself forward; Peter resisted and said, almost wryly, "I *did* say I'd be the first through the door."

Manasseh nodded then, and said softly, "I don't suppose he would invite his daughter in if there were any danger."

Sam Gray stepped aside, and Peter and Elspeth and Manasseh entered the jailhouse. Barrow, looking uncertain, chose to remain atop his horse.

Inside, the guard room was cheerily lit by a fire in a large hearth, and an older man sat there in fine clothes and an old-fashioned wig. He had a book opened in his lap, and he was just in the act of laying a ribbon between its pages before closing it. "Come in, come in," said this elderly fellow, "I am acting the host at jail tonight."

Peter was astonished to see Captain Clayden sitting there, and it was his first thought to pull his father's hat over his eyes and hope that his father's coat disguised the clothes that must be familiar to the old man. There were two other men sitting nearby, and they looked a shade less certain than Sam Gray and a good deal less certain than Captain Clayden.

"Do you know Moses and Enoch Donnell, gentlemen?" asked Captain Clayden. "I hear, from your conversation, that you know Samuel Gray. Pardon me, I beg you, if I don't stand; I suffer the gout some in this old foot, and the ride from Newcastle has set it to shouting." He pointed to one shoeless foot that was raised on a rude-looking stool. He shut the book in his lap and held it up, saying, "I couldn't bear to leave this behind, as I just obtained it, so I've been reading selections to my companions here."

"He was quite a man, that old Long Jaw," said Sam Gray, who apparently admired the reading. The Donnell brothers continued to look less definite about matters in general.

Peter took off his hat. "Good evening, Captain Clayden," he said.

"Who's that?" said the old man. "Who's that?" and then, surprised, he leaned forward a little and said, "Mr. Loon? Is that you, young man?"

"It is, sir. It's Peter Loon. I left Beam in New Milford so no harm would come of her."

"That's very good of you, lad, but Mr. Leach tells me that *you* were supposed to stay there yourself. Were you the fellow banging on the door and bellowing about peaceable means?"

Peter was stunned to hear that Parson Leach had, as some suspected, returned to Captain Clayden's after leaving New Milford, and he could imagine the muttering outside if Barrow's men caught this revelation. "You saw Parson Leach, then?"

"Yes, and it was he that convinced me to get these Liberty Fellows out of here. And what's this?" he said, taking note of Elspeth. "A young woman?"

"She's my daughter, Captain," said Sam Gray.

"Well, this is an odd mob, make no mistake," said the elderly captain.

"I don't understand, sir," said Peter. "Where are the other prisoners?"

"Drifting down the Sheepscott, I shouldn't wonder. There's a brig waiting for them off Macmahan, on which they'll run to the South Seas, I've been told. But what does that crowd intend, out there? Those fellows behind you seem more warlike than peaceable. Is that a ram they have ready?"

Peter was aware of torchlight casting his shadow before him on the plank floor, and he looked over his shoulder to see several heads peering in after him. "It's Nathan Barrow and his men," said Peter.

"What?" said the old captain, suddenly bristling. "The villains who chased after little Nora? The devil you say! This is not the company I expected you to keep, young man."

"It's that company and yourself that the lad has put himself between," said Manasseh Cutts.

"He's come only because I insisted on coming myself," explained Elspeth.

Peter flinched slightly, for this was not entirely the truth, though the effect upon Captain Clayden was gratifying, as it seemed to corroborate his opinion of Peter.

"So Mr. Leach has arranged for the other prisoners to take ship?" said Manasseh, who was weighing what Captain Clayden had already revealed.

"He is a persuasive man, is our Mr. Leach," said Captain Clayden, "and he was himself persuaded that the backcountry was suitably roused—and in enough numbers—to break the jail by violent means if the prisoners were not first released by peaceful ones. He spoke rather eloquently in favor of Mr. Gray and the Messrs. Donnell as well, and it was decided by several of us, including the sheriff and the jailer, that justice might best be served if these three were not chased so far away as their Liberty Fellows."

"Is this what happened?" asked Manasseh of Sam Gray.

"The lot of them took horse after dark," said the man.

Manasseh Cutts found the matter pleasing.

"Captain McQuigg never consented to this," said Peter.

"He knew nothing of it," said Captain Clayden, "though, fortunately, Mr. Kavanagh was amiable to the design."

"Was he?" said Peter, startled by the thought.

"Mr. Kavanagh does love to altercate," said the old man, "but he's a fair sort of fellow. And he's more than a little fond of our Martha, so he was amenable to my theories upon the matter."

"What's going on in here?" demanded a peevish voice. Nathan Barrow had finally raised his courage, it seemed; he strode into the guard room and focused his displeasure on Captain Clayden. "Let's free our men and burn this place to the ground."

Manasseh Cutts, who had no desire to reply directly to Nathan Barrow, walked past the man to speak to the mob outside. "It's all been done before us," he called to them. "Parson Leach has arranged freedom for them all. The seven will be aboard a brig presently, and the three who were not present at the incident with John Trueman have been given leave to go home."

Nothing could have confounded the entire company more than to discover that their principal mission had been accomplished without them. They gaped at one another, amazed, and embarrassed perhaps that such pains and such energy had brought them far from home for so little reason.

"Why didn't he say something and save us the trouble of coming here?" wondered someone nearby.

"Who among you would have let him go to Captain Clayden's and discuss it?" returned Manasseh.

Nathan Barrow followed Manasseh among the waiting men, and he was yet filled with fury and spite. "It's a lie," he said, then, "Let us burn the place!" he shouted, and snatching the torch from one of his men, he would have laid fire to the jail, however successfully, if Crispin Moss had not clutched him first by the shoulder, the wrist, and finally by the scruff of the neck. Barrow tried to drive the end of the torch into Crispin's face, but the weapon was knocked from his grasp and the big woodsman shook the preacher as a dog would a rat.

There was a general uproar; some of Barrow's men rushed to the aid of their chief, and the mob shifted from uncertainty to separate levels of outrage and movement when a rider crossed from the road before the jail to the perimeter of the crowd, raised a pistol, and fired it in the air. Captain McQuigg's militia followed him like a flood tide, and there was a confusion of rearing mounts, shouting men, and cocked weapons.

Captain McQuigg thrust the discharged pistol into his belt and retrieved a second weapon. His horse had shied back at the report, and the old warrior nudged the animal back against the line of Liberty Men. Having pushed through the other riders, Edward Kavanagh now anxiously spurred his horse before the Captain, so that the old fellow drew back his extended arm for fear of striking his own man with the muzzle of his pistol. "Fall back, man!" ordered the Captain. "I'll blow down the first who points a weapon at us!"

"They are *all* pointing weapons, Captain," said Kavanagh.

And indeed, despite their surprise, the Liberty Men looked more ready to serve a volley than did the Captain's militia. Elspeth had hurried from the jail after her father, and Peter wrestled himself in front of her, though he was himself unarmed.

Crispin Moss had unshouldered his own musket and Nathan Barrow took advantage of this to scurry away, screaming, "So much for your Mr. Leach! Here we are betrayed!"

"It's your torches betrayed you," pronounced Manasseh Cutts evenly.

"No, it was I," said Edward Kavanagh grimly, "and Mr. Loon's aunt."

None of the company was familiar with Peter's aunt and they looked to him for an explanation. Peter was dismayed by the attention and attempted to say something.

"You did very well by him," interrupted Kavanagh, "till he claimed to be carrying the alarm to the wife of his lost uncle. There are no Winslows in Wiscasset, to my reckoning, Peter, so I turned us around. It was a close thing."

Peter was not proud of himself for having lied to the man, no matter the reason, but Kavanagh's expression was not hard when it fell upon him.

"What is this?" declared Captain Clayden, as he hobbled out from the guard room and into the torchlight. "What has happened? Edward, what is this?"

"You are more trusting than I, Captain Clayden," said Kavanagh. "I do beg your pardon. I could let the prisoners go to ship, but I couldn't rely on this mob to behave peaceably because of it. If anything happened to you, I wouldn't have been able to look your family in the face. Peter, however, nearly fooled me into thinking we could thwart these fellows on the road."

"Good Heavens! This isn't right at all!" declared Captain Clayden. "Where's Mr. Leach?"

"Not right, indeed!" sputtered Captain McQuigg. Wild-eyed, his horse danced nervously in the small space between his militia and the Liberty Men. "What *about* this Leach?" demanded Captain McQuigg. "What do you mean, Edward, about prisoners taking ship?"

"They're gone, sir," said Kavanagh. "They've been released and are taking leave for the south seas."

"How is this possible?" shouted Captain McQuigg. "Captain Clayden, I demand an explanation!"

Captain Clayden limped further from the door and the mob stepped aside so that he might approach his mounted counterpart. "As there was evidence, Captain McQuigg," said Captain Clayden, "that some of the prisoners had been arrested under false pretenses, it was decided that they should all be released."

"Why, it is illegal!"

"But it seemed like justice, sir."

"The sheriff will be wild!"

"The sheriff assisted Mr. Leach in taking them to the wharf."

Captain McQuigg looked to have a hundred more declarations and questions, and his face was more red than could be explained by the torchlight. His whole form shook with wrath and emotion. "Edward!" he bellowed. "Why wasn't I told of this?"

"You would have tried to stop us, sir," said Mr. Kavanagh, and with a degree of respect that the words themselves could not convey.

For a moment, nothing more was said. The torches crackled. The horses shifted feet. Men on both sides relaxed their guard. "It is the only wise thing you've said all night," declared Captain McQuigg to Edward Kavanagh. The old man swore mightily under his breath.

Nathan Barrow had, by this time, wormed his way behind some of his men, and he spoke in something more than a whisper, "Now is the time to start the war. Shoot that old devil from his saddle!"

Those who could not hear the words understood their essence, and there were several of the lay preacher's men who looked ready to comply.

"*I'll* shoot the first man that offers to," said Manasseh Cutts before Edward Kavanagh had the opportunity. Crispin Moss put punctuation to his friend's words by looming at Manasseh's side.

Kavanagh, whose hands were empty of anything but reins, slid down from his mount as a token of peaceful intention. Peter would not have credited the man with such action; he looked from the dismounted horseman to Crispin Moss and thought the men were like the dark and light sides of the same person—both of them tall and broad shouldered, both of them quick to active purpose *and* good humor.

"If there is any question of justice," said Captain McQuigg, speaking to the mob before him, with more reason than anger, "you will certainly be beyond it, were you to kill me."

"There wouldn't be a man of you left to testify against us," answered Nathan Barrow. "You are completely surrounded."

The lay preacher was first among them to sense the gathering of Liberty Men below. Drawn by the torchlight, the unexpected movement of the mob upon the hill, and finally by Captain Mc-Quigg's single pistol shot, the companies that had been left to guard the approaches to jail hill had risen from all quarters and left their posts to spread themselves in a regimental line, just beyond the province of light. Peter could see them, barely limned against silvered fields, only shadows in the moonglow.

"There is not a house below us," said Captain McQuigg evenly, "but has a man or men waiting with musket primed. You'll face the whole town, and finally the whole district for such infamy." He was undaunted, though he might be the first to fall, and Peter felt a fierce admiration for the old fellow.

"We'll hold the high ground," came a new voice, and Peter saw Joshua Cargin raise his contentious head. Just beyond Cargin was an old man with a musket leveled and a dog beside him, and Peter thought every moment of fear that he had experienced that night had redoubled itself and found home in his heart.

The sound of horses, and then a voice came from below the line of men on the shadowed slope of the hill. Three riders materialized into the torchlight, and perhaps the greatest surprise of all was to see the sheriff of the county Edmund Bridge, Mr. Pelligue, and Parson Leach riding together.

Parson Leach drew up between Captain McQuigg and the

Liberty Men. Edward Kavanagh, who had been standing before the old captain, stepped around Mars. Sheriff Bridge also moved into the crowd of horsemen. "Thank you, Captain McQuigg," he said, "but I have matters in hand, now."

"I would respectfully disagree, sir," said Captain McQuigg.

The sheriff did not reply. Mr. Pelligue stepped down from his horse and nodded to Manasseh. "No," said Mr. Pelligue, in answer to the unasked question, "I didn't know about this till moments ago myself."

An unusual stalemate had formed in the jailyard, so that there seemed only the one question among them, and that was who dared turn their back and leave the first.

"It's been a useless tramp," said someone among the Liberty Men.

"You are all alive," said Parson Leach. He leaned forward wearily in his saddle. "And that is compensation to me, at least." Mars, too, looked like many miles, and the two of them seemed ready to fall in their traces. The parson's long face was touched with his typical humor, however, and it was hard to feel warlike watching him. "Your task is proven," he said to the Liberty Men. "Your fellows are free and you have demonstrated your determination and your numbers. Praise God you haven't paid a sterner toll for the night's journey."

"This is *your* devil's design from the start!" declared Nathan Barrow. "So let *you* pay the toll!" The man was struggling with something beneath his coat, and several things seemed to happen in the same instant: A pistol came out in Barrow's hand, the weapon erupted in a charge of flame, and Parson Leach was jerked from Mars's back like a lifeless doll.

271

Barrow's own man, beside him, was the first to act, for he hauled his musket back and struck his chief in the face with the butt of it. The pistol flew from Barrow's hand as his head snapped back, and for good measure, the man drove the butt of the musket into Barrow's chin before Barrow crumpled at his feet.

A great shout went up—a mix of anger and dismay that Peter hardly heard for the roar in his own ears. He pushed several men aside, rushing toward the fallen parson, and scrambled around Mars to find the tall man rising to his feet and thanking Edward Kavanagh. The sound of Barrow's pistol shot echoed off the buildings below them, and from the further shore of the Sheepscott.

"I'm glad the stitches in your coat held," said the brawny Kavanagh with a smile of relief, but his face was pale and he still clutched at the tail end of Parson Leach's blue wool garment, as if he might be called upon to pull the man from danger again.

25

*How Peter Loon Returned to New Milford
and How He Left There Again*

NO MAN'S MOTIVE FOR WAR OR REBELLION IS WHOLLY LIKE AN-other's, and every man returns home at his own pace, with his own sense of loss or victory. The Liberty Men who dispersed to their farms and their forests from Wiscasset were more of one mind than most veterans of conflict, for they were all a little confounded by the night and the machinations of such amicable men as Parson Leach, Captain Clayden, and Edward Kavanagh. It is much easier to fathom "stand to and fire at will."

They were weary from their tramp and their emotions. Some trudged home without rest, some lay down in the forest and slept half the next day. Some went to New Milford to bring the news, hoping that in telling it, they might come to understand what it meant. Some scoffed at the entire business and went home. One or two scoffed at the entire business and pulled up stakes for deeper wilderness. At least one scoffed at the entire business and paid the local Proprietor what was demanded for the land he had settled, even if he didn't believe he owed it.

Nathan Barrow's unconscious form was arrested for attempting to murder Parson Leach. None of his followers objected. He woke the next morning in jail and asked for a drink.

Peter was offered the tavern floor to sleep on at the Whittier. Elspeth and her father slept on the other side of the room. Peter woke to an early light and considered the young woman. She was wrapped in a shawl and looked like a child in her sleep, her hair spilled over her brother's coat, which she had used for a pillow. Her father lay on his back and snored.

Parson Leach came in soon after Peter was awake. He and Captain Clayden had slept at the sheriff's and the parson was now going to escort the old fellow home. Peter half-wished to go with him and see Nora Tillage, or the young Clayden women. He walked out onto the tavern green with Parson Leach and nodded uncertainly to Captain Clayden.

"I beg your pardon, Captain Clayden," he said, with his head down, "for wearing your son's clothes in a pursuit against your own."

"I believe last night proved that our pursuits are not so different, Mr. Loon," said the old fellow graciously.

"It proved that Peter should have listened to me and stayed in New Milford," said the parson, though without real reprimand in his voice.

"I will remember," said Captain Clayden, "that Peter's was the first voice through the door and that he spoke of peaceable means, and that he was the first *man* through the door and carried no weapon." He gave Peter his hand, which was more than Peter felt he deserved. "You were right in escorting Mr. Gray's daughter."

The parson must have understood that Peter was ready to qualify this praise, for he cleared his throat and mounted Mars. "You can come with us to Newcastle if you like, Peter," he said, "if you still want to search for your uncle."

"I should go home, I think, and see how my family fares. They buried my father the other day. But I have to return Beam."

"Ride home, Peter," said Captain Clayden. "Bring her back, or send her home when chance offers." One of the tavern keeper's sons helped the old man onto his horse.

"But your son's clothes," said Peter.

Captain Clayden waved this off. "Emily thinks you should sign on to her father's ship when next he's home."

"God speed, Peter Loon," said Parson Leach and the two men trotted from the tavern yard.

Peter watched them disappear past the three elms and around the corner of the Whittier. He described half a circle doing this and found himself regarding Elspeth Gray, whose own wavery image watched him from a tavern window.

"I thought you would go with them," she said when Peter went back inside.

"I thought so, too," he said.

Peter had thought, also, that he would have the chance to see Manasseh Cutts and Crispin Moss, before he left Wiscasset, but he could not find them, nor gain any knowledge of their whereabouts in a short and awkward circuit of the town. He came back to the tavern to discover that Captain Clayden had paid for his and the Grays' breakfast, which they were not shy about eating.

They were on the road to New Milford before the morning was very old, with Elspeth on the family horse and her father and Peter on foot. Elspeth thought that little had been accomplished the night before, and said so. Peter was offended for the sake of her father, whose life and freedom had been preserved, but Mr. Gray himself appeared more amused than angry with his daughter. The man reminded Peter of Parson Leach just then, and he could understand that Mr. Gray and the clergyman were friends.

"The peculiar thing is," said Sam Gray, "that I have nearly enough coin to secure my acres if I'm not dunned more than once for it."

"Does Mama know this?" wondered Elspeth.

"Lord in Heaven, no!" said her father. "She thinks a coin to the proprietors is a coin to the devil himself."

"Did you tell the sheriff when he arrested you?" she pursued.

"The matter wasn't raised," said Mr. Gray.

Elspeth thought about this for a while, and when they had been traveling for half an hour or so, she let out a short growl and spurred the horse to a trot.

When she was some yards ahead of them, Peter looked ready to pursue her, but Sam Gray laid a hand on the young man's shoulder, saying, "Let her go, lad. The backcountry is harder on women, mostly, and it makes them angry at times, when they consider it." Soon, she was out of sight.

"*You're* not angry," said Peter, thinking the man had more right to be, who had been thrown in jail unjustly and who had a daughter prone to wrath.

"Perhaps I should be," admitted Sam Gray. "Her mother will think so. But it was almost restful there, once Mr. Leach and Captain Clayden arrived. And that old knight the Captain read about was more than I could have imagined. I don't know when I've laughed so."

Peter told Mr. Gray about the angler Parson Leach had read about on the way to Balltown, and the older man thought it sounded a queer sort of conversation, between the angler and the hunter and the falconer. He said he would have liked to have heard it. Talking about the road to Balltown led Peter to describing others of his adventures and he was amazed himself what had happened to him in a few days, and how much greater it seemed than everything that had happened to him before it, besides the death of his father.

There were other men upon the road and Peter and Mr. Gray were a little concerned about Elspeth riding alone. They thought they spotted her, though, once or twice, waiting behind an imperfect screen of trees, or pausing on a rise in the distance before disappearing down the further slope. They had report of her from those men they caught up, and they fell in or left off with these fellows as their separate destinations required. Peter had little to say about the preceding night, or about his own deeds, but he was interested in what other men had to say and they seemed happy to fill his ear.

"Men do have opinions, Peter," said Mr. Gray when they found themselves alone upon the road again.

The woods held little mystery, now, that was not already endemic to an October day. A hint of rain followed the wind through the trees. The call of something strange came from above them, but like the ducks, days ago in Patricktown, Peter could not discover the source of the sound.

As they drew nearer to New Milford, and in particular, when they left the woods and crossed a field to ford the Sheepscott River, Peter dreaded seeing Elspeth again, and also feared that he would not. She was waiting for them above the Star and Sturgeon, but while he retrieved Beam's saddle and gear from the stable and readied the horse in the field, she stayed well away. Mr. Gray held Beam's bridle while Peter secured the cinches and gear.

Mr. Gray shook Peter's hand before the young man mounted and turned Beam's head about. Above them, in the field, Elspeth sat astride her horse like a man, dressed in men's clothes; but she had taken off her hat and untied her kerchief so that her dark hair spilled down her shoulders, and very little could have struck Peter with more force. He felt an inner tug that almost caused him to spur Beam in her direction, but he stopped himself, and experienced an unexplainable sense of vertigo—as if he had almost fallen off a bad height.

Elspeth's father had offered him room in his barn as long as he wanted it, but Peter demurred, and he pointed Beam home. Peter raised his hand in a wave. He thought for a moment that Elspeth would not respond, or that she would simply turn her horse and ride toward her home. But after some thought, she raised her own hand and watched him as he spurred Beam to the west, in which direction he had been told he would come to a crossroad and meet a discernable road north.

26

How Peter Journeyed Home and What He Found There

WHEN HE CONSIDERED RECENT DAYS AND THE MILES HE HAD TRAV-
eled, not to mention the people he had seen—more people than he
had known his entire life—Peter was amazed that he could make
his way home in a day and a half's ride; and though he was concerned that he might lose his way he was glad of another route to
travel home as he had no desire to return by way of the Ale Wife
Tavern and Nora Tillage's father at the head of Great Bay.

He reached the western settlement of Balltown before noon,
and here he crossed the Sheepscott by an ancient ford and found
a tavern, where a meal could be had for the price of his story concerning doings in Wiscasset. He related the business as if he had
been but a witness, and raised the reputation of Parson Leach and
Captain Clayden whenever opportunity arose. His tale was good
for commerce there since the tavern keeper and those of his patrons who heard Peter could tell the tale again, and many were the
tankards filled that night as others received the story at second
hand or more.

In his leisure at the tavern Peter thought to ask after his Uncle
Obed, and was amazed that several of his listeners knew of someone named Winslow, that each of these Winslows was someone
separate from all the others, and that each of them had some ex-

traordinary story attached to them. One had tried to murder his wife in a jealous rage, and another had owned a horse that could pick apples from a tree and drop them into a basket without breaking the skin, while yet another had had a vision of the devil on a lake up north and hadn't known his right mind since. There were a peculiar lot of people in the world, Peter thought, and a lot of peculiar people.

Peter had no idea how far spread were Nathan Barrow's companions, and as he continued his way home he was uneasy of being seen when he found himself nearing farms and houses. He hoped his horse was outstripping most of the Liberty Men on their way home, or that they were from other towns, or that he and Mr. Gray had already passed them the day before.

His path took him along the Sheepscott River Valley, and he traveled most of the afternoon in sight of the stream. A short storm of wind and rain rose out of the southwest and wet him thoroughly before it blustered off. From a low hill overlooking Pleasant Pond he could see the dark cloud and its attendant rain as a shadow racing away, north and east.

It was here, riding the perimeter of a small acre of hardwood, that he first saw a thread of smoke to his right. He hesitated before riding from behind the cover of the trees, but could see no direct way to avoid whoever was responsible for the fire. The smell of smoke reached his nose when its source was not yet apparent, and before he was properly ready, he came round a rocky knoll and into the presence of Mr. Klaggerfell and his dog Pownal.

The old man sat with his back against the granite protrusion of the hill and his dog stood opposite him by the fire. The animal was already waiting for Peter before he appeared, its hackles up, its throat rumbling ominously. Peter pulled Beam up, with a surprised "Ho!" and let her shift back a step or two.

"Don't mind old Pownal," said Mr. Klaggerfell.

"You will pardon me, but I do," said Peter.

The old man gave him a serious look then, and said, "You're the young fellow with the preacher I met the other night."

"I am."

"Yes. Well, all is for nothing. The people here are not up to fighting, it seems."

"I would guess that that was more than nothing," said Peter.

"You would?" said the old man with hardly an inflection.

"And to many purposes, in fact."

"They are not mine."

"I hope so," said Peter, and he was startled by his own words.

Mr. Klaggerfell rose to his feet; the motion held no threat in it, only the activity of an old man using sore bones. He looked off to the northeast. "That squall, just went by, didn't damp my fire," he said, which observation the young man could not immediately connect to their conversation.

"Goodbye, Mr. Klaggerfell," said Peter. The old fellow set Peter's teeth on edge, and he wanted to quit him as soon as was polite—or sooner, if possible.

"That preacher of yours is a lucky man," called the man after Peter.

Peter did not wait for the old warrior to explain his meaning. Beam happily (and even thankfully, Peter thought) took him down the slope in the direction of a small settlement between the river and Pleasant Pond. Peter did look back, now and again, and though he could see the old man and his dog and the smoke of the fire dwindling behind, he had the uncanny feeling that some-thing of them clung to his back like a leech. Peter was glad to be rid of even the sight of them.

In the hamlet below there was less offered in the way of vict-uals and more in the way of suspicion concerning Peter in his fine Clayden clothes, and he did not stay long. He had only to follow the Sheepscott north, skirt the Deadwater Slough, west of Great Pond, and he would be within a quarter mile of home.

Night came on and he found a bed of leaves. Beam was teth-ered nearby, and he hoped the horse would whinny if there were other creatures in the vicinity. It rained in the gray hour before dawn and he rose from his soaked bed and, walking Beam, picked his way alongside the river.

All the way he had only the company of his own thoughts, and he spent many a stretch considering Nora Tillage, and Emily and Sussanah Clayden, and Martha, and Elspeth Gray. He was old enough to think of the rest of his life, but he was not wiser for his deliberation. His life at home occupied him as well, and he was in-creasingly anxious to see his family, and particularly little Amos.

It was mid-morning, with the skies overcast and peevish with fitful rain, when he rode Beam up a stump-covered slope and came upon the fresh grave. Three other markers lay beyond and he knew them by the names of his sisters and a brother who had died in years before.

The new mound dismayed Peter, however, and he fell off Beam as much as he dismounted. Someone had taken the time to fashion a presentable headboard, with his father's name, his age, and the date of his death. Peter recognized the work of a neigh-borhusband by the handsome willow tree carved into the wood

above the name of Silas Loon. What would his father have made
of Peter being away? What would Silas Loon have made of the
clothes his son wore beneath his own coat and hat?

Peter hunkered in the misty rainfall and shook a little. His eyes
were closed tight. How his father would have liked Parson Leach,
he thought, and he wept for that missed meeting as much as anything else.

Some time later, he rode down the eastern slope, picking his
way among the stumps and tromping over the harvested furrows.
There was a small barn, where he put Beam, and he wondered
that no one had seen him and come out to greet him.

On the short porch of the house, he scraped mud off his
boots, opened the door and stepped inside. He knew immediately
that something was strange within. It was as if he had come to the
wrong house—as if he had only dreamed of his family here, and of
his mother sending him away.

The first face to greet him was that of a young man his own
age, who sat at the kitchen table. Then he saw his sister Sally Ann,
standing by the hearth. He could not tell if she were more astonished to see him or the clothes he wore. The day was dark and little light penetrated the tiny windows; they seemed to cast more
shadow than light and Peter squinted into the main room of the
house after his other siblings and his mother.

Sally Ann moved across the room and put her arms around
Peter with something like a sob. Looking over his sister's shoulder,
Peter recognized the young man at the kitchen table as Job
Winslow from the bottom land north of the Loon's farm.

"Where's Mama?" asked Peter. "Where's Amos and Deborah
and—"

"Peter," said Job Winslow, looking uncomfortable. He nodded formally.

"They're gone," said Sally Ann. "Peter, what happened to you?"

"Gone? Where could they be gone?" He hardly hugged his sister back, he was so dazed.

"They've gone off with Job's Uncle Obed," said Sally Ann. She stood back from Peter and searched his face for a reaction to this news, then looked more closely at Captain Clayden's clothes.

"*Job's* Uncle Obed?" he said.

Sally Ann and Job exchanged glances before she looked back at her brother and said, simply, "Yes."

"Obed *Winslow?*"

"Yes."

"But Mama said he was *our* uncle. I asked her if he had anything to do with the Winslows down on the bottomland, but . . ." He thought back on the business between himself and his mother that night, and tried to remember what had been said. "But she didn't really answer me," he decided aloud.

"Job went to him when Papa died," said Sally Ann.

"Why would you do that?" wondered Peter in Job's direction; then to his sister he added, "Why would Mama send me off looking for him if he was one of Job's people?"

"She didn't know . . ." began Sally Ann. "Oh, she knew he was Job's uncle, of course. But she didn't know that Obed had been taking news of Mama and our family for years. Job's father used to send word or go down to Bowdoinham himself sometimes. But he sent Job in late years and when Papa was killed, Job took his father's horse and raced down to tell his uncle."

"But what's this Obed Winslow to us?" wondered Peter. He sat down at the kitchen table and leaned toward Job. "What did he want with news of us?"

"He knew your people, I guess," said Job. "He'd known your mother and been friends with your father, when they were boys." The young man looked up at Sally Ann for help.

"He was in love with Mama, years ago, when she and Papa married, and she might have married Job's uncle but for some decision he and Papa made. And Obed left Sheepscott Great Pond for Wiscasset, then Bath, and then Bowdoinham where he owns some land and a shingle mill. But Mama never knew, and when he came the other day, while you were gone, she packed up the children and left with him."

"To Bowdoinham," said Peter quietly.

"Bowdoinham," she said, and their voices had descended almost to whispers.

Peter looked about, as if he might yet catch sight of Amos, or Deborah, or Hannah running to jump into his lap.

"I would have gone with them," said Sally Ann in a sudden rush, "but Job was here when we were getting our things and he asked if I'd be his wife and Mama said you were to have the farm if you wanted it, and we were to take the stake you began up north, betimes, but you'd let us live here perhaps while Job set up a little cabin for us. And Job and I are together now and we'll have the first preacher that comes through do it proper . . ."

"Did she think I wouldn't let her go?" wondered Peter aloud.

"She'd have gone anyway," said Sally Ann. "And you never saw her so strong on anything, Peter, I swear it. But she was going to take us all."

"Did she think I wouldn't have let Amos go, or Hannah?"

"It wasn't why she sent you," said Sally Ann.

"She never knew where he was," said Job, and Peter believed him. "Uncle Obed never let us tell a soul. She couldn't know he was coming for her."

"She wondered if you'd even come back," said Sally Ann in a guilty hush. Clearly their mother had passed this doubt along.

"She's so lost herself," said Peter a little bitterly, "I can't imagine what she thinks she knows about *any* of us."

"She said you were to have the farm if you want it."

Peter truly saw his sister for the first time since he came into the house, and he turned to look at her new husband, who was sitting at what Job might have more obviously hoped would become his own kitchen table. Job looked unconcerned, however, and Peter liked him for it. His sister, he thought, was beautiful and clever and a good catch for a backcountry boy, but if Obed Winslow owned land and a shingle mill, he would have been able to put a stepdaughter in finer clothes than she was wearing now. Put Sally Ann in a new dress and she would have held her own against the Clayden women. She would have had a mob of suitors, no doubt. She could cook, as well, and she had inherited their father's good nature. She smiled, as a rule, but now she only looked distressed and uncertain.

"I feel a little lonely," said Peter in a matter-of-fact way.

"The house does feel still without the little ones," she said. "It's a wonder you didn't pass them on your way."

"I'm sorry I wasn't here to bury Papa," said Peter.

"We could hardly figure where you were," admitted Sally Ann. "When Mama finally thought to explain it all, I thought I would hit her, sending you out in the middle of the night." She sat at the table beside Job and her husband took her hand, which made Peter like him more. "I think she was a little sorry for it," said Sally Ann.

"People understood, though, when they were told," Job assured Peter.

"What did you do, Peter?" asked Sally Ann. "Have you made your way so fast?" she wondered, amazed all over again at the fine things he wore. She was filled with questions. "What did you see? Mama says that there's a powerful lot of people out there in the world."

Peter did not respond to this immediately, but when he did it was with surprise, as the meaning of Sally's words struck him. "Did she?" he said. "It wasn't what she told me. But God knows, there are. There are a lot of people out there."

27

Concerning Peter Loon's Decisions and also What Was Decided for Him

PETER HAD NEVER KNOWN ANY HORSE VERY WELL BEFORE, BUT HE had grown to like Beam, so that he hated to give her up and wondered if after more than a month, Captain Clayden had done so himself.

Snow had fallen early in November, but the woods were not full of it yet and he felt it was time to make the journey before it was made impossible, and the roads impassible, by a real storm. Thin ice gripped the marshes and lined the streams so that he took great care at crossings; he walked Beam cautiously over rocky ground. All the leaves had fallen, except from the slender beeches, but otherwise the slopes of hardwood gave a traveler license to peek through their bare branches at further hills and trees. The forest seemed wider, and less dense, and the world larger to Peter. It took him three deliberate days to reach Newcastle.

On the first day he traveled the woods in which he had once met the deer herd, and then he rode alongside the river which he had crossed when he last passed. On the second day, the sky drew up gray clouds and snow fell in the afternoon. The third day came off bright, and near to evening he reached the short bank above the Clayden farm and, just looking at the smoking chimneys, he nearly felt warm enough to unwrap himself from the quilt he wore over his shoulders. He might have been an Indian trader.

When he first came over the rise, he could see the figures of Ebulon and James, of Sussanah and Emily, and Martha, and even, he was sure, of Nora Tillage, dashing about the yard with snowballs flying in every direction. Laughter carried in the crisp bright air.

He was still a quarter of a mile away when they saw him, and he was surprised that he had been recognized. Two of them hurried inside the house, and he could imagine that Captain Clayden had been roused from his den and that Mrs. Magnamous would be stoking the kitchen fire and warming stew in a pot.

They came out to meet him and they seemed happy and excited; there was James and Ebulon before any of them, then Sussanah and Martha and Nora, and finally Emily looking more solemn than the others. The boys were filled with questions, for it seemed that the Captain had told them something of Peter's involvement with the adventure at Wiscasset. Sussanah insisted that her brother show some manners to their guest, and allow him to get inside and warm before peppering him with demands and queries. Martha's eyes sparkled in the light when she smiled and greeted Peter.

But Nora Tillage was a revelation to Peter, for he swore she was rounder in the face and fuller in her frame; everything about her, in fact, seemed fuller and more certain than when he and Parson Leach left her weeping hysterically in the parlor. The red in her hair had disappeared some with the retreat of the sun. Could such a brief sojourn with these people cause this change? She walked through the snow to Peter and Beam and stroked the horse's muzzle. When she regarded Peter, it was with a brave face and he did not even think to dismount, which would have been polite.

"I fear, Mr. Loon," she said, "that I have not thanked you properly for all you have done for me." Now Peter could see the practice that had gone into her new demeanor, and he was both heartened and saddened by it. She had prepared her own place of bravery within her when she first decided to flee her father and Nathan Barrow, but it was yet a thin construct, behind which he could easily detect the stirrings of her old apprehensions.

"It was Parson Leach," he said awkwardly.

"But thank you," she said, and her courage left her for a moment, so she dropped her gaze.

Martha took Nora under one arm and announced that they must all go in to warm themselves by the fire and drink chocolate. She tugged at Nora and pulled her toward the farm, with Sussanah close in tow. Peter swung from Beam's back and found himself walking alongside Emily, who had yet said nothing to him.

Ebulon stepped up to take Beam, but Peter said he would like to stable the horse himself, and Emily suggested that Ebulon find something else to do. Martha and Nora had disappeared in the house, and Sussanah called from the step to her sister. "I'm going to show Peter my cat," shouted Emily across the yard, with more vehemence than the statement might have called for.

"It's Mr. Loon," said Sussanah, before she stepped inside.

"That's all right," said Peter to Emily over Beam's back. "I hardly know enough to answer to Mr. Loon."

The barn was dark. The heat and the earthy smell of animals took the edge from the November chill. Emily closed the door behind them and watched while Peter found an empty stall, pulled the saddle and gear from the Beam's back and found a curry comb to brush the horse with.

"I hope your grandfather doesn't mind I had her so long," said Peter. He was a little doubtful about those pale blue eyes as they reflected the light from the window behind him, so he concentrated on Beam's coat and the rhythm of his brushing.

"Mr. Moss has been by," said Emily suddenly, without a change in her expression.

"Crispin Moss?" said Peter, and he stopped what he was doing.

"Yes. He's been here several times."

"Has he?" The knowledge puzzled Peter. He couldn't imagine what Crispin Moss and Captain Clayden had in common, but he would be happy if he had the chance to see the woodsman again. He paused in his attentions to Beam, lost in thought.

Emily reached over and took the curry comb from him; then, as she leaned into Beam's side with the comb, she said simply, "He's come to see Nora."

"Oh," was Peter's cogent reply.

Emily's words matched the rhythm of her strokes with the curry comb. "I think if he comes a time or two more," she continued without looking at Peter, "he'll ask her to marry him."

Peter looked surprised.

"And I believe that she is disposed to say yes," added Emily. Then her words came quickly. "Grandfather says that under the circumstances he has as much right to give her away as anyone and that he'll provide her with something and if her father comes to make trouble he'll have at him with a cane."

Emily was looking at her own feet before she was through, but Peter almost laughed. "That's very nice for the both of them," he said. "Crispin and Nora."

"It *is?*" Emily looked over Beam's back with an expression that Peter could not decipher.

"Of course," he said. The notion had lifted a weight from Peter, and he did look happy. "Nora is a brave sort of girl and pretty, and Crispin is a stout fellow to have beside you in any circumstance."

"Oh," said Emily. Peter thought she looked very keen and wise for a fifteen-year-old girl. "You're not jealous?" she asked, which seemed to be what was troubling her now.

"Not at all."

"We thought, since you had rescued her . . ."

"But Crispin was there, as well," he said. He did have a flash, however, of Nora at the river bank, and how it felt to be kissed by her and to feel her slim body pressed against him. The dénouement of that instance was quick on this memory's heels, and he went from a pang of loss, to a physical memory of Nora's fit of shivering, to a sudden consciousness of the freckles across Emily's nose and the ernest expression in her eyes. "And Parson Leach and Manasseh Cutts," he finished, and she could hardly be aware of the series of thoughts that had run through him. "It was Crispin who pulled the both of us to safety."

"Oh," said Emily again. "You don't mind, then, that he's come courting?"

"I gave neither of them reason to think I would."

"Sussanah is very pretty," said Emily suddenly.

Peter could not think what this meant, and he gave Emily a wary look. "Yes, she is," he said cautiously.

"But she changes her affections from day to day, I warn you."

"You needn't—" he began, then stopped himself and said, "Thank you."

"Mr. Kavanagh will marry Martha, we're sure."

"I hope he does."

Emily nodded, though more to herself, it seemed. She took a breath or two, as if she were ready to dunk her head under water. She stopped combing Beam's side and looked over the horse's back at Peter again. "Then you shall marry me," she pronounced, as if she were arranging the seating at the evening meal.

Peter was seventeen, but Emily was only fifteen and too young to be marrying anybody, even though Peter's newly wed sister *was* hardly older herself. He gaped at the girl and she must have known what he was thinking for she said, "Not now, of course," and her words came tumbling out again. "I won't marry till I'm eighteen, at least. But when my parents are back, my father will take you on as crew and you can work your way up rank as he did, and I am very much like my mother and will sail with you when the time comes and you have your own ship."

Looking over Beam's back into those pale blue eyes, Peter could almost believe it would happen in just that way. He laughed quietly, and a little uncertainly, but there was such a look of profound hope on Emily's face, that he became serious as he contemplated her. She was very pretty herself, and he had rather liked her way of taking charge from the start. He thought he might have some fairly stiff disagreements with someone like Emily before all was said and done, but it didn't seem to him all that terrible a fate. And she *was* very pretty, and promised to be prettier still when she blossomed into a woman. And she looked very soft and vulnerable with such a look of hope splashed across her face.

"Yes," he said, "I suppose I could at that."

Emily frowned.

"I would like to, I am sure," he amended. "To marry you, in time."

She nodded then, and after a look of relief passed over her face, she looked serious again and said, "Mama and Papa will be home soon. Grandfather watches for their ship every day now. But they won't be leaving again for a few months, I think."

"I have to go visit my family in Bowdoinham," said Peter. "I have to see my little brother Amos."

She nodded again. Something about what he had said seemed to confirm her opinion of him, and she looked pleased.

Peter was feeling uncomfortable, suddenly, alone in the barn with his prospective bride, however far in the future or *quixotic* that prospect might be. He hurriedly grained Beam, threw some fresh hay into the stall and went out into the snowy yard with Emily. She touched his hand, but just briefly, then walked ahead of him till she was half way across the yard.

She was frowning, just a bit, when she looked back at him and said, "You think Nora's pretty?"

Something about this question gave Peter an unexpected sense of comfort. His heart was very conscious in his chest, as he considered the pale face in its dark frame of hair and the dark arched eyebrows over pale eyes. "Yes," he said, "when I first met her I did. But I thought our farm at Sheepscott Great Pond was beautiful till I came here."

Emily smiled at this. She turned, and like a child, she ran into the house ahead of him.

AUTHOR'S NOTE

It was while reading Van Wyck Brooks's *World of Washington Irving* some years ago that I first became fascinated with postrevolutionary America. His series of books on American art and letters are beautifully written, filled with insight as well as riveting biographies of American writers and artists, and the enterprise and adventure of our country's early days. The first seeds of this story were planted as I read these histories, and I am grateful to the late Mr. Brooks.

Equal gratitude goes to Alan Taylor, author of *Liberty Men and the Great Proprietors: The Revolutionary Settlement on the Maine Frontier, 1760–1820,* which is probably the most important work concerning this little-known period in Maine's history. Other histories and biographies, including *Colonial Entrepreneur: Dr. Silvester Gardiner and the Settlement of Maine's Kennebec Valley* by Olivia E. Coolidge; *Maine in the Early Republic: From Revolution to Statehood* edited by Charles E. Clark; and *Maine in the Making of the Nation: 1783–1870* by Elizabeth Ring contributed to my understanding of the era, but Mr. Taylor's fine volume was most important in understanding the mind set of the settlers and the bitterness of carving a farm out of the Maine wilderness. Anyone who cares about the issues central to this novel should know and read Mr. Taylor's book.

Also of great importance was *The Jails of Lincoln County:*

1761–1913 by Prescott Currier, as well as many of the books listed in the Author's Note for *Daniel Plainway.* I would also like to acknowledge the importance of certain ideas posited in Alan M. Dershowitz's *Genesis of Justice: 10 Stories of Biblical Injustice That Led to the 10 Commandments and Modern Morality and Law.*

It was not many years after the period of this story that the Liberty Men did fall into lethal violence and lost their broadbased support because of it. Despite their suspicion of politics, the backcountry people almost backed into elected offices and helped to raise the profile of the Jeffersonian Party on a state and national level. In many instances, something like compromise assuaged the tension between settler and "landowner."

———

On a personal note, I would like to thank again my agent Barbara Hogenson and her assistant Nicole Verity, as well as my editor at Penguin Putnam, Carolyn Carlson, and her assistant, Lucia Watson. Thanks to the copy editors and production people. Thanks to reader Arthur Addison for making my words come to life on audio tape. These are the folks that make an author look and read and sound good. And a special thanks to my friend Marty Lodge.

Continued best wishes to Sarah Fieder and Michael Driscoll.

Thanks go to Nick Dean (Historical Resource Extraordinaire), Doug Stover (the Man of Ten Thousand Biographies) and James L. Nelson (the Great American Nautical Novelist) for their interest, support, and friendship.

More gratitude to DeDe Teeters of Armchair Books in Port Orchard, Washington; Susan Holloway of Good Books, and the folks at the Common Reader; Peggy Hailey of Book People in Austin, Texas. Someday, when I'm able to travel, I hope to meet you all.

Thanks to all the folks who have communicated with me by way of www.moosepath.com; and added thanks to my friends Scott Silverman, Dane Hartgrove, and Johnny Pate.

Most especially, thanks to Jane and Mark Bisco, Susan and Barnaby Porter, Penny and Ewing Walker, Pat and Clark Boynton, Trudy Price, Susan Richardson, Frank Slack, Joanne Cotton, Tyler Dobson, Devon Sherman, Hester Stuhlman, and all my other friends and colleagues at the Maine Coast Book Shop in Damariscotta.

Finally—and most importantly—nothing is ever accomplished alone and I couldn't write a word without the extraordinary support and encouragement of my family, the joy of my children, and the inspiration of my wife.

Moxie! to all.